www.TheNewHereos.co.uk

For Bliz & Murt

First published in Great Britain by HarperCollins *Children's Books* 2006

HarperCollins *Children's Books* is a division of HarperCollins*Publishers* Ltd

77-85 Fulham Palace Road, Hammersmith, London W6 8JB

The HarperCollins Children's Books website address is

www.harpercollinschildrensbooks.co.uk

1 3 5 7 9 8 6 4 2

Text copyright © Michael Carroll 2006

ISBN-13: 978-0-00-721093-0

ISBN-10: 0-00-721093-0

The author reserves the right to be identified as the author of the work.

Printed and bound in England by Clays Ltd, St Ives plc

THE NEW HEROES

SAKKARA

MICHAEL CARROLL

HarperCollins *Children's Books*

TEN YEARS EARLIER...

THE LARGE-CALIBRE bullets slammed into Paragon's armoured chest and knocked him to the ground. He scrambled forward, took hold of Quantum's arm and dragged him back to the shelter of the fallen tree.

"You hit?" Paragon asked.

No answer. Quantum was barely conscious, his eyes rolling, but otherwise appeared uninjured.

Paragon checked his friend's pulse. It was strong but erratic. "Come on, man! You've got to stay awake!"

A voice came over his communicator. It was Josh Dalton, a member of The High Command. "We've got Dioxin," Josh said. "Energy was right – the girl was able to stop him. We've handed him over to the marines."

Titan's voice said, "Are you nuts? What could the marines do to stop Dioxin? The man's a walking acid factory!"

"True, but he's not bullet-proof. They could shoot him in the head."

"Enough chatter!" Paragon said. "Josh, get back here ASAP. We need to take out that tank!"

Titan yelled, "We can't make a dent in it, Paragon! *You're* the mechanical genius; any ideas on how we can stop it?"

"Find a weak spot," Paragon replied.

"We've tried. Can't find one."

"Then we're going to have to *make* a weak spot! Someone cover me – I'm going in!" Paragon activated his jetpack and soared towards Ragnarök's battle-tank, zooming low over the ground.

Ahead, close to the hundred-metre-long machine, Paragon could see the arcs of lightning issuing from Energy's floating body. The gun turrets on the battle-tank were firing at her, but somehow Energy remained unharmed.

Then Paragon noticed a pale blue blur zipping through the air around Energy: before the bullets could reach her, Titan was stopping them. Possibly even *catching* them.

Another volley of gunfire from the tank ripped into Paragon's chest plate, knocking him off balance. He zoomed up, out of the line of fire, and activated his communicator. "All right, people... This is what we're going to do. We need to tear a hole in that tank's armour and get Titan inside. Energy? I'm going to take out its main cannon – you just keep me covered and Titan will cover you!"

Paragon zoomed towards the battle-tank, its heavy gun turrets swinging in his direction. Missiles and plasma bolts streaked towards him, vaporised by Energy's powerful bolts of lightning.

He dodged left, then right, as the tank's twin flame-throwers scorched the air around him, then tucked his feet up just as he crested the rear of the tank's hull, the toes of his boots brushing the roof of a small jet-like pod.

There! That's the one! Fires in twenty-second bursts, then a gap of eight seconds before firing again. He pulled his last grenade from his belt and set down on the roof of the tank next to the powerful turret. This close, few of the tank's weapons could target him without hitting each other.

The cannon let loose with another deafening volley and Paragon counted down: *Three. Two. One.* The firing stopped. He rushed around the cannon towards the barrel, its heat blistering his skin even through his armour. He activated the grenade, dropped it down the barrel, then hit his jetpack's afterburners, pulling himself from the tank as fast as possible.

Energy allowed herself a quick glance at the battle-tank as its cannon exploded, then refocussed her concentration.

All around her, she could feel the energy from the

7

tank's plasma bolts, the heat radiating from its engines, the light from the midday sun, even the kinetic energy from the tank's weapons. She concentrated, channelling that energy into herself, converting it, letting it stream back out of her in the form of lightning, aimed at the ragged tear in the hull where the cannon had been.

"Come on!" she muttered through clenched teeth. *"Burn!"*

She sensed a sudden shift in the ambient energy levels around her. "I'm almost through!" she shouted to Titan. "It's starting to melt!"

Energy allowed herself to float closer to the tank. From here, she could feel the heat radiating from the white-hot metal – she absorbed that heat and converted it back into lightning.

"You did it!" Titan shouted. "Get to safety! *Now!*"

"No, you need someone to cover you!"

Then she felt Titan's strong hands gripping her arms, throwing her straight up into the air.

Still soaring, Energy spun about, watched as Titan rocketed towards the battle-tank and crashed his way through the weakened hull.

Seconds later, everything went cold.

❂

A voice screamed through Paragon's headset. "Somebody help me! I can't fly! I'm falling!"

Paragon looked around quickly, then spotted Energy far above, tumbling down through the air.

He angled towards her and surged through the air. "Spread your arms and legs out!" he yelled. "Try to slow your descent!"

Can't slam right into her! Got to match her speed!

He arched high into the air, above Energy's position, then flipped over and dived head-first for the ground. He could see the ground rapidly approaching, and put on another burst of speed. *I'm not going to make it! No time to be subtle about this!* "Grab the line!" he shouted.

Paragon aimed his suit's grappling gun and fired. Energy spun about and grabbed hold of the thin cable as it shot past her.

Paragon set his jetpack to hover, then reeled in the cable, slowing Energy's descent. *She's still going to hit the ground, but she'll live.*

Energy landed feet first, tumbled once, then collapsed. Paragon dropped down next to her. "Are you OK?"

"No. I... I don't know what happened! It was like everything was just turned off! My power... It's gone!"

"Oh God," Paragon muttered. He activated his communicator. "Situation report!"

Silence.

"Max? Apex? Titan?"

Energy took hold of Paragon's arm and pulled herself to her feet. "Titan's inside the tank. You've got to go after him, Paragon!"

Paragon nodded, then pointed towards the west. "I left Quantum over that way. Find him!"

At least the firing has stopped, Paragon thought as he ran towards the battle-tank, ignoring the stream of Ragnarök's men who were now fleeing from it, some of them carrying or dragging unconscious comrades.

The machine was still lumbering forward, its enormous wheels gouging deep tracks in the dry ground.

When he was twenty metres from the tank, Paragon flew the remaining distance, straight through the ragged hole where the cannon had been.

He landed in a large room, the walls lined with pipes and tubes. In the middle of the room were the remains of a complicated-looking piece of machinery, now mostly in pieces. At its centre was a large metal ball. *Never seen anything like that before*, Paragon thought. The engineer in him wanted to know what the machine was, but right now he had more important things to worry about.

As he scouted the room he heard a faint buzzing from a computer set into one wall. One glance at the read-out was all he needed. "Aw *hell*!" He activated his communicator. "Anyone who can hear me! Get out of the area ASAP! In three minutes this thing is going to self-destruct!"

Dioxin felt sick. He swayed, almost fell.

The three US marines guarding him backed away. "Don't trust him!" one of them shouted. "Down on the ground!" he roared at Dioxin. "Now!"

Dioxin couldn't remember the last time he'd felt sick. His pock-marked, acid-seeping skin was starting to itch. He looked down at his hands. *What's wrong with me?* He dropped to his knees, leaned over, retched. A thick stream of bile spilled from his mouth, the acid instantly scorching the ground. *Oh God. It's my own poison! I'm not immune to my own poison any more!*

Then one of the marines shouted, "Sarge! He's burning!"

Dioxin could feel his skin starting to blister and bubble. *The acid... Need to dilute it.* Dioxin looked around in panic, then spotted a large ornate fountain in the middle of the small town's square. He tried to push himself to his feet. *The water...*

The marine sergeant cocked his gun. "One more move and you're a dead man!"

If I can't get the acid off my skin I'm a dead man anyway! "Help me! The acid... It's killing me!"

The sergeant paused. "Yeah? Now you know what it felt like for all your victims."

"Paragon!" Titan's voice shouted as the armoured man entered the dark room.

Paragon could see one of Titan's legs protruding from beneath a piece of fallen machinery.

"I'm here!" Paragon said. "Where's Ragnarök?"

"Gone," Titan said. "I don't know what happened... It's like I've lost all my powers! I think my leg is broken."

Paragon looked around, spotted a thick steel beam and grabbed it. "Hold still. I'm going to get you free." He wedged one end of the beam under the machine. His muscles straining, Paragon pushed up on the beam. The machine raised a centimetre, then another.

Groaning from the pain in his shattered leg, Titan pulled himself free.

Paragon dropped the beam, allowing the heavy machine to crash to the floor. "We've got less than a minute. Can you stand?"

"I don't think so."

"OK... Nearest exit?"

"The roof…" Titan pointed to a metal ladder leading to an open hatch in the ceiling.

The armoured man reached down and lifted Titan up, threw him over his shoulder. He grunted. "You're damned heavy for a man who can fly."

Paragon pulled himself up the ladder and on to the roof. "Hold on to my legs!" he yelled at Titan, then activated his jetpack. They soared away from the battle-tank just as it exploded in a two-hundred-metre-high ball of flame.

⁂

Dioxin saw his chance: the marines were staring off into the distance at the fireball. Pain coursing through every inch of his body, he pushed himself to his feet, grabbed hold of the nearest soldier and put his hand on the man's neck. The soldier dropped to the ground screaming.

Before the others could react, Dioxin was on them, pressing his venomous, acid-dripping hands against their bare skin.

Then he turned towards the fountain and ran, painfully aware that his own skin was now beginning to peel away. He was sure that if he looked behind he'd be able to see his own blood-stained footprints.

Get to the water, wash the acid off! If I'm lucky, I won't be too badly scarred. Since it happened – whatever it was – there hasn't been any new acid.

I'm cured.

The fountain – filled with life-giving water – was only a few steps away when something hard and heavy ploughed into Dioxin's back, knocking him face first to the ground. He screamed and rolled over on to his back.

Paragon stood over him, his armoured fists smouldering from the acid. "Stay down, you goddamned psychopath! You just murdered those men!"

Dioxin tried to crawl backwards away from him. "No! You've got to let me…"

Paragon slammed his fist into Dioxin's face. "Let you what? Let you get away?"

Dioxin kicked out at Paragon's legs, leaving a smoking, bloodied streak across the armour. "I'm not immune to my own acid any more! It's killing me!"

Paragon glanced towards the fountain. *He wasn't trying to escape. He was trying to get to the water…* For a moment, he considered letting the man burn himself to death.

Then he reached down, grabbed hold of Dioxin's arms and threw him into the fountain. The water hissed and bubbled as it splashed down over Dioxin's skin, turned red with blood and gore.

Dioxin collapsed, unconscious.

Paragon waded into the water and propped up Dioxin's head. *Don't want him to drown before he can go on trial for murder.*

As Paragon was stripping off his now-ruined armour, a dark green army truck screeched to a halt a hundred metres away. A thin, grey-haired old man climbed down. He was wearing an immaculately-pressed uniform with four silver stars on the shirt's lapels.

Paragon took off his helmet and walked over to the truck. "General Piers. What the hell happened here today?"

"I wish I knew. Our people are going over what remains of the tank. We've already picked up most of Ragnarök's men. And we've got your friends. They're all in a bad way. Looks like they're not superhuman any more. What about you?"

"I never was a superhuman, General." Paragon looked back towards the fountain. "What about Ragnarök?"

"He's gone. There was an escape pod on the roof of the tank. Moved too fast for us to track."

The general patted Paragon on the shoulder. "You did good work here today, son."

"General, you've got to keep all this secret. We can't let people know that the superhumans have lost their powers. It might only be temporary. But if not…"

"There'd be chaos. I understand. Every crook on the planet would think that all his birthdays had come at once. Max Dalton said the same thing."

A soldier approached. "Sir? Dioxin..."

"What about him, soldier?"

"He's..." The man looked sick and pale. "He's gone, sir. There's nothing left of him. Dissolved by his own acid."

"Can't say I'm sorry to hear that," the general said. "All right. Get a crew on to it and start mopping up. Treat it as a level-one biohazard situation. I want every remaining particle of that man's body bagged and labelled." He turned to Paragon. "So what next?"

"Someone has to follow that tank's path, find out where it came from. I want to know how something that big could have come this far without anyone noticing it. Then we've got to find Ragnarök and finish this once and for all."

COLIN WAGNER RUSHED towards the burning toy store. Even from a hundred metres away he could feel the heat of the fire.

It was late December, a little after five-thirty in the evening, the streets packed with rush-hour traffic, the pavements blocked with shoppers carrying bags.

Colin and Renata had been on the other side of town, just about to start their Christmas shopping, when Colin heard the screams. They'd run to a deserted alley and changed into their costumes; Colin was wearing his father's old Titan costume, which his mother had repaired and cut down to size. Renata was wearing black jeans, a black long-sleeved T-shirt under a short red leather jacket she'd bought for a fiver in the local charity shop, and a mask.

Now the two teenage superhumans pushed their way through the crowds. From far away, Colin could hear the sirens of half a dozen fire engines, all slowly trying to get through the dense Christmas traffic.

"Excuse me!" Colin said to a large man who – like hundreds of others – had stopped to watch the fire engulf the toy store.

17

The man glanced at Colin, then did a double-take when he saw his costume and mask. "You're Kid Titan! I saw you in the paper!"

Out of the corner of his eye, Colin saw that Renata was having better luck: she had leaped over the crowd and was now running across the roofs of the slow-moving cars, straight towards the burning building.

Colin ducked past the man, spotted a gap in the crowd and ran for it. He jumped on to the bonnet of a taxi, then on to the roof of a stalled Toyota. The Toyota driver beeped his horn in anger.

Ahead, Renata had reached the building. A frightened-looking, soot-covered woman in a scorched store uniform was talking to her. As he ran, Colin listened:

"We got everyone out of the ground floor, but there's still people trapped upstairs. Part of the ceiling collapsed! The stairs are burning and there's no way for them to get out!"

"OK. Get everyone back as far as possible. See if you can get someone to clear the way for the fire brigade."

The woman nodded and turned back to the crowd.

Colin reached Renata just as she kicked her way through the remains of the burning wooden doors. "What happened?"

"She didn't know. Said she was working in the

18

storeroom at the back when the alarm went off. She got everyone out of the ground floor. But there's—"

"More upstairs. I heard that." Colin squinted around, trying to peer through the thick black smoke. "Stairs are over that way."

"That woman said the stairs are burning."

"We don't have a choice," Colin said. "Take a deep breath and run for it, OK? I'll go first."

"No, let me. I can always turn myself solid if the heat gets too much."

They ran through the blackness towards the stairway, tearing their way through the displays of burning teddy bears and melting model kits. Renata took the stairs three at a time, with Colin close behind her.

Ahead of them was a wall of flame; Colin could feel the heat beginning to singe his costume. Without hesitating, Renata plunged into the fire. Colin followed and seconds later he crashed into something cold and hard.

Renata had turned herself solid.

Damn it! Colin thought. *The heat* was *too much for her!* They were still in the middle of the flames. Colin grabbed Renata's solid form around the waist and picked her up. He continued up the stairs, moving a little slower now.

He emerged from the flames at the top of the

stairway and took a moment to breathe. Ahead was a locked fire door and he could hear something pounding on the other side of it. Knowing that time was crucial, Colin didn't waste any looking around for something to smash open the door. He muttered, "Sorry about this!" to Renata, then ran straight for the door, using her solid form as a battering ram.

The door crashed open and Colin saw a scared, red-faced man on the other side, holding on to a baseball bat. His name-badge read, "Hi, I'm Dave!"

Colin let Renata drop to the floor and pushed the door closed. "You can't go that way! The fire's too hot!"

"What are we going to do?" the assistant screamed. "The sprinklers didn't come on! We used the extinguishers but they didn't make much difference."

Colin looked around. The room was thick with smoke, the only light coming from the fire at the far end of the room. A small bunch of people were huddled together in the middle of the room, coughing, keeping low to the floor where the air was a little more clear. "How many others up here?"

"Five, including me," the man said. "I tried to break the windows with this..." He waved the baseball bat. "They've got wire mesh in them."

On the ground beside them, Renata turned back to her human form and got to her feet. Colin could see that her hands and arms were covered in large white blisters. "Sorry," she said. "I panicked."

"Punch out the windows," Colin said. "I'll try to find something I can use to lower everyone down." To the assistant, he said, "Dave, round up everyone. Get them over to the windows. Tell them to keep low."

All right, Colin said to himself as Renata ran towards the windows. *What's on this floor? Dolls, action figures, books, puzzles... Nothing I can use.*

There was a crashing sound as Renata punched and tore her way through the wire-mesh glass.

What can I do to get everyone out? Need a rope or something... He yelled out to the assistant, "Dave! Skipping ropes!"

"Downstairs, next to the register!" the man called back. "Actually, there's a special on this week... Sorry. Force of habit."

"Great," Colin muttered. He listened carefully: the fire engines were still a few minutes away. Then, from the floor below, he heard a series of small explosions. *The paint for the model kits*, he realised. *It's flammable!* "We have got to get out of here *now!*" he yelled to Renata.

"It's too far for them to jump!" she called back.

With a *crack*, the roof at the far end of the room collapsed, showering them with white-hot sparks.

"*You* jump!" Colin said to Renata, running over to her. "I'll drop everyone down to you!"

Renata nodded, then vaulted out of the window. As Colin lifted up the nearest woman, he caught a glimpse of Renata's skin and costume glistening as she turned solid. Seconds later, he heard her call, "I'm ready!"

The woman in Colin's arms began to panic as he lifted her over the window ledge. "No! It's too far!"

"Just close your eyes," Colin said.

"Can't you just *fly* us down? What the hell kind of superhero are you?"

"The kind who can't fly," Colin said, then dropped her. Below, Renata was waiting with her arms outstretched. She caught the woman and lowered her to the ground. The watching crowd clapped and cheered.

"Next!" Colin yelled.

A second section of the roof collapsed, sending the flames surging towards them. Colin turned back to see that Dave was lifting a teenage boy – not much older than Colin – in his arms. Dave dropped the boy down to Renata.

A coughing, wheezing elderly man was next. As carefully as he could – knowing that old people's bones could be very fragile – Colin lifted the man up. "Hold on to my hands, OK? Can you do that?"

Still coughing, the man nodded.

Colin lifted the old man out and – gripping on to his hands – leaned out of the window and lowered him down as far as he could go.

"Do it!" Renata shouted. "I'm ready!"

Colin let go, but the old man twisted somehow at the last second, swung away. Renata made a grab for him... And missed.

There was a gasp of shock from the crowd when he hit the ground. The man's left leg was bent at an unnatural angle. Renata crouched beside him, but he waved her away. "No, help the others!"

A young woman was next. Renata caught her easily, helped by the teenage boy.

Colin looked around. "Who's next?"

"Me," Dave said. "I'm the last one." He was already climbing on to the ledge. "Kid Titan, isn't it?" He smiled. "We've been watching you on the news... Just this week we must have had thirty people coming in looking for action figures of you and Diamond!"

Before Colin could respond, there was a loud creak from the roof above them. He lashed out, pushing Dave out of the window just as the rest of the roof collapsed on top of him. At the same time, the floor gave way.

Colin coughed and blinked rapidly. *Blacked out for a second.* He was flat on the floor, face down, covered in burning toys and ceiling tiles. He could feel a heavy steel girder across the back of his legs.

Then he heard Renata rushing into the store. She

pulled the girder off him, threw it to one side, then lifted him to his feet. "You all right?"

Colin groaned. "I'm never shopping *here* again. How's Dave?"

"The assistant? He's OK. I caught him." Renata suddenly jumped. "Your arm's on fire!"

Colin slapped the flames out, then looked down at his costume. It was covered in burns and rips, and his cape was in shreds. "My mother's going to *kill* me!"

"Come on, let's get out of here before the rest of the place caves in."

"Wait! Is my mask on straight?"

"It's fine."

They made their way out of the shop and into a sudden flurry of camera flashes. The crowd was cheering wildly, shouting "Kid Titan! Kid Titan!" over and over. A few – mostly teenage boys – were trying to drown the others out by shouting, "Di-a-mond! Di-a-mond!"

"My fan club is here," Renata said.

"What, both of them?" Colin said, his white grin spreading across his soot-blackened face.

A TV reporter rushed up. Without asking their permission, he pushed his way between them, turned to face the camera and began speaking. "Barney Macintosh here with the new heroes known as Diamond and Kid Titan, at the scene of a daring rescue. Diamond, if I can turn to you first... What were your thoughts as you selflessly entered the burning building?" He pushed his microphone up to her face.

Renata said, "No comment," then turned and walked away.

"Er... Kid Titan! Do you have anything you'd like to say?"

Colin nodded. "Yeah. My name is Titan, not *Kid* Titan!" He turned his back on the reporter and followed Renata.

❁

As they were making their way across the rooftops, to the alley where they'd stored their civilian clothes, Renata said, "We did good tonight."

"We shouldn't have let that reporter talk to us. The camera was pretty close."

"Col, you're wearing a mask and your face is covered in soot. No one would be able to recognise us." Renata paused. "Sorry about what happened on the stairway. The heat was just too much for me."

"That's OK. Sorry about using your head as a battering ram," Colin said as he used the end of his cape to wipe his face.

She laughed. "Danny's going to love that one!" They approached the edge of the roof. "Where are we now, exactly?"

"Bishop Street." It was an easy jump to the building on the other side of the alley, not much more than the length of large car. Colin stepped back, took a short run and cleared the gap.

Renata landed next to him.

"So you think Danny's *ever* going to get his powers back?" Colin asked.

"How would I know?"

"Well, you've been a superhuman for longer than we have. Besides," he added cautiously, "you and him have been spending a lot of time together."

"Yeah, well... He needs us around. It's not easy for him. I don't mean about his powers or his arm. All that stuff with his dad."

"You mean his real dad or Façade?"

"Façade. I don't think he should have told Danny's mother the truth."

"Renata, he wasn't legally married to her! He pretended to be her husband for *years*!"

"If he hadn't told her, she'd never have thrown him out of the flat."

"Can you blame her? No relationship can survive that sort of lie! What if you were her, and you found out that for eleven years you'd been living with a former supervillain who..." Colin paused, listening.

"What is it?"

"A scream, somewhere behind us. Come on!"

They turned and ran back the way they came, racing across the flat rooftops, jumping across the alleyways and narrow streets.

"There!" Colin said in a loud whisper. He pointed down into a dark alley, six storeys below. "Four men, mugging a young couple. Think you can jump down there?"

Renata didn't bother to answer: she just threw herself off the edge.

Colin watched as her skin suddenly glistened and turned transparent. There was a crash as she hit the ground. He saw the four large men spin to face her, one of them holding a knife.

Colin stepped back, took a deep breath and ran. He launched himself across the alleyway and landed on the metal fire escape three floors below, then vaulted over the edge and dropped to the ground next to Renata just as the knife-wielding man charged.

Renata lashed out with a side kick, knocking the knife from the man's hand.

There was a moment's pause, then Renata yelled at the muggers' victims: "Get out of here! Phone the police!"

The man grabbed the woman's arm. "C'mon, Jackie! Let's go!"

"No, but..."

"Come on!"

The couple rushed past Colin and Renata, and stopped when they reached the street. "Great," Colin muttered. "They're hanging around to watch."

"Forget about them," Renata said. "Let's just sort these guys out."

One of the men – large, muscled, bald – advanced on them. "What's this? It's a little late for Halloween, kids. Turn around and go home."

"No," Renata said. "We're taking you in. Citizen's arrest."

The men laughed. The one nearest Renata – a short, stocky man in his early twenties – reached out to grab hold of her arm.

Renata spun about, knocking his hand aside.

"Damn, that hurt!"

There was a brief pause, then the stocky man shouted, "Get 'em!"

Something crashed into Colin's back, almost knocking him off balance. The bearded man had rushed him from behind and locked his arms around his chest. The one with the shaved head swung his fist at Colin's face. There was a loud *crack* and the man gasped.

"*Oh God*! My hand!" He collapsed to his knees.

Colin had felt the force of the punch, but no pain. He grabbed hold of the bearded man's arms, quickly ducked down and flipped the man over his shoulder, slamming him heavily to the ground.

Colin looked around to see that Renata was holding the fourth man by the throat. On the ground next to her, the stocky man was groaning and clutching his stomach.

"Are you going to play nice?" Renata asked.

"Please don't hurt me! I'll do anything you want!"

"Good." She opened her hand and he dropped to the ground. "Stay put and keep quiet!"

"What *exactly* are you trying to do?" Colin asked the bearded man, who was now repeatedly punching him in the face. He grabbed hold of the man's fist and twisted his arm around, forcing him down.

The stocky man suddenly scrambled to his feet and made a run for it. "I'll get him!" Renata yelled as she chased after him.

Colin let go of the man's hand and stepped back, pleased with himself. *Not a bad night's work,* he said to himself. *Now comes the tricky part.* He'd have to keep these men here until the police arrived, then get away before they could ask too many questions.

He looked around to see that the young couple were still at the entrance to the alley, peering in. The woman was using her mobile phone. "Yes! Four of them! And these two kids flew down out of the sky and just beat the hell out of them! No, I am *not* making this up!"

There was a groan from the ground beside Colin. He turned to see the bald mugger slowly getting to his feet.

"Stay down if you know what's good for you," Colin said. He put his foot on the man's neck and applied a little weight.

The man coughed into the dirt. "Who... who *are* you?"

"Who am I?" Colin replied. He had been waiting for this moment. "I'm the one the bogeyman is afraid of. I'm the new face of justice. I'm your worst nightmare."

He crouched down, leaning closer to the man. "You'd better warn the rest of your low-life friends that there's a new hero in town. You and your kind won't be tolerated any longer."

Colin stood up and folded his arms. He wished there was a breeze that would make his cape flap about a little. "Who am I? I'm *Titan*."

And that was when one of the other muggers hit Colin across the back of his head with a plank of wood.

※

Colin felt someone slapping his face and he shook himself awake. "What? What happened?"

Renata pulled him up into a sitting position. "Looks like your powers took the wrong moment to desert you. You OK?"

He reached up and gingerly touched the back of his head. "Ow! What hit me?"

"I don't know. I lost the other guy, and when I got back the rest of them were gone."

Colin turned towards the entrance to the alley. "What happened to the onlookers?"

"They're gone, too. Think you can stand?"

"Yeah. Yeah, I'm fine." He jumped to his feet, picked up the plank and crushed it in his hands. "See? Powers back and everything. Now let's go and hunt those guys down."

Renata put her hand on his arm. "No. We're going to call it a night. Get you back home."

"Why?"

"Check your face."

He frowned. "I'm not bleeding, am I?"

"Colin... your mask is gone."

2

"FINALLY! THE LAST ONE!" Danny Cooper took the dripping dinner plate from the washing-up rack and placed it on a tea towel that he'd spread out on the kitchen counter. He used a second tea towel to carefully dry the top of the plate, then put down the tea towel, turned over the plate, picked up the tea towel again and dried the plate's underside. Then, one by one, he put the small stack of plates into the rack above the sink.

He glanced at the clock. Washing and drying the dishes had taken him forty-three minutes, a new personal record. Before he'd lost his right arm, he could do it in ten minutes.

He sat down at the table and resumed flicking through his magazine, just as his mother pushed open the kitchen door and slammed it behind her. Danny instantly knew what had happened: Niall had blabbed.

He didn't look up, but he could sense his mother glaring at him.

"I cannot *believe*," she began, "that you were planning to deliberately go behind my back and bring your brother to see that man!"

Danny simply said, "I didn't think you'd find out."

"That's the best you can do?"

Danny finally looked up from the magazine. "Sorry."

"Sorry you were going to do it or sorry I found out?"

"Sorry you found out." He pushed the magazine aside and stood up. "What did the little squirt say?"

She glared at him, arms folded, a grim look on her face. "He did his best not to tell me. And don't call him that!"

"Façade is his father," Danny said. "Despite what he did, he's still Niall's father."

"That man..." Mrs Cooper swallowed. "He..."

"I know. He lied to all of us. But he thought he was doing the right thing."

"How *dare* you defend him!"

"I'm not defending him, Mum. I'm as mad at him as *you* are. I don't know if I'll ever forgive him. But..." Danny's shoulders sagged. "If he hadn't agreed to take my real dad's place, then Max Dalton would have used what he thought was his only other option."

Fourteen years ago when Danny was born, his real father – the superhero known as Quantum – had had a vision of the future in which Danny was responsible for a huge, devastating war between the humans and the superhumans. Max Dalton had concluded that the only way to avoid that war was to either kill Danny as a baby or strip all the superhumans of their powers.

Max had persuaded the shape-shifting villain Façade to masquerade as Quantum, while the real Quantum worked with Ragnarök to create the power-stripping machine. The machine had worked: for ten years there had been no superhumans. Then, a couple of months ago, both Danny and his friend Colin Wagner had discovered that they were the offspring of some of the most powerful superhumans of all: Colin's parents were Titan and Energy.

Mrs Cooper filled the kettle and turned it on. Without looking at Danny, she said, "I don't want you to see him again."

"But..."

"No! I mean it, Danny! That man ruined our lives! And you're grounded for a month."

Danny muttered, "It's not like I ever go anywhere anyway."

"And when I say grounded, that means you can't have your friends over either. Do I make myself clear?"

"Perfectly," Danny replied. "But just listen to me for a second, OK?"

"Why? Why should I listen to you when I know you're only going to lie to me anyway? God knows we've had enough lies in this house!" She glared at him again. "All right then. Go ahead. As if there was anything you could say that might make a difference."

Danny hesitated for a second, then decided to plunge ahead. "He's in love with you."

"What?"

"Dad. I mean Façade. He phoned yesterday when you were out. He told me that he loved you from the moment he first met you. That was one of the reasons he agreed to take my real dad's place. He says that he has always loved you and he always will."

Mrs Cooper said nothing.

Danny chose his next words carefully. "Did you ever notice anything? Any clue that Façade had taken your husband's place?"

His mother glanced towards the spot on the wall where, until recently, there had been a family photo. "He... He was always a little unstable. Your real father, I mean. I thought that was because he knew that at any moment he might have to run off and save someone. But after Façade took over, he seemed to have calmed down a lot. Then that thing with Ragnarök happened and for the first time he seemed to be genuinely happy. Sometimes I wish he hadn't told me." She gave her son a weak smile. "But if I'm going to wish for things, I should be wishing that you hadn't lost your arm."

Danny glanced down at the stump of his right arm. His shirt sleeve was folded over and pinned up.

"You're going to have to go back to school soon."

"I know. But there's only another couple of days before Christmas. I'll go back with the others in January."

Mrs Cooper walked over to the table and picked up the magazine Danny had been reading. "You did the Sudoku puzzle." The little squares had been filled in with Danny's shaky left-handed writing. "And the crossword."

Danny flexed his left hand. "It's still hard to write, but I'm getting better. I keep reaching for the pen with the wrong arm."

"And you always had such lovely handwriting!" She looked as though she was about to cry.

The kitchen door opened and Niall walked in. "Colin's on the telly," he said.

"What? *Our* Colin?" Danny asked. "Colin Wagner?"

"Yeah. And he's dressed up as Kid Titan, too."

Danny and his mother exchanged a glance. "Must be someone else, Niall," Danny said.

"See for yourself then if you don't believe me!" Niall said.

They followed Niall back to the sitting-room.

"See?" Niall said, pointing at the screen. Two newsreaders – a man and a woman – sat behind their desk. On the screen behind them was a photo of Diamond and Titan. Niall turned up the volume.

"...when a blaze broke out at the store less than an hour ago," the man was saying. "Though the cause of the fire itself is still unknown, there are some fears that it might have been started deliberately. But the most remarkable aspect of this story is the rescue of five people – one member of staff and four customers – who had been trapped on the upper floor." The screen cut to a shaky, grainy image of Renata and Colin running into the building. The words 'Amateur film' appeared in the corner of the screen. The newsreader continued: "The teenage superhumans known as Kid Titan and Diamond – seen here entering the building – braved the intense heat and managed to get the trapped shoppers to safety by knocking out a window and dropping them…"

Danny pulled the remote control from Niall's hands and hit the mute button.

"Told you," Niall said. "That's Colin."

"Rubbish!"

"It is!" Niall insisted. "And Diamond must be his girlfriend Renata."

"Renata is *not* Colin's girlfriend!" Danny said.

"Well, she lives in his house and she's always hanging around with him."

"Sweetheart, Renata is Colin's cousin from America," Mrs Cooper said, lowering herself into her armchair.

Niall gave her a look that made it clear he didn't believe that. "Even so. That doesn't mean they're not Diamond and Kid Titan."

The screen changed again, this time showing Kid Titan and Diamond leaving the building and being ambushed by the reporter. This film was a lot clearer than the previous one, but luckily the two heroes were both covered in so much soot that it wasn't any easier to recognise them.

"See?" Danny said. "He's nothing like Colin!" He waited until Colin and Renata had left, then turned the sound back up.

"So there you have it," the reporter said, trying to hide his embarrassment. "Two brave young heroes, risking their life to save others. They're clearly not seeking publicity or fame, but it seems that their selfless actions will bring them fame regardless. This is Barney Macintosh, reporting for Channel 6 News."

The screen switched to show the newsreaders in the studio. The woman said, "That report from Barney Macintosh. Prior to this evening, only a handful of blurred images of these new heroes had emerged, leaving many people to believe that they were nothing more than a hoax, but as our exclusive footage has just shown, no one can now doubt the existence of Diamond and Kid Titan."

The male newsreader chuckled. "Don't you mean *Titan*, Diana?"

She returned his chuckle. "That's right. He doesn't

seem to like being called a kid. Well, I think his actions today have proved that though Titan might be young, in some ways he's very definitely a grown-up!"

Watching this, Danny didn't know whether to be happy for Colin or jealous. *If I hadn't lost my powers... I could have been there with them. In fact, I would have been so fast that by the time Renata and Colin arrived at the scene I could have rescued everyone and put the fire out all by myself.*

He looked again at where his right arm used to be. In the past few days, Danny had taken to wondering whether losing his arm was worse than losing his powers. *I was only a superhuman for a couple of days,* he thought, *and my speed wasn't even reliable, but...*

Then there was the vision. He hadn't told anyone about it. Not Façade, not Renata, not even Colin.

He had seen a vision of himself – not that much older than he was now – leading an army that could destroy the world. They were running from... someone. The vision had been too vague for him to make out many details. But one thing was certain: in that vision, Danny's future self had a mechanical right arm.

Danny's mother said, "Oh, not *him* again."

Danny looked back at the television set. On screen, standing at a podium in front of an American flag, was a tall, overweight, bearded man. The caption below the screen read 'Trutopians' new leader Reginald Kinsella'.

Kinsella was responding to a question. "No, the Trutopian movement has always been dedicated to the better qualities of humanity and always will be. We *have* no political agenda. Not in the way that you mean. That is not going to change under my leadership. If you've read our press releases you'll already know this. We accept all races, all creeds. All we ask is that anyone wishing to join our society should be willing to obey our rules. Yes, we do strictly enforce those rules, but there's nothing outlandish. They are simply a set of codes by which most decent, law-abiding people already live."

Another man raised his hand. "Mr Kinsella, what about the reports that your followers are—"

Kinsella interrupted him. "*My* followers? The people who've joined our movement are not following me, Mr Lincoln. They're following the Trutopian principles." He counted off on his fingers. "One: do no harm. Two: help the less fortunate. Three: pay your taxes and pay your bills. Then you will be taken care of."

"But what about people who *can't* pay their taxes, Mr Kinsella? Suppose someone joins the Trutopians, moves to one of your gated communities and then loses his job? What then?"

"Then we will give that person work until he can find a job that suits him. You know the statistics: over twelve per cent of our people work in security. We have the safest communities in the world. There has yet to be a single crime committed by a member of the Trutopian movement. We have no crime, no poverty, no bigotry."

Another hand was raised. "So what's the point of having the largest private police force in the world if you don't have any crime?"

Kinsella took a deep breath, held it, then let it out slowly. "We don't have any crime *because* we have the largest private police force in the world."

The same man asked, "So is that why you want to recruit the new heroes? You want them to work for you?"

"I want them to work *with* us, not for us. That's the purpose of this session. No one knows how to get in touch with them, so I'm making a public appeal." Kinsella turned towards the camera. "Diamond, Kid Titan... If you're watching this, I'm asking you to get in touch with your nearest Trutopian community. Join us and we will provide you with all the assistance you will ever need. We will house your families, provide them with good jobs and unparalleled education. The Trutopian goal is in the name: Truth and Utopia. We are aiming to make this world a better place – *for everyone.* Join us. Save the world."

With that, Kinsella stepped back from his podium.

Danny looked at his mother. She was looking back at him. "No way," Danny said. "I know what you're thinking."

"It sounds…"

"It sounds too good to be true. That usually means that it's not true. Besides… I can't do anything any more."

"They might still be interested. It could be worth phoning them. Just to see."

"What are you talking about?" Niall asked, looking from one to the other.

Before Danny could reply, the television once again cut back to the newsreaders in the studio. "Breaking news just in," the male newsreader said, clearly excited, "another Channel 6 exclusive! It seems that following this evening's rescue of five people from a burning toy store, new heroes Diamond and Kid Titan saved a young couple from four men attempting to mug them. Apparently, the heroes managed to scare off the muggers, but not before Kid Titan was knocked unconscious."

Danny suddenly sat up straight.

The newsreader continued: "One of the muggers' intended victims – part-time nurse Jacqueline Caldwell – used her mobile phone's built-in camera to take this photograph of Kid Titan."

The screen showed a grainy, low-resolution photo of Colin, unconscious and unmasked, lying on the ground.

Niall squealed and was practically jumping up and down with excitement. "I told you Colin was Kid Titan!" he shouted at Danny. "I *told* you!"

3

ALMOST FIVE THOUSAND miles away, in the Chinese city of Jiamusi, a gunman lay on the balcony of his luxury hotel room, a high-powered rifle in his hands.

The gunman was in his mid-forties, though little about his physical features gave that away. He was completely bald – lacking even eyelashes – and his pallid, mottled skin was a network of thick red and white scars. He was tall, but slightly built, with long wiry arms ending in thin, nailless fingers.

He had not moved from his position since before dawn, staring through the rifle's telescopic sight, which was fixed on a specific window of the apartment block across the busy street.

Through the sight the gunman could only see a small portion of the room opposite, but he had chosen his location carefully: that portion of the room contained a mirror, and reflected in that mirror he could see part of an occupied bed.

Then the occupant of the bed stirred, reached out to shut off an alarm clock.

Finally, the gunman said to himself. Barely moving, he

43

reached into his shirt pocket and removed a single bullet-shaped pellet. He used his teeth to tear open the pellet's plastic coating, slipped the pellet into the rifle and waited, finger on the trigger.

Two minutes later, the apartment's window opened – as he knew it would – and directly in his line of sight was a woman's bare arm.

He squeezed the trigger. The rifle made a faint *phut!* sound and the arm was instantly pulled back.

The gunman waited long enough to watch – through the mirror – the woman climb back into bed, yawning.

Now – move! He quickly crawled backwards, into the hotel room, disassembling his rifle as he went.

Getting to his feet, he dropped the rifle's components into a black canvas bag, slung it over his shoulder, then quickly and quietly darted from the room.

The gunman silently raced along the corridor and dashed quickly past the room occupied by the businessman who – for some unfathomable reason – never fully closed his door.

As he ran, the gunman pulled a forged key-card out of his pocket. The previous day, he had picked the pocket of the guest staying in room 1102, duplicated the card then left the original where it could easily be found in the hotel's lobby.

Directly ahead was room 1102: the gunman slipped

the card into the lock and stepped through.

Inside, a startled man was sitting cross-legged on the bed, eating toast and reading a newspaper. He barely had time to say, "What...?" before the gunman emptied the contents of a small aerosol canister into his face.

The man collapsed backwards, unconscious.

The gunman checked the hotel guest's pulse. *Good. Strong and steady. He'll sleep for about four hours and won't remember a thing.*

The gunman opened the balcony doors and peered out. His car was parked in the alley below, ten floors down. He pulled a thin rope out of his canvas bag, connected the quick-release hook to the balcony's railing and vaulted over the edge.

Hand over hand, he quickly rappelled down the rope, dropping the last two metres. A quick, sharp tug on the rope and the hook above automatically disconnected. He caught the hook, then ran for his car, coiling the rope as he went.

He had his car keys in his hand and was reaching for the lock when the car's windscreen suddenly shattered.

The gunman instantly vaulted over the car, just as a hail of silenced bullets ploughed through the air, barely missing him.

Damn it! I knew they'd try something like this!

Then a voice called out, "Mr Jackson? You would do well to surrender!"

"Perfect," he muttered to himself. "It's Junior."

"We know your methods, Mr Jackson! We know you never carry any lethal weapons on a mission where you're not expected to kill! We have you outnumbered. There is nothing you can do!"

Right, the gunman thought. *You think you know me. You think I'm some honourable assassin who always plays by a set of rules. Well, if you think I didn't see this coming you've just made the biggest mistake of your life.*

He reached into the canvas bag and pulled out a Heckler and Koch P7K3 semi-automatic pistol, a small snub-nosed weapon that in the right hands could be deadly accurate.

Lying flat on his back, the gunman crawled halfway under the car and looked out. He could see three pairs of feet. Two of his would-be killers had their feet spread apart: the stance of someone proficient with a powerful hand-gun. *Junior's bodyguards.*

He aimed and fired four times in quick succession, hitting the bodyguards' ankles. The men fell to the ground screaming.

The remaining set of feet shuffled, then turned and ran.

The gunman rolled out from under the car and charged after the young Chinese man.

Junior had almost reached the entrance to the alley when the gunman floored him with a flying kick to the small of his back.

He pulled Junior to his feet, pressing the muzzle of the gun into his neck. "Whose idea was this? Your father's?"

Junior shook his head. "No!"

The gunman dragged Junior back towards his car and handed him the keys. "Get in."

Shaking, Junior unlocked the car and climbed into the driver's seat.

"Start it up."

As the car rumbled to life, Junior asked, "Where are you taking me?"

"Nowhere," the gunman growled. He reached in, grabbed Junior around the neck and pulled him out of the car. "Just wanted to make sure you didn't have a bomb wired to the ignition." He forced the young man to his knees. "You hire me to put your rival out of commission so she'll miss today's meeting. You don't want her dead because that would bring her gang into conflict with yours. That's good thinking. I applaud that. She misses the meeting and suddenly it looks to everyone that her people don't care about your precious trade agreements."

"Mr Jackson, I—"

"Shut up. I'm not finished. So all on your own you

decide that instead of paying me my two million dollars, you and your friends will kill me and keep the money for yourself. And Sheng Senior will never find out, right?"

"No, it wasn't like that!"

"Then what *was* it like?"

Junior Sheng didn't have an answer.

"I thought so. Junior, your old man is a fool if he believes that one day you're going to be able to take over his organisation." The gunman laughed. "You actually thought you could kill me. You hired me because I've got the best reputation in the business. I have never failed to take down a target, but somehow you thought that you and your goons would be able to stop me."

He stepped back. "Get up. I'm not going to kill you."

Holding on to the car to steady himself, Junior Sheng got to his feet. "I'm sorry, Mr Jackson!"

The gunman raised his eyes. "You can't even get my *name* right!" He shook his head. "You're in serious trouble, Junior, you know that? Sure, I did the job. Your rival will sleep for about six hours and there is absolutely no evidence of foul play. The knock-out pellet I hit her with will already have dissolved into nothing. But you had to come after me. How's that going to look? She misses this important meeting and on the same day there's unexplained gunfire in the alley behind the hotel closest to her apartment."

The young man swallowed and stared at his feet.

"Listen, Junior, you just tell your father that I'm coming to see him today and that I want him to give me my money in person. Plus a little extra... This is a hired car and I'm damned if *I'm* going to pay for a new windscreen. If I don't get my money, I'm going to kill him. If you or any of your organisation tries to pull another stunt like this, I'll let him live but I'm going to kill *you* and every other member of your family. Got that?"

Junior nodded vigorously. "I am sorry, Mr Jackson! It won't happen again! I swear!"

The gunman put his gun away. "Yeah, I'm sure it won't, Junior. And for the last time, my name is *not* pronounced Jackson. It's Dioxin."

4

WARREN WAGNER ANGRILY stabbed at the buttons on the remote control. "It's on every channel!"

Sitting on the sofa next to Warren's armchair, Colin groaned inwardly. *This is all my fault! If I hadn't been showing off, if I'd been paying attention, that guy wouldn't have knocked me out and none of this would have happened!*

Warren flung the remote control on to the coffee table and – without looking at his son – said, "Colin, how many times over the past few weeks have I told you to be careful?"

"I know, Dad! I'm sorry!"

"Sorry isn't good enough! We have to find a way to fix this... I don't know, maybe get someone else to wear the Titan costume and arrange it so that the two of you can be seen in the same place at the same time. If Danny Cooper still had his powers..."

"It wouldn't work, Dad. Danny's taller than me and his hair's the wrong colour. Plus, you know. His arm. Anyway, he *doesn't* have his powers and there's no way we can fake them."

Mrs Wagner and Renata came into the room. "Renata just had an idea," Caroline said to her husband. "Why don't we start phoning everyone, saying things like, 'Did you see how Kid Titan looks just like Colin?' A pre-emptive strike. It would be better than people calling us about it."

"It's not *Kid* Titan," Colin said. "Just Titan."

"I really don't think the name is what you should be focussing on right now," his father said. He turned to Renata. "Let me take a look at your hands."

She sat down next to him. Warren carefully unwrapped the bandages on her hands and examined the blisters. "You're healing fast," he said. "You'll be OK in a day or so. Any pain?"

"A bit," Renata said, "But it's not bad. Look, maybe Titan could make a public announcement, saying that he has the power to change his face, like Façade could, and that it's just a coincidence that the face he chose looks like Colin."

Warren shook his head. "And when he's asked to demonstrate this power, what does he do then?"

The phone rang. Everyone looked at each other.

"That's the first of them," Caroline said, biting her lip.

Colin stood up. "I'll get it. If it *is* someone asking whether I'm Titan, I'll just laugh at the idea. Or something." He went out into the hall and picked up the phone. "Hello?"

"Col?" It was Brian McDonald; along with Danny, Brian was Colin's closest friend.

"Hi, Brian... How's it going? Hey, were you just watching the news?"

"Yeah! That's why I'm phoning. Kid Titan looks just like you!"

"I know. Now everyone will think I'm a superhero!"

Brian laughed, then said, "You're not, are you?"

"Oh, I wish!"

"You're going to have everyone bugging the hell out of you now! Still, maybe some girls will finally notice you!"

"Oh, thanks a bunch."

"Not that you need to worry on that score," Brian said after a short pause, "you've had a hot babe living in your house for weeks. Pity she's your cousin."

"I don't think of her as a hot babe, though," Colin said. "Just as someone who eats all the biscuits and forces us to watch girly movies."

"You know," Brian said slowly, "she does kind of look like Diamond."

"Brian, I think I'd know if my own cousin was a superhero!"

"I suppose. Anyway, I'd better go. I just phoned Danny but his mum wouldn't let me talk to him. He's been grounded or something. See you tomorrow, right?"

"Sure," Colin said. "See you." He hung up. *Maybe I*

should have told him ages ago. He wouldn't have told anyone else. Probably.

The phone rang again. Colin hesitated for a second, then picked it up. "Hello?"

"Colin? Is that you?" A girl's voice asked.

"Yeah. Who's this?"

"It's me! Judy Morris! Don't tell me you don't recognise my voice!"

How could I recognise it? Colin thought. *You've hardly ever looked at me, let alone talked to me!* He could hear whispering and giggling in the background.

"So listen, we were just watching television and guess what we saw?"

"You saw someone who looks like me. Yeah, you're not the first one to let me know. How did you get my number, anyway?"

"Adam Gilmore told me. So it's not you, then? Kid Titan, I mean?"

Colin resisted the temptation to say that the name was Titan, not Kid Titan. "What do you think? That I'm secretly a superhero? I wish I was."

"He does look a lot like you, though. And we were thinking, OK, that he hangs around with that girl superhero Diamond, and she looks kinda like that girl staying with you."

From the sitting-room, Colin could hear his mother's

mobile phone ringing. "Judy, it's just a coincidence that Kid Titan looks like me."

There was a brief pause. "If you really *were* him, you wouldn't tell me anyway, would you?"

Damn it! Colin thought. "Probably not. I mean, I barely even know you."

"Well, that's because you never talk to anyone. You're too shy. You know my friend Emma? The short one with red hair? Well she fancies you!"

Another voice squealed, "Don't tell him *that!*"

Despite the seriousness of the situation, Colin couldn't help being drawn in. "Really?" He'd seen Emma around and had always thought she was sort of cute.

Behind Judy, Emma was saying, "Oh my God! Oh my God!"

"Yeah," Judy said. "You could actually try *talking* to her sometime. Hold on, I'll put her on."

Colin began, "No, wait…" but it was too late.

Emma came on. "Erm… Hi, Colin." She was almost drowned out by a loud burst of giggles.

"Hi," Colin said, thankful that he was on the phone and she couldn't see how much he was blushing.

At that moment, the sitting-room door opened and his father stepped out. "Hang up the phone."

Colin covered the mouthpiece. "In a minute!"

"*Now*, Colin!"

With his father standing there watching him, Colin

said into the phone, "Sorry, Emma, I have to go."

"Oh. OK then."

"Bye," Colin said, then hung up and instantly regretted it. *I should have said that I'd see her soon or something like that! Now she's going to think I don't like her!*

Mr Wagner reached out and unplugged the line from the phone. "We've been talking, Colin. We're all going to have to leave here. It won't be long before someone figures out that Renata must be Diamond. Then someone will realise that your mother and I used to be Energy and Titan." He shrugged. "If that happens none of us will be safe."

"There must be something we can do to sort things out!"

"There's nothing. There's no going back. I'm going to phone Joshua Dalton, tell him to arrange transport out of here and somewhere for us to stay. Ever since California, he's been asking us to go and work for him."

"What does he do, anyway?"

"I'm actually not sure. Some kind of top-secret work for the US government."

"So... We're going back to America?"

Warren nodded, then smiled. "Yeah. But at least *this* time we're not being kidnapped."

After much badgering from Danny, his mother had finally agreed to allow him to take Niall to see Façade. She laid down the rules: "You are not to stay for more than an hour. You are to go straight there and come straight back. Do *not* invite him for Christmas dinner – I don't care how lonely he seems! And don't go telling him that everything will be all right and that I'll give in eventually!"

Having agreed to all the rules, Danny and Niall pulled on their winter coats and set off for the bus stop.

Danny was thankful that the bus was nearly empty because Niall couldn't stop talking about his discovery that Colin Wagner and Renata Soliz were superheroes.

By the time they got to the last stop, Danny was just about ready to throttle his little brother.

"Right," Danny said, taking Niall aside. "There's lot of people around, so do not talk about Colin or Renata, OK?"

Niall nodded. "OK. But, right, what if…"

Danny raised his eyes. "Niall, just keep quiet, OK? And stick close."

They made their way through the market square. As Christmas was approaching, most of the shops were still open, and the square was filled with people either laden with packed bags or carrying absolutely nothing and looking like they were on the verge of panic.

Danny shuddered as a freezing wind whipped through

the square. He glanced down at the zipper on his coat. *Should have worn the other jacket. Buttons are a lot easier to manage with one hand.* "Niall? Help me out here, OK?"

As Niall zipped up the coat, Danny tried to ignore the looks of the people passing by. He heard a muttered comment, "That poor boy!"

I didn't know how lucky I was when I had two arms. I tied my shoelaces every single day and never even thought about it. I could open a bag of crisps without having to use my teeth. Now it's all I can do to get dressed in the mornings.

Danny's mother had bought him a new pair of trainers with Velcro straps. That should have made things easier, but it only made him more aware of what he had lost.

As they passed Morton's Electrical Goods, Niall stopped and stared. The window was packed with dozens of television sets, all showing the same film: Kid Titan and Diamond rescuing the shoppers from the fire.

"Come on," Danny said. "We don't have time to hang around."

They were just about to turn away when the screens changed to show the photo of Kid Titan without his mask. *Oh God*, Danny thought. *It's not going to be easy for him. But at least the photo's not great quality, so I suppose things could be worse.*

And then a caption appeared below the photo: "Colin Wagner, 13, AKA Kid Titan."

Danny's blood froze. "No..." he whispered.

Niall turned to him. "What does AKA mean?"

"What?" Danny asked numbly.

"AKA Kid Titan, it says."

"It stands for Also Known As."

Around them, people had stopped. Someone in the crowd said, "Colin Wagner... Doesn't he go to school with our Philip? His mother's one of the teachers there, right?"

Danny whispered to Niall, "Let's just go. Quietly, OK?"

They turned away, stepping carefully through the growing crowd. Niall kept glancing back towards the store.

"Come *on*!" Danny said. "Niall!"

His brother had stopped walking and was staring open-mouthed at the largest wide-screen television.

The screen now showed a decade-old photograph of Titan and Quantum. The caption beneath read, "Titan, AKA Warren Wagner. Quantum, AKA Paul Joseph Cooper."

For the first time in his life, Danny swore in front of his little brother. He grabbed Niall's arm and tried to pull him away.

At that moment the screen changed once again, and showed the same captions over much more recent photos of Warren and Façade.

"Danny! Look at that! It's *Dad*!"

Danny quickly glanced about: a lot of people had heard Niall and turned in their direction.

Niall kept talking: "It's Dad and Mr Wagner! Danny, it's saying that they used to be—"

Pushing Niall ahead of him, Danny said, "Just shut up and run!" *How did this happen? How could someone have found out so quickly?*

A man stopped to block their path. It was Mr Leopold, who lived in a neighbouring flat. "Danny and Niall! Did you see that? About your dad? It's not true, is it?"

"No," Danny said. "Of course not!" He tried to dodge past his neighbour. "We've got to go..."

"Is that why your mother threw him out? She found out about his past?"

Danny looked around. More and more people were stopping to stare at them. They knew his father was the manager of the local supermarket, and everyone would have heard about how PJ Cooper's son had lost his right arm in an accident.

"Your friend Colin," Mr Leopold was saying, "he's Kid Titan, so then that cousin of his must be Diamond. What's her name again?"

Niall stepped closer to Danny as the crowd advanced.

"It's all just some stupid hoax," Danny said, thinking quickly. "There's a guy who works in the TV station who used to go to school with our dad. They're always playing pranks on each other."

Someone said, "You expect us to believe that?"

If I had my powers, Danny thought, *I'd just pick Niall up and run away from this lot faster than they could see.*

A woman Danny didn't recognise pushed her way through the crowd. "Listen... I'm having some trouble with gangs of kids in the area, always hanging around. Maybe your dad could do something about it?"

"I don't like this," Niall said in a low voice. "I want to go home!"

Me too, Danny thought. Aloud, he said, "It'll be OK, Niall. Just stick close to me."

Then an elderly man approached. "Quantum saved my life, about fifteen years ago! Pulled me out of the way of a speeding truck. I never got a chance to thank him!" He stretched out his right hand, offering it to Danny to shake, then instantly pulled it back when he saw that Danny didn't have a right hand of his own. "Oh. Sorry."

"Please," Danny said. "Let us go! It's all a mistake! My father is *not* Quantum!"

A man asked, "You're Quantum's kids? For real?"

"No, we're not!"

"Ten years since the superheroes all disappeared," the man said. "Ten *years*! We all thought they were dead, but now..." The man's face took on a snarl. "I *know* PJ Cooper!

I used to work for him in the supermarket! Four years back my sister was knocked down by a couple of drugged-up joy-riders. She's going to be in a wheelchair for the rest of her life! If Quantum had been around, he never would have let things get that bad."

The man next to him yelled, "Where the hell were your dad and his mates when my estate was being terrorised by junkies? Did they just decide that normal people weren't worth saving any more?"

"Of course not!" Danny said. "I'm telling you, this is all a mistake!"

"That's what happened, isn't it?" a young woman asked. "They gave up on us. They think they're better than we are!"

Mr Leopold said, "All right, everyone just calm down! I've known the Coopers for years! They're good people and taking your anger out on these boys won't solve anything!"

"Yeah!" someone in the crowd yelled. "Quantum and Titan and the others saved the world dozens of times! They don't owe us anything! We owe them!"

Danny looked around. He and Niall were completely surrounded. *There's hundreds of them!*

Then a large man pushed his way to the front of the crowd, shoving people aside. He stopped in front of Mr Leopold. "Outta my way!"

Mr Leopold swallowed. "What do you want?"

The man pointed at Danny. "His old man owes *me*.

61

Caught me breaking and entering. I was inside for four and a half years! Du you have any idea what that was like, Cooper?" he roared at Danny. "It was *hell*! Day after day of eating the same tasteless crap, sleeping in a cramped, rat-infested cell, knowing that at any minute you could be stabbed in the back by some moron who's got a grudge against you!"

Danny said, "You can't blame my father for that! If you were stupid enough to break into people's houses then you deserved to be in prison!"

"So it *is* true!" The man stepped closer. "Don't think that just because you're missing an arm I'm going to go easy on you!"

There was a gasp from the crowd, but the man ignored it.

Oh God, this guy is going to flatten me! The man charged, his powerful fists raised. Danny pushed his brother to one side. *Come on*, he told himself. *Use your super-speed! The power might not be completely gone!* He tried to remember what it had felt like to switch into slow-time mode: a prickling sensation at the back of his head, the way everything else seemed to slow down, the way the sounds became quiet and low.

It wasn't working.

He quickly stepped aside, out of the man's reach for the moment, and glanced around. There was a ripple of excitement running through the crowd, but the people closest to him didn't seem inclined to help.

Only one thing for it, he decided. He took a deep breath, squared his shoulders and stared the large man in the eye. "Before you do anything, I have to warn you."

The man snarled at him. "What are you talkin' about?"

"Yes, my father was Quantum. He could move faster than anything you can imagine. He was able to move so fast that he could pass through solid objects. And superhuman powers can be inherited. Now, I understand your anger, so I'm willing to let this go. You turn around and walk away right now and we'll say no more about it. But if you really want to return to prison, then go ahead. Hit me, if you can. If you're willing to pay the price."

The man hesitated.

"Or you can do the wise thing, the *right* thing, and turn away now." Danny was vaguely aware of a greater commotion in the crowd, but didn't want to take his eyes off the large man.

The man barked a short, cruel laugh. "You little punk! You almost had me going there for a second! And for that, you're going to pay!" He lashed out at Danny with his fist.

Danny flinched and closed his eyes, but the fist didn't connect. *Did I do it? Did I just dodge his fist?* He opened his eyes to see that the large man was now lying on the ground, face down. Standing over him was a tall, powerful-looking man in steel armour.

The crowd of people had backed away considerably, but now began to surge towards the armoured man.

"Stop right there!" the armoured man's voice boomed out.

Everyone froze.

"These boys are under my protection! Anyone who wants to hurt them will have to go through me first!" The armoured man turned to Danny. "Mr Cooper? Pick up your brother and hold on to him."

Danny did so, then the metal-clad man scooped the two of them up in his arms. There was a brief flare from the man's jetpack and suddenly they were soaring away from the crowds.

The armoured man looked down at Niall's terrified face. "Hi there. You must be Niall. My name is Solomon Cord. Or, if you like, you can call me Paragon."

5

"**GOD, IT DIDN'T** take long for the word to get around," Renata Soliz said, peering through a gap in the sitting-room curtains.

Outside, the normally quiet street was filled with people: friends, neighbours, reporters and police officers trying to hold everyone back. An enterprising ice cream man had stopped his truck across the road and was doing great business despite the freezing weather.

Mr Wagner had been forced to disconnect the doorbell, but that hadn't stopped people from banging on the doors and windows. It was only when the local police sergeant had stationed two officers outside the front door and another two in the back garden that the crowd had finally calmed down a little.

Renata turned to Colin. "Bags all packed?"

"Yeah. Everything I could think of. You know what's going to happen, don't you? Once we're gone and the police leave, that lot are going to break in and look for souvenirs. Someone's going to make a lot of money flogging our stuff on eBay."

She smiled. "I think we might need a good lawyer."

"*I* was thinking that what we need is a good agent."

Renata collapsed into the armchair and turned on the television set. Almost every channel showed a different view of the Wagners' house. "Hey! He's not a reporter! He's the weather man! They're *all* getting in on the action!"

Colin's mother entered, carrying two small bags. "Is this all you have, Renata?"

"That's everything, Mrs Wagner. For once I'm glad I don't have much stuff."

"How did they find out about you and Dad?" Colin asked his mother.

"I wish I knew."

"You didn't wear a mask when you were Energy," Renata said. "Maybe someone *always* thought that you looked like her, and when they found out about Colin..." She pointed to the television set. "Col, isn't that one of your friends from school? He's giving an interview!"

"Yeah... And look: that kid in the background. That's little Peter what's-his-name from down the road. God, I hope they don't let *that* slimy little turd on the television!"

Renata turned up the sound. Malcolm O'Neill was talking to the reporter and kept glancing at the camera. "Yeah, I've known Colin for years and years. I'm probably his best friend."

"Some friend!" Colin said. "He nicked half a Mars Bar from me last year!"

"And did you know about his powers?" the reporter asked.

"I always suspected that he was different," Malcolm said. "Colin can't kick a football to save his life, you know? I mean, he's definitely the absolutely worst player in the whole school. Ever. Which is saying something because nearly all of them are crap, except me. So what Colin was probably doing was just pretending to be rubbish so that no one would suspect that he's a superhuman."

"That's not true!" Colin said. "I genuinely *am* rubbish!" He paused and frowned. "No, that's not what I meant."

The reporter asked, "And what can you tell us about Diamond, Kid Titan's girlfriend?"

Renata and Colin both yelled, *"Girlfriend?"* at the same time.

"I only met her once," Malcolm said. "Her name is... uh... Romana, I think. She's supposed to be Colin's cousin, but she puts on, like, a really fake American accent. As if anyone would be fooled by that."

Renata turned off the television set. "Idiot!" she muttered.

"You OK?" Colin asked.

"I will be, once we get to the States. I'll finally be able to go home."

Caroline said, "We've been over this before, Renata. It's not going to be that simple. Your parents don't know that you're still alive."

"We have to tell them at some stage!"

"I know, love, but not yet. Maybe when all this calms down."

"If it ever *does* calm down," Colin said.

❊

Mr Sheng's bodyguards stepped aside as the scarred man strode into the office. They knew he was unarmed; they also knew that being without weapons didn't make him any less dangerous.

Sitting behind a polished ebony desk on which was nothing but a large flat-screen computer monitor, a keyboard and a mouse, Mr Sheng smiled. He was old and extremely thin, with an abundance of loose, hanging skin around his neck, the sign of someone who had lost a lot of weight much too quickly.

Behind him stood Junior, pale and nervous, unable to look Dioxin in the eye.

"All is well," Mr Sheng said. "The meeting was abandoned. Our rival failed to appear. This has made her appear uninterested in the agreements. We will capitalise on this, use it to our advantage."

"Glad to hear it," Dioxin said, "considering the stupid stunt your son here pulled this morning."

"He will be punished accordingly."

"And?" Dioxin asked.

The old man frowned.

"I'm waiting for an apology for his actions."

"My son has already apologised to you. I do not believe that an apology from myself is necessary."

"It wouldn't hurt," Dioxin said. He leaned forward, spreading his scarred hands on the desk. "Look, Sheng. It's business. I understand that. But your son not only tried to kill me – which is bad enough – he also insulted my intelligence *and* my reputation. So... don't apologise if you don't want to. I don't care. But you should at least thank me for allowing him to live."

"Then you have my thanks, Mr Dioxin."

"And can I have my money, too?"

At a signal from Mr Sheng, one of the bodyguards handed Dioxin a slim white envelope.

"Two million US dollars, as agreed," Sheng said. "Plus one thousand dollars to pay for the damage to your automobile."

Dioxin opened the envelope and pulled out a single slip of paper on which was printed two seventeen-digit sequences of letters and numbers. He pulled the keyboard closer and swivelled the computer monitor so that it was facing him. The screen already showed the website of the international bank Sheng used to transfer funds. Dioxin quickly entered his details, then keyed in the two sequences of numbers. Seconds later, the balance in his account increased by two million one thousand dollars.

"A pleasure doing business with you, Sheng. Next time, the price is doubled."

The old man nodded. "Of course."

Using the mouse, Dioxin clicked on the website's 'Log-off' button, and was about to push the monitor aside when he spotted something in the corner of the screen, in a small box labelled 'RSS News'. Among the Chinese characters there was a single English phrase: 'Titan Unmasked.'

"What the hell...?" Dioxin clicked on the link and a window opened to show an old photograph of Titan and Energy, side by side with the wedding photograph of a young married couple.

Dioxin turned to Junior Sheng. "What *is* this?"

"Internet."

"I know that. What does it say? Translate for me."

Haltingly, Junior translated the text on screen: "Mr Warren Wagner, revealed today as the true identity of the long-missing superhero Titan. His super-powered son is the new Titan. Also revealed are the two sons of Quantum, rescued from a crowd by the former hero Paragon. Mr Reginald Kinsella, newly-appointed leader of the Trutopian organisation, has offered the new heroes sanctuary among his people, in exchange for their help in saving the Earth from evil, poverty and corruption."

"Enough." Dioxin turned back to the old man. "Let's make a deal, Sheng. You get me all the information you can on these people, and arrange for immediate passage to the US, and I'll transfer the money back to you. Hell, I'll even forget that your boy tried to kill me."

Mr Sheng considered this. "Agreed. But what interest do these new heroes have for you?"

Dioxin stared at the screen. "I've got some old scores to settle..."

⚙

Warren Wagner ended the call on his mobile phone, then turned it off so that no one would be able to ring through. "Good news, for a change," he said to his family and Renata. "Josh says that our passage has been fully cleared by the government. The transport's already on the way. One of his people is going to stay here and take care of the house until we can arrange to sell it."

"What about the Coopers?" Colin asked.

"Danny and Niall were picked up in town and their mother's about to be collected from the flat. There'll be someone watching their place, too."

"Mr Wagner," Renata said, "I don't really like the idea

of working with Josh. Not after what happened with his brother."

"Josh is a lot different to Max," Warren said. "He's OK. You met him, didn't you? I mean, before you were frozen."

"Yeah. We captured Dioxin together." Ten years earlier, Renata had been in her solid form when Ragnarök's power-damping machine had stripped all the superhumans of their powers. She had remained frozen until a couple of months ago, when Maxwell Dalton had tried to duplicate Ragnarök's machine: an accidental power-surge from the machine had somehow freed Renata from her solid state. Now, Renata was technically twenty-four, but physically still only fourteen. "Josh was only about twenty-three then, I think. But everyone thought that Max was OK, too and look how that turned out. He was prepared to kill thousands of people just because of one of Quantum's visions."

Colin said, "I'm willing to give Josh a chance. You can't judge someone just because his brother is a nutter. Besides, it was Josh who sorted everything out after what happened in California."

"What about the Trutopians?" Renata asked. "From what Reginald Kinsella was saying, we might be better off going to them instead. They're trying to save the world without using violence."

"Good luck to them," Colin said. "But they can do it

72

without *my* help. There was a documentary about them the other week. You know how they keep the peace? They have a system of points. You park your car illegally, that's one point. Nick something from a shop, that's three points. Play your stereo too loud, that's another point. If you build up ten points, they throw you out. They just barge into your house, round up the whole family, put you on a truck and drive you to the gates. You know what that is? A dictatorship!"

"It's not a dictatorship if there's no dictator," Renata replied. "It's just peace at the cost of a little freedom. And it's not like the people don't know all that when they join."

Colin's mother sighed. "Can't the two of you agree on *anything*?" To her husband, she said, "Two days ago they had a fight over whether the top part of a slice of bread was better than the bottom part!"

Warren laughed.

"Oh, *that* helps!" his wife said.

Under his breath, Colin muttered, "Top."

"Bottom!" Renata said. "And I'll tell you *why*—"

"Enough!" Caroline said. "The two of you, go upstairs and check your rooms one last time. Make sure there's nothing there that you can't leave behind."

Reluctantly, Renata and Colin trudged up the stairs. They stopped on the landing and Renata said, "I think your mother is really worried."

"The two of them are. I suppose we should be, too. But it'll all turn out all right, won't it?"

"How would *I* know?"

Colin shrugged and went into his bedroom. He stood just inside the door, looking around. *Schoolbag – won't be needing that for a while.* He dropped to his knees, fished around under the bed and pulled out Toto, the ancient, frayed teddy bear that he'd had since his first birthday. Toto was covered in dust and cobwebs. Colin stared at him for a few moments, wondering whether he should be feeling some sort of sentimental attachment, then shrugged and tossed the bear aside.

He resumed searching and found a bundle of comics, two Matchbox cars with only three wheels between them and a lot more dust.

"Find anything?" Renata said from the doorway.

Colin stood up. "Nah."

"Oh, you have a teddy!" She picked it up off the floor and tried to brush the dust off.

He blushed. "Oh, that old thing. I was going to throw that out."

"What's his name?"

"Toto."

"After Dorothy's dog?"

"Probably. I can't remember. I've had him a long time." He noticed the way Renata was holding the bear.

"He's yours, if you want him."

"Well, he's not in bad condition. It'd be a shame to throw him out. I could give him to my niece, if I ever get to meet her. I told you that Samantha has a two-year-old, didn't I?"

"Yeah. Your sister's, what, twenty-two now?"

"And my brother is nineteen. Which means that he's five years older than me and he's five years younger."

"All your friends will be grown up, too."

Renata nodded, hugging Toto close. "I know. But I try not to think about it too much."

Colin smiled. "Does that work?"

"Not really. I keep thinking that it must be absolutely *hell* for my parents. Every year the whole world has a great big celebration for Mystery Day and all they can think of is that it's the day their eldest daughter disappeared."

"You went missing on the same day that all the other superhumans did, so maybe they figured out that you were a superhuman, too."

"No, they didn't. Josh said that a lot of families contacted the authorities after Mystery Day, asking whether their loved ones might have been superhumans. My family didn't. It probably never crossed their minds."

"You're going to go home even if my parents and the others don't think you should, aren't you?" Colin asked.

"They wouldn't be able to stop me; I'm probably the strongest person in the world. You're the only one who even comes close and I know *you* won't try to stop me. Will you?"

Colin shook his head. "Of course not! But you have to..." Colin froze. His superhuman hearing picked up a familiar sound from far away. "Transport's here."

They ran back downstairs, Renata still clutching the bear. "It's here, Dad!" Colin shouted from the hall, as he picked up the largest of the suitcases.

He opened the front door and ignored the sudden onslaught of camera flashes and the cheering. The two police officers turned to look at him.

"Thanks," Colin said.

"That's what they pay us the big bucks for," one of them replied. "But I should be thanking you. My wife's cousin Dave was one of the people you rescued from the toy store tonight."

"The shop assistant?"

"That's him. You and Diamond saved his life."

"Is he OK?"

"Cut and bruises, a few minor burns. He's a lot better than he would have been if you two hadn't been there..." The police officer's voice trailed off as he became aware of a low rumbling noise. He glanced upwards and saw a large black vehicle descending slowly from the night sky.

"What on earth is *that* thing?"

"That's a StratoTruck," Colin said.

"I want one of those!"

The StratoTruck was about the size of a transport helicopter, but shorter and wider. It had short wings at the back, and was powered by four large turbine engines that could pivot to provide forward thrust as well as lift.

As Colin's parents and Renata filed out behind him, the StratoTruck gently settled on the road, the down-draft from its powerful turbines blowing dust over everything. The craft was immediately surrounded by neighbours and reporters, all taking photographs or trying to touch it.

The StratoTruck's hatch opened, and a burly man wearing combat gear and full body-armour climbed out and strode up to Warren. "Titan?" he asked, his voice gruff and low.

"That's me," Warren said, shaking hands with the man. "So you're house-sitting for us?"

The man nodded. "Four tours of duty with the Marines. I'm an expert in weapons and security. I'm the best man for this job. I give you my word that while I am here, no unauthorised person will gain access to your home."

"That's nice to hear," Caroline said. "There's food in the fridge and I've left a list of phone numbers just in case anything happens."

Colin said, "You can use the video if you like but you're not allowed to have your friends around."

Renata laughed, but the soldier didn't.

"Get in," Warren said to the teenagers.

Colin climbed on board and saw that Danny's mother was already there. "Where's Danny and Niall?" he asked as Renata passed the bags to him. Mrs Cooper didn't reply; she looked extremely angry about something.

Then the StratoTruck's pilot turned around and said, "We're going to pick them up next."

Colin almost dropped one of the suitcases. "*Façade*? What are you doing here?"

"Don't worry, I know how to fly this thing."

"That's not what I meant! I just thought..."

"I'm as much a part of this as you are, Colin. Now get the others on board and strap yourselves in."

Warren and Façade exchanged reasonably courteous nods, but Caroline refused to even look at him.

"All right then," Façade said. "Everyone ready?"

As the hatch swung closed, and the StratoTruck's powerful turbines whined into life, Colin peered out through one of the little windows and realised that he was almost face-to-face with Brian McDonald, who was staring back at him with a betrayed look on his face. Colin felt a knot twist in his stomach. *Oh God... I should have told him!*

The police officers began to usher everyone away from the StratoTruck.

Colin looked at Brian one last time and mouthed the words, "I'm sorry. Goodbye."

Then the StratoTruck lifted off the ground, spun about and soared into the night.

6

AFTER DANNY, NIALL and Paragon had been picked up, Façade piloted the StratoTruck to the west and ramped it up to full speed.

The interior of the vehicle was not large, but it was just about able to accommodate all the passengers, including Niall, who had fallen asleep shortly after take-off and was now stretched out across two seats.

"How fast *is* this thing, Dad?" Danny asked. He noticed his mother glaring at him and quickly added, "I mean Façade."

"Top speed is a little over MACH two," Facade replied. "MACH one is the speed of sound at sea level; seven hundred and sixty-one miles per hour. We can travel twice that fast."

Renata asked, "What's our destination?"

"Kansas."

"So what's in Kansas?"

Solomon Cord said, "You'll find out when we get there. Until then, no more questions!"

"Just one," Colin said. "Why did you decide to become Paragon again?"

Solomon Cord stared out of the hatch's tiny window. "I thought I could escape the past, Colin. I was wrong. After Max Dalton betrayed us, I realised that he knew everything about me. *Everything*. He knew where my daughters went to school, who their friends were, where my wife's mother lived, what my brother did for a living."

"But you told me you'd destroyed your armour."

Cord nodded. "I did. It was practically ruined after the last battle against Ragnarök anyway. This" – he thumped the armour on his chest – "is just a prototype." He smiled. "The new version will be much more powerful. Now everyone get some sleep! We've got a long journey ahead of us."

Ignoring his mother's disapproving look, Danny climbed into the co-pilot's seat. "Façade... How do you know how to fly something like this?"

Façade smiled. "I used to be in the US Air Force. I was a test pilot."

"Seriously?"

"Seriously."

"But—"

"Danny!" Solomon Cord said. "I said no more questions!"

Gradually, Colin became aware that someone was saying his name. He opened his eyes and looked around. Danny was staring at him. "What?"

"We're almost there."

Colin looked out of the StratoTruck's window, but all he could see was darkness. He concentrated, focussing his eyes. He still wasn't sure how his night-vision worked, but somehow it did: the landscape outside became brighter, almost as though a weak sun had suddenly appeared.

"What can you see?" Danny asked.

"Everything's covered in snow. It's pretty flat out there... There's a lot of fields, a couple of lakes, a few small hills."

Façade's voice called out, "Hold on tight! We're about to bank to the right! You should be able to see the lights of Topeka on your left, about twenty-five kilometres away. That's a little over fifteen miles."

Colin climbed into the co-pilot's seat. "There are some hills ahead. Can't see much else. Wait! There's a platform in the middle of them and there's a guy standing on it. He's freezing. Stamping his feet to keep warm."

"You can *see* him?" Façade said.

"Sure."

"Amazing... But that's not a platform. That's a roof."

Façade picked up the radio. "Josh... Hit the lights."

The StratoTruck crested the top of a small hill, just as the building ahead was illuminated. Through the thick flurries of snow, the passengers could see their destination: an enormous snow-covered stone structure with sloping sides. It looked almost like an Egyptian pyramid with the top third removed. Close to the top of the building were two rows of large windows, and far below, at ground level, was a covered entrance.

Manoeuvring slowly and carefully through the snow storm, the StratoTruck touched down on the wide, flat roof. "All right," Cord said. "It's freezing out there so no hanging around! Grab your bags and let's go, people!"

The hatch opened and the wind howled through the vehicle. Colin was the last to leave – it didn't seem all that cold to him – and took a few seconds to look around. He guessed that the roof of the building was about the length of a football pitch in each direction. It was almost featureless except for a wide stairway that led down to a set of steel doors and a hangar that was just large enough to take the StratoTruck.

"Come on, Colin!" his father shouted from the top of the stairwell.

Colin hurried over to the others and followed them down to the doors.

As he got closer, he saw that the man he'd spotted

from almost a mile away was wrapped in a thick coat. He was smiling at them, his cheeks red with the cold.

"Hi, I'm Josh Dalton." Josh was in his early thirties, with thinning hair and a touch of flabbiness around his face and neck. "So everyone's here? Great!" He pointed to a glowing glass panel next to the doors. "Hand-print reader," he explained. "These doors are impossible to open to anyone not registered on the system. Right now, you're all being scanned to check your identities. It'll take a couple of minutes."

"What other security does this place have?" Warren asked.

"Very thick walls," Josh said, with a sly smile. "Seriously. The whole shell of the building is four-foot-thick concrete reinforced with steel beams. Its pyramidal shape means that structurally it's very sound. The windows are two-inch Plexiglas, completely bullet-proof. Nothing short of a nuclear weapon is going to breach this building. This is the *only* way in; the doorway on the ground level is fake. Inside, every room has only one doorway and all the doors can be sealed remotely. In the unlikely event of someone breaking in, we just seal all the doors and they're trapped."

"What about people? I mean, actual human security guards?"

"We have two security specialists; they're the men

84

currently guarding your homes." Josh smiled. "With our system, we don't really *need* security guards."

Rose Cooper said, "That's all very well, Mr Dalton, but locking all the doors doesn't sound too safe if there's a fire!"

"Every room is equipped with at least two CDH delivery systems. CDH is Carbon Dioxide Hydrate. If a fire is detected the system shoots out hundreds of tiny CDH pellets. They react to the heat and release water and carbon dioxide." Josh smiled again. "Trust me on this, Rose... Your boys will be safe here!"

The glass panel beeped once and a green light came on. Josh pressed his hand against the panel and the doors slid quietly open. "Ladies and gentlemen, welcome to your new home, headquarters and general base of operations. Welcome to Sakkara."

7

WHILE THE OTHERS were being shown to their rooms, Solomon Cord took Colin, Renata and Danny on a brief tour of Sakkara.

Their first stop was what Cord called "Nostalgia Central" – a large, mostly empty room that contained a dozen life-sized mannequins, each in its own glass case. Most of the mannequins were bare, but three of them wore replicas of the costumes once worn by The High Command.

"Josh says he's been planning to turn this room into a sort of superhero museum," Cord explained. "If you ask me, it's a little self-indulgent."

Colin stopped in front of the mannequin wearing Max Dalton's costume. "Doesn't look much like him."

"Yeah," Danny said. "Shouldn't it be wearing a prison uniform?"

Renata walked around the blank mannequins and said, "Hey, most of these things have names on them! Apex, Titan, there's Energy over there! What's this empty one for...? Oh." Her face fell.

"What is it?" Danny asked, walking over to her.

"It's me." Renata pointed to the small plaque on the base of the empty glass case. "Diamond. Real name unknown. Why is there no mannequin in it?"

Solomon Cord said, "When you got frozen, everyone thought you were dead. Josh was going to put you there."

Renata shivered. "God, that's just creepy!"

"Max had put your body into storage. Josh said that he'd never been able to figure out a way of getting you back without alerting his brother as to what he was up to."

"So Max didn't know that Josh was involved?"

"No," Cord said. "Max was too well-known to be brought in. With a place like this, even the slightest hint that something is going on and it would become public knowledge."

Cord led them back out into the stark, empty corridors. "Josh knows a lot more about the history of Sakkara than I do. But I can fill in some of the background for you... A little over forty years ago the US government established a facility for research into superhuman activities. They tried to understand why some people developed powers. Was there any connection between these people? Perhaps some similarities on a genetic level? Had any of them been exposed to unusual radioactive or biological substances?"

"And that's this place?" Colin asked.

"No. After the attack on Ragnarök's battle-tank, when the superhumans all lost their powers, that facility was officially disbanded. The people who ran it were blamed for everything that Ragnarök did."

"Right," Renata said. "Because he was their prisoner and they let him escape."

"That's just the *official* story," Solomon said, then paused. "The man who became Ragnarök was not a prisoner. He worked for the facility. He was the only one who had any real understanding of how the powers worked. He was involved in certain experiments – I'm not sure exactly what, Josh won't tell me – and he wanted to take those experiments further. When he was refused permission, he left. Disappeared for years before resurfacing as Ragnarök. At some stage before the last battle, much of the research carried out at the facility somehow found its way into Max Dalton's hands. It's generally assumed that the information was stolen by Quantum, under Max's control."

"Damn it," Danny muttered.

"Regardless of how it happened, the truth is that the facility was not disbanded. This place was built and everything was relocated here. Outside of those who work here, only a handful of people in the political and military world know of Sakkara's existence."

"Sakkara..." Renata said. "The name sounds familiar."

"Well, it's not a name I would have chosen," Cord said. "About four thousand years ago Sakkara was part of the necropolis of Memphis, the Egyptian capital during the first and second dynasties."

"A necropolis," Danny said. "Remind me again what that is?"

"A tomb. Whoever chose the name Sakkara was obviously a fan of ancient Egypt. Either that or they didn't know the names of any other pyramids."

"So how *did* Josh get involved?" Colin asked.

"He's a smart guy, plus he used to be a superhuman, which made him doubly qualified." Solomon paused. "He wasn't their first choice. I was, but I didn't want the job. Until a couple of years ago, Sakkara was run by an Air Force man, General Scott Piers. When he retired, Josh was appointed Chief of Operations. His primary goals are to continue his research into the superhuman phenomenon, and to track down and investigate any other potential superhumans."

Renata said, "Mr Cord, I don't like the idea of working for a government."

"Right now there's no other option," Solomon replied.

"There's the Trutopians. That guy Kinsella wants us to work for him."

"You don't know anything about him, Renata."

"We don't really know much about this place either," she replied.

"At Sakkara we have resources and equipment you wouldn't believe. We will train you three and the others. Trust me: this is the best approach. Between myself, Warren, Caroline, Josh and Façade we have a *lot* of superhuman experience."

Their next stop was a large dining hall that took up half the top floor of the building. Some of the tables were occupied by people in white coats, who couldn't help staring at the teenagers as they stood in the doorway.

"Dining hall," Cord said. "All the meals are served here. There are forty-six people in Sakkara, so it can get pretty crowded at times."

Danny walked over to one of the large windows and looked out. He could see the lights of Topeka, the capital city of the state of Kansas. The heavy snow clouds above the city were orange and yellow from the city's lights. "Sol, I can't believe that a building this large – and this close to a city – could stay a secret."

"The people who designed this place were smart; they landscaped the entire area so that unless you're right next to it, the building can only be seen from the air. And if anyone *does* see it from the air, it looks just like a water-treatment plant. In fact, part of the facility is given over to that function, just in case anyone ever investigates. We take a minimal amount of power from the local grid; the rest of it is supplied by a geothermal energy converter."

"A geo-what?" Colin asked.

"It takes the heat from deep within the Earth and converts it to electricity."

Renata asked, "Couldn't someone just find the place by following the StratoTruck?"

"We're right in the heart of a no-fly zone; any aircraft coming within two miles will be ordered to change course by air traffic control."

"And if they don't?"

"Then there's an Air Force Base not far from here. The ATC people think that's what the no-fly zone is protecting. Everything we need – food, clothing, electronics, whatever – comes to us through disguised channels. Basically, unless you actually work here, there's no way to tell that it exists."

Colin said, "I know I'm going to hate myself for saying this, but... what about school?"

"We have a full-time tutor," Cord replied. "And your mother's a teacher, too, right? She'll be able to make sure you get all the education you need."

Renata turned to him. "Mr Cord, how long are we going to be here?"

Cord shrugged. "I don't know. Come on, I'll show you the rest of the place."

He led them to a dark, windowless room in the heart of the building. It was filled with large white metal objects, each over two metres tall. "The computer room," Cord explained. "Seven custom-built machines linked to a bank of Cray XD4s. I'm told that this is the single greatest concentration of computing power in the country."

"Wow!" Colin said, walking around one of the featureless white boxes. "What do you need them for?"

"Number crunching and data processing. We have permanent high-speed links to NASA and most of the large universities in the US. Josh tells me that's one of the ways this place can keep running: we process their data for them and charge them for it. There's stuff that goes on here that even *he* doesn't have access to."

"Yeah, but can you play games on them?" Danny asked.

Renata walked over to one of the computer terminals. On screen was a complex, rotating, three-dimensional image. "What's this?"

"DNA analysis," Cord said. "That's one of Josh's pet projects. They're still trying to figure out whether superhuman powers come from your DNA or somewhere else."

"Where else *could* the powers come from?"

"Aliens," Danny said. "At least, that's what Niall thinks."

"Hey, look at this!" Colin called from the far side of the room. "There's lots of videos of the old superheroes back when they had their powers!" He used the computer's mouse to select a video from the list. "It's..." He looked up at Danny. "It's your father. It's Quantum."

Danny and Renata watched over Colin's shoulder. The computer monitor showed a paused video of a dark room with a single, white-clad figure sitting in the middle. Quantum's hood had been pulled back and he bore a startling resemblance to Danny.

"How old is this?" Danny asked.

Colin checked the date in the corner of the screen. "Fourteen years and..." Colin paused. "This is the day you were born."

Cord said, "Wait a second! That terminal should have been locked!" He leaned over Colin's shoulder. "Danny, if that video is what I think it is, it might not be a good idea to watch it. It concerns the prophecy."

Danny bit his lip. "The one about me?"

Cord nodded.

Colin looked at Danny, his finger hovering over the mouse's button.

Danny nodded. "Play it!"

Colin hit the button and the video began to play.

On screen, Quantum was rocking back and forth. A voice from an unseen person asked, "What happened?"

"Twenty-two minutes ago," Quantum said, his voice weak. "Eight pounds exactly. A boy. He's perfect. Ten fingers, ten toes. He didn't cry. That's strange, isn't it? Don't all new-born babies cry? He's..."

"He's what?"

"We have to do something, Max. My son... I saw something when I held him."

"What did you see, Paul?"

"The end. The end of everything. He was there, leading them. None of us were there. None of us. Do you understand what that means?"

"I'm afraid I..."

"You *should* be afraid, Max. We should all be afraid. The end is coming and my son is at the heart of it." Quantum stopped rocking, leaned his head back and closed his eyes. "There's war and death. The skies are black with smoke and dust. The ground is red with blood. The seas are burning. There's anger in him, a raging fury that nothing can stop. No, his friends are there. They fight for those who can't fight back."

"When will this happen?"

Quantum shook his head. "Difficult to say... He's tall, strong, muscular. A teenager at least. But not much older than that. Why can't I see his eyes? No, he's gone now... But there's something else. A rip."

"A rip?"

"A chasm. Something is torn."

"Paul, that doesn't make any sense."

"Ah... I see him again. He knows, Max. The war is coming and he knows that he's at the heart of it. Billions of deaths on his hands."

"How can we prevent this?"

"We can't," Quantum said. He paused, then added, "*We* can't. We won't be there."

"Is this war inevitable?"

Quantum frowned. "I can't see anything beyond the war."

"Tell me about your son, Paul! What can we do to prevent him from starting the war?"

"He doesn't *start* the war, Max, but in some ways he's responsible for it. We all are." He opened his eyes. "Especially you."

"Paul, you've got to concentrate! What else can you see? Where does the war take place?"

"Everywhere. Cities in flames, the survivors starving to death, people killing each other over scraps of rotten food. The human race..." He laughed. "The race will be won, but you and I will be dead before that happens. The writing is on the wall. Literally."

"Paul, is there *anything* we can do to prevent this?" Max's voice asked, sounding desperate.

"The future is already there, Max. We just haven't

95

caught up with it yet. We can't change it. I know that. Just like I know that you are going to die in absolute agony and I'm going to die at my son's hand."

"So if we..." Max hesitated. "If we were to..."

"No. You cannot avoid this by killing my son."

"If this war is as bad as you say it will be, then what choice do we have?"

"Take the powers away. The energies that make us superhuman... The blue lights. They drift about, cluster around certain people, enhance our abilities."

"Where do these energies come from?"

"The chasm."

"Again, what does that mean? Where is this chasm?"

"I don't know. That's all he will tell me."

"Who?"

"Ragnarök. He's the only one who knows how to do it, Max. He understands the superhuman energies. He will build a machine that will strip all of us of those energies, make us human again."

"Will that work?"

"Yes."

"And that'll prevent the war?"

Quantum shrugged. "I don't know. But if there are no more superhumans..." There was a blur, then Quantum was standing on the other side of the room. Another blur and he was standing directly in front of the camera, staring into it. "He's watching me now. In the future."

Danny jumped back. "Oh my God!"

"He's there with three others. A black man... It's Paragon. Did you know that Paragon is black, Max? I never knew that. I couldn't tell underneath that armour. His name is Solomon Cord. He's not a superhuman. I didn't know that either. You have to find him. He's going to be important. And there's a boy there. My son's best friend. He hates you, Max. He *really* hates you." Quantum frowned. "And a girl. That's strange... She's... She's powerful, Max. She doesn't know yet just *how* powerful."

Then there was another blur and the room was empty. A few seconds later, the video ended.

Colin turned to look at Danny. "You OK?"

"Not really, no." To Cord, he said, "He *knew* I'd be watching him! Is there any more like that?"

"I don't know." Cord pushed past Colin and began tapping on the keyboard. The words 'Terminal Locked' appeared on the screen. He stepped back and said, "All right... The three of you, look at me. *Look* at me!"

They looked.

"Do not talk about what you've just seen, not even among yourselves. We are not meant to know the future. That's what pushed Quantum over the edge." Cord glanced at his watch. "All right. There's something

I have to show you now. Come with me."

Silently, they followed Cord to a set of doors on the far side of the building. "This is the gymnasium. You'll be spending a lot of your spare time in this room." He took a deep breath. "Ready?"

Renata said, "We've all seen a gymnasium before, Mr Cord!"

"I know. But the gym itself isn't what I want to show you." He reached out and hit the switch on the wall, then the doors unlocked and slid open. "Go in."

Renata leading the way, the teenagers walked into the brightly-lit room. A voice said, "Oooh! They're here!" and Renata looked to see two girls of about her own age approaching. They were followed by a tall, well-built teenage boy.

"You'll have plenty of time to get to know each other properly," Cord said. "But for the moment I thought I'd just introduce you."

The six teenagers looked each other up and down.

Colin began, "So, uh..."

"I'm Yvonne," the nearest girl said. She was short, slim and – Danny and Colin couldn't help thinking – extremely good-looking. She had a pleasant smile and a massive shock of jet-black hair. "You're Colin, right? We saw you on the news. This is my sister Mina and this is Butler."

Mina was slightly taller than Yvonne, with short blonde hair. She nodded briefly and looked down at her feet.

Butler was about Danny's height, but had a much broader build. He had close-cropped black hair and dark eyes.

"Nice to meet you," Colin said. "This is Renata and Danny."

"Quantum's son, right?" Butler said. He stretched out his hand to Danny, then pulled it back. "Woah, sorry, kid!"

Renata said, "So who *are* you guys? What are you doing here?"

Solomon Cord said, "They're here for the same reason you are. They're superhumans."

8

DANNY AND NIALL were given rooms on either side of their mother's. Danny's room was stark and functional, containing only a bed, a chair and a single built-in wardrobe. Aside from one small mirror, and two white boxes marked "CDH" that were fixed close to the ceiling, the walls were completely bare.

As Danny was unpacking his suitcase, Colin appeared in the doorway.

"The exact same as mine," Colin said, giving the room a quick once-over. "Except mine has a telly."

"This room had, too, but Niall wanted it."

Colin paused for a second. "So we're not the only superhumans around." He shook his head. "I suppose it makes sense, but it's still a bit weird. I wonder how many others there are out there? For all we know, there could be dozens of us."

Danny shrugged. "Maybe." He stopped what he was doing. "I've got a weird feeling about this place."

"Like what?"

"It just doesn't feel right. I've been wondering about what Sol said, about how the old facility used to run

100

experiments. I hope he didn't mean that they were experimenting on superhumans. Do you trust him?"

"Sol? Absolutely. I'm not sure I trust Josh though. I'd still like to know how the press found out about our parents. The information had to come from somewhere. Not all of Max's people from the mine were caught. One of them might have sold the story to the newspapers." Danny grimaced. "Listen, about what Quantum said on that video..."

"Sol said we weren't to talk about it," Danny said.

"I know. But I wouldn't worry about it if I was you. I mean, the war won't happen now. And anyway, who's to say that it wasn't all just... well, insane ramblings?"

"He knew we would be watching him, Col." Danny sighed and closed his suitcase. "Unpacking can wait. Let's go exploring."

Closing the door behind them, they walked along the brightly-lit corridor. "It's like being in a hospital," Colin said. "Everything's so clean and lifeless."

"I was thinking the same thing. Which way is it to the dining hall? I'm starving."

"Down this way and then up the stairs."

They rounded a corner and almost bumped into the other teenage boy, Butler.

"Hi," Colin said. "It's Butler, right?"

The boy nodded, but didn't speak. He was staring at the stump of Danny's right arm.

A little uncomfortable at the silence, Danny said, "So, have you been here long?"

"A few months," the boy said.

"What's your second name?"

"Redmond."

"What can you do?" Colin asked.

"I'm strong, fast. I can make an invulnerable forcefield around myself." With that, a thin, transparent bubble appeared around him and spread slowly outwards.

Colin pressed his hand against the forcefield. It was cold and yielded a little, but the harder he pushed the stronger the forcefield became. "That's pretty cool," Colin said. "How did you discover your powers?"

The boy shrugged and the bubble disappeared. "Gotta go." He stepped around them and walked off down the corridor.

"Nice talking to you," Danny muttered. To Colin he said, "*He's* going to be a barrel of laughs to have around."

"Speaking of laughs," Colin said, "I can hear Renata in the dining room and she's talking to... It sounds like the two girls."

They resumed walking. "That always freaks me out a little bit," Danny said. "You can hear anything you want to, all the time!"

"Not *all* the time," Colin said. "I have to sort of switch it on. Any sign of your own powers coming back?"

"No. I made my arm intangible and pushed it inside a machine that was designed to strip superhuman powers. They're not *going* to come back, Col. Probably just as well, too. If I'm not a superhuman any more then that means that Quantum's prophecy can't possibly come true."

They pushed open the doors of the dining room and saw that the large room was empty except for one table in the corner, which was occupied by Renata and the two teenage sisters, Mina and Yvonne.

"Can we join you or is this a girls-only meeting?" Danny asked, and was about to sit down when he noticed that the table contained five mugs of coffee. "Who else is here?"

Colin froze. He could hear the heartbeats of two people behind him and turned around to see two other girls approaching.

Yvonne said, "Alia and Stephanie Cord. Solomon's daughters."

Stephanie gave Colin a smile that made him instantly blush. "So you haven't forgotten me then?"

❀

The coast of Oregon was still in darkness when an ancient fishing boat pulled into the harbour of a small town ninety miles to the south-west of Portland. The fishermen began to unload their catch, then one of them slipped away.

Wearing a heavy overcoat, and with a woollen hat pulled down to cover as much as possible of his scarred head, Dioxin slung his bag over his shoulder and silently and quickly made his way through the port and on to a quiet street.

Ahead of him, standing next to a large expensive car that was parked beneath a streetlight, a short, nervous-looking man was watching him.

Dioxin slipped his hand into his overcoat's pocket and took hold of his gun.

As he neared the car, the short man said, "I was sent to meet you."

"You've got the wrong man, buddy."

"No, no I haven't. You were smuggled out of China on a private jet. You parachuted out twenty miles from the coast and rendezvoused with that fishing boat. That's how Mr Sheng operates."

"So who are you and what do you want?" Dioxin asked. He pulled off his hat and stepped into the light.

The nervous man gasped at Dioxin's face, then quickly looked away. "My employer has a job for you, Mr Dioxin."

"I'm here on personal business. I'm not taking on any work right now."

"We know everything about you, Dioxin. We know all of your secrets. We know all the details of every single crime you've committed since you disappeared ten years ago. What would happen to you if all of that information became public knowledge? Think about that: all of those people you helped put into power, all of those terrorists you've worked for, the crime lords, the drug barons. They would all know that you were the one responsible for airing their secrets."

Dioxin considered this. "For a little guy you sure talk big."

"Do I have your attention or not?"

"I haven't killed you yet. That means I'm interested."

The man opened the car's passenger door. "Then get in. We've got a jet waiting for us."

"Who are you?"

"My name is Evan Laurie."

"Never heard of you."

"No reason you should have. But like I said, we know everything about *you*. You're here to kill Paragon. Ten years ago, you lost your superhuman abilities. You were no longer immune to your own acid. If Paragon hadn't slowed you down, you could have washed the acid off before it scarred you. How many operations has it taken, Dioxin? Twenty? Thirty? If it hadn't been for Paragon, you would be able to live a normal life without people flinching when they saw your face."

Dioxin said nothing.

"So you will work for us and we will give you something invaluable in return."

"And what's that? You can give me back my face?"

"No. But we can tell you where Paragon is."

9

AT BREAKFAST ON his first full day at Sakkara, Colin made his way to the dining hall, which was half-filled with people he hadn't seen before. He realised that most of them were in their thirties or forties, which made him feel even younger.

He spotted Renata and Danny sitting in one corner, and was about to wander over when he heard his father's voice. "Colin? Come here a minute!"

As he walked over to his father's table, he saw Façade sitting on his own. He was the only person in the whole room not to be sitting with someone. *If he hadn't helped us in California we'd all have died,* Colin thought, *and in return he lost his family and his friends.*

"Colin," his father said, "you've met Sol's wife Vienna, haven't you?"

"Not officially," Colin said. "We were never introduced." He shook hands with her. "It's a pleasure to meet you."

Mrs Cord smiled. "Aren't *you* the polite one?"

Warren said, "Lock them in the coal shed for a week at a time and they learn manners soon enough." He tilted his head in the direction of Renata and Danny. "Go on, join your friends. I'm sure you don't want to be stuck here with the old fogies."

As Colin wandered over to the others, Stephanie Cord intercepted him and steered him to the large buffet table at one side of the room. "Just help yourself to whatever you want," she said.

None of the food looked very appetising. "Isn't there, like, cornflakes or something normal? What's *this* stuff?"

"Corn hash with bacon bits and cream cheese."

"People actually *eat* that? For breakfast?"

"Some do."

Colin made a face. "It looks like it's been eaten before."

"It's loaded with essential somethings and recommended other things." Stephanie handed him a plate and began spooning the mixture on to it. "Everything a growing boy needs to build up his strength."

"Stephanie, I don't think I can face it. I think I've got jet lag. I woke up about five hours ago and couldn't get back to sleep."

"Danny said the same thing." She piled more food on to the plate: waffles, strips of bacon, small round green things that Colin couldn't identify and slices of raw onion.

She's winding me up, he thought. "I'm not that hungry, Stephanie. I can't eat all this."

"So?" She took the plate from him. "This is for me! You thought I was serving your food for you? What am I, your maid?"

Colin poured himself a large glass of orange juice and followed Stephanie over to the corner table where Renata and Danny were sitting. They were soon joined by Butler, Yvonne, Mina and Stephanie's sister Alia. Niall had chosen to stay in his room and watch cartoons.

Colin couldn't help noticing that Yvonne was by far the most talkative one at the table. As they ate, she filled them in on the gossip about every one of Sakkara's technicians and scientists, or "labcoats" as she called them.

Stephanie whispered to Colin, "We've only been here a couple of weeks and I've already heard all of her stories. What have *you* been up to since we last saw you?"

"Mostly just trying to get used to the idea that I'm a superhuman. So you and Alia didn't know that your dad was Paragon?"

"Not until the day you showed up. After Dad took you to California, Mom told us all about it. We were in a safe house that Max set up, but when we heard that Max was behind everything we left the place and went into hiding. We haven't been back home since that day. My friends probably have no idea what happened to me!"

"What about, you know, your boyfriend?" Colin found his mouth had suddenly gone dry and he took another sip of his orange juice.

"You mean Sam? Oh, we brought him with us." Stephanie pointed to the far side of the room. "That's him over there."

Colin almost swivelled around to look, then stopped himself. "Nice try."

"OK, you caught me!" Stephanie smiled. "How could you tell?"

"I've noticed that you bite your bottom lip just after you tell a lie."

"I do? Seriously? So *that's* how my folks always know!"

"Actually, *I* was lying. I just guessed. Now you know what it feels like."

At the far end of the table, Danny suddenly whispered, "You *love* her, Colin! You want to *kiss* her and *marry* her!"

Colin almost coughed his orange juice all over the table.

"You OK?" Stephanie asked.

Colin nodded. "I'm fine, thanks." He quickly looked around the table. If any of the others had heard, they hadn't reacted. Danny was looking down at his plate, a huge grin on his face.

"What's he smiling about?" Stephanie asked.

"Er... dunno."

110

"So Danny and Renata are an item, are they?"

"I'm not sure."

"He's your best friend! How could you not be sure?"

"We don't really talk about stuff like that much." To change the subject, Colin said, "It doesn't seem like a lot of fun here."

"No, it's not exactly Disneyland. Josh marches about and tries to order me and Alia to do things. He keeps forgetting that we're not superhumans."

"You could still be a superhero though," Colin said, risking a quick look at Stephanie's incredible brown eyes. "Your dad never had any powers. You could take over from him. Or Alia could. Either of you, I mean. Or both."

Shut up! You're babbling like an idiot!

Stephanie flashed him another smile.

God, she's gorgeous! And not really that much older than me. Only a year.

Colin suddenly realised that an uncomfortable silence had fallen over the group. He glanced over at Renata; she was staring daggers at Butler, as was Mina.

Speaking slowly and deliberately, Renata said, "*What* did you just call him?"

Butler shrugged and resumed shovelling scrambled eggs into his mouth. "Just kidding."

Stephanie whispered, "Butler has the superhuman ability to put both feet in his mouth at the same time."

111

Yvonne stared at Butler. *"Apologise. Right now."*

Butler turned to Danny. "Sorry I called you 'Stumpy'." He glanced at Yvonne. "Happy now?"

"You don't *sound* sorry," Renata said.

"I have trouble expressing my emotions. Trust me, I'm crying on the inside."

Renata leaned close to the large boy and whispered, so softly that no one but Colin could hear, "You ever say anything like that to him again and you'll be *bleeding* on the inside. Get it?"

Butler nodded, the smirk vanished from his face.

The uncomfortable silence continued for a few moments until Yvonne said cheerfully, "So. Let's compare powers then! Colin? How much can you bench-press?"

"I have absolutely no idea."

"On a good day, Mina can lift over five hundred pounds. But it's not reliable, is it, Mina?"

The girl shook her head.

"It sort of comes and goes spontaneously," Yvonne explained. "The labcoats here have been trying to figure out a way to make it happen all the time, but nothing seems to work."

"What about yourself?" Danny asked.

"I'm a little stronger and faster than a normal person, but my IQ is off the charts. Or so they tell me.

They keep giving me tests and I keep passing them."

Butler laughed. "Yeah, you don't want to play poker with this one. She can always figure out who's holding which cards. *And* she can remember things. She can read a book once and recite it back word for word."

"How long have you been here, Mina?" Colin asked.

Yvonne answered for her. "Oh, we've been here forever."

"Which is?"

"We've never lived anywhere else."

"You're serious? What about your families?"

"We're the only family we have," Yvonne said.

Renata said, "For sisters, you don't look that much alike."

"That's just because of our hair. Mina says we're very closely related. She can sense these things."

"Auras," Mina said. It was the first thing Colin had heard the blonde-haired girl say.

"She can see them," Yvonne explained. "That's how she knew immediately that Façade wasn't Danny's real father. But he is *Niall's* father."

"You can see auras," Danny said to Mina. "Sorry, but that's..."

"A big pile of crap," Butler finished for him.

"I was going to say it was strange."

113

"It's a big pile of *strange* crap then," Butler said, ignoring Mina's glare. "There is no such thing as an aura. What Mina's seeing is probably caused by a sort of low-grade telepathy that somehow triggers a visual manifestation."

Yvonne said, "God, those big words must get lonely rattling around in that empty skull of yours." To the others, she said, "He was drummed out of Oats' Military Academy in Alaska because of what they called 'unsatisfactory performance'."

"*That* is a lie," Butler said, jabbing his finger at her. "And it's none of your damn business."

They all stopped talking when Solomon Cord approached the table. "All right, boys and girls. You might have noticed that you're the only people left in this room. No one – no matter how special they think they are – needs a two-hour breakfast. Time to hit the gym, troops."

"Aw, Dad!" Alia said.

"Move it. Now. And everyone has to clean up their own mess, Danny Cooper!" he added, as Danny walked away from the table.

"I was going to!" Danny said and walked back.

"Alia, you take care of Colin's tray. Colin, you're with me... *Now*, Colin! Front and centre, son! Get the lead out!"

As Colin got up from the table, he whispered to

Stephanie, "Is he like this at home?"

She replied, "From now on, *this* is home."

❋

"I'm relying on you to hold them together," Solomon said as he led Colin down a wide staircase.

"Why me? I'm the youngest one here, except for Niall."

"Danny's got enough troubles of his own, as does Renata. That guy Butler is a real handful; he's got a big ego and an even bigger mouth. Yvonne and Mina... The jury's still out on them. You're the only one of the new heroes I know I can trust."

"Where are we going?"

"The machine room. There's someone you have to meet and then you're going to the gym with the others."

Solomon opened the double doors to the machine room and ushered Colin inside. They were on a narrow platform overlooking a room that was three storeys high. Colin was impressed; he'd seen smaller shopping centres. Below, at least two dozen people in white coats were working on various pieces of machinery.

Suspended from the ceiling by huge chains was what looked like a two-seater version of the StratoTruck. "Still in the design stage," Solomon explained as they

115

descended the metal staircase. "We don't have the time to work on it right now."

Against one wall was an unfinished steel skeleton, over two metres tall. "What's that?" Colin asked.

"The framework for the new Paragon armour."

"But it's *huge!*"

"It'll be a powered exoskeleton. We're designing a new kind of lightweight armour plating to go over it. Wearing that, I'm going to be much stronger and faster than a normal man. It's not so much a suit of armour; it's more a robot that you wear." He shrugged. "If we can ever get the damn thing to work."

"What's wrong with it?"

"The mechanics are coming along fine, but a machine like that needs a lot of computer technology to control all the functions. But that's not why I brought you here." He pointed to one of the technicians who was hunched over a circuit board. "That young man is turning out to be a real asset. He has a natural aptitude for mechanics. He didn't even realise it himself until I put him to work on the weapons for the new armour."

Solomon picked up a rubber band from the nearest workbench and flicked it at the technician's head. The man jumped and looked around, then grinned when he spotted Colin. "I do not believe it!" He dropped the circuit board and almost ran over to them. "Colin Wagner, the son of Titan!"

Colin frowned at this stranger, then suddenly realised. The last time he'd seen him, the man had had long, ragged, bleached-blond hair and a goatee beard. Now, he was clean-shaven, his hair neatly tied back. "Razor?"

10

"I **DON'T KNOW** why Sol keeps making *me* do this," Razor said. "I'm just a labcoat. I don't need to go to the gym!"

Razor and Colin were both wearing white T-shirts, shorts and trainers. As slowly as they could manage, they walked in the direction of Sakkara's gymnasium.

"Maybe he thinks you're out of shape," Colin said. "So how did he persuade Josh to take you on? I mean, with your track record..."

"Just because I boosted a few cars doesn't mean I'm a bad guy," Razor said, then laughed. "This is a sweet deal, Col. I owe you. If you hadn't tricked me into driving you all the way to Sol's house in Virginia, I'd probably be living on the streets now. I turned eighteen two weeks ago. They don't let you stay in the runaways' shelter once you're officially an adult."

"Actually, I owe *you*," Colin said, as they approached the doors to the gym. "I'd never have found Sol without you, and then Max Dalton's plan would have worked and I'd be dead, and so would Danny and Renata, and thousands and thousands of other people."

Solomon Cord stepped out of the doorway and yelled at them: "What *is* this? A mutual admiration society? Get in here!"

Colin looked around; Renata was lying on her back on a bench, lifting weights. He couldn't see how much she was lifting, but it looked like a lot. Butler Redmond was standing behind her, ready to catch the weights if necessary. Danny, Yvonne and Mina were taking turns to use a springboard to leap over a vaulting horse. Colin was surprised to find that Cord's daughters were also in the gym; they were wearing karate suits and sparring with each other. They looked like they knew what they were doing.

"Razor, do your warm-ups. Colin, see that rope?" Cord asked.

"I see it."

"Climb up it, using only your hands."

"OK."

Colin walked over to the rope suspended from the middle of the ceiling and began to climb, hand over hand, his legs swinging free. He quickly reached the top and looked down. The floor was five metres below. "No problem!" he shouted to Cord.

"Now let go!"

"What?"

"Let go!"

"Are you nuts?" Colin yelled. "My powers still aren't

119

completely reliable! Suppose they disappear when I'm halfway down?"

"Yeah? And suppose your powers disappear when you're in the middle of fighting some bad guys and, say, they knock you out and someone takes a photo of you without your mask?"

Under his breath, Colin muttered, "You're not such a nice guy now, are you?"

"Let go! I want you to land on your toes, knees bent slightly."

Here goes, Colin thought. He opened his hands, and the floor suddenly rushed up to meet him. He landed lightly on his feet and remained standing. *That wasn't too bad!*

"That was terrible," Cord said. "Now do it again. But this time, when you land, I want you to bounce, OK? The moment your toes touch the ground, somersault forwards and land on your feet."

Again and again, Colin climbed the rope, allowed himself to drop and tried to somersault. It took him twelve attempts to master it.

Cord seemed satisfied. "You're getting better. That'll do for today, but within a week I want you to be able to flip over as you're falling and land on your hands."

"You're kidding, right?"

Cord didn't respond to that. He called out, "Everyone?

Stop what you're doing and gather in the centre of the room, please! Anyone who's wearing sneakers, take them off!"

When they had all gathered, Cord said, "We're going to try some simple hand-to-hand combat. Alia?"

The girl walked forward and stopped in front of him.

"Block!" Cord said and swung his fist at his daughter's head.

She swung up her left arm and blocked the punch.

"It's a simple move," Cord said. "Just sweep your arm up and knock your opponent's hand aside. If they punch with their right, you block with your left, sweeping to the right. Why? Because that'll move your opponent to their left, which means that they can't then throw another jab with their left hand. But it also means that you can't easily hit them with *your* right hand. Later, we'll look at ways around that. Now pair off: Renata and Butler, Steph and Razor, Yvonne and Colin, Alia and Mina. Danny, you're with me. Take turns punching and blocking. And don't actually try to *hit* your opponent – we don't want any casualties!"

As he sparred with Yvonne, Colin kept glancing over at Danny; with only one arm, Danny was finding it tough.

Sol's not going any easier on him, Colin thought. *You'd think that—?*

121

Wham! Yvonne's fist collided with Colin's jaw, sending him staggering backwards.

"Oh my God! Are you OK?"

Colin could see spots in front of his eyes. "Yeah, I'm all right. I think. My fault – I wasn't paying attention."

They were interrupted by the arrival of Niall Cooper, who was wearing a karate suit that had been cut down to size.

"I'm ready!" he announced cheerfully.

Cord said, "Sorry, Niall. You'll have to sit this one out."

"Aw! Just teach me some of the moves!"

Butler laughed. "Who feels brave enough to take on the shrimp?"

Niall gave him a dirty look. "I know I'm small, but I won't always be! One day I'll be a superhuman, too, like my dad was, and I need to be ready!"

"Yeah, but your dad was one of the *bad* guys. How do we know you won't be just as evil as he was?"

"That's enough, Butler!" Cord shouted.

Oh hell, Colin thought. To Yvonne, he whispered, "Didn't anyone tell him that Niall doesn't know?"

"Josh told us yesterday."

"What are you saying?" Niall demanded, marching over to Butler. "My dad used to be *Quantum*! He was the best!"

"Kid, that man you call your dad was never Quantum.

He was Façade. He worked for the bad guys."

Niall clenched his tiny fists and made a run at Butler, but Danny stood in his way.

He put out his hand to calm his brother, then turned to Butler. "Tell him that's not true."

Butler smirked. "But it *is* true. He's got a villain for a father and a murdering cripple for a half-brother."

"Redmond!" Cord said, advancing on him.

Butler turned to Cord and gave him a look of contempt. "Stay out of this, Solomon. This is between me and Lefty here."

Colin moved closer to them. *If Butler's as strong as he says he is, he could knock Sol's head clean off his shoulders. He knows it, too. They both know it.*

"What is your problem with me?" Danny demanded.

Butler's forcefield suddenly appeared around him and expanded outwards, forcing Danny to step back.

Butler sneered. "My problem? My problem is that you're a nobody, Cooper. You don't have any powers. Sure, your old man was something else in his day, but he's doing the pine-box waltz now. And *you* put him there. *I* got sent to military school because I beat the crap out of a guy who was trying to mug me, but you murdered your own father and no one has done a thing about it."

"That was an accident!"

Enough! Colin decided. He walked over to Butler and

stepped between him and Danny. "I don't know whether you're stronger than me, Redmond, but we're going to find out if you don't back away right now!"

"Hey, I'm not going to touch him! It wouldn't be right, him being a powerless cripple and all."

"Hit the showers, Redmond," Cord said. "You're done for the day."

Butler looked around at everyone, then nodded. His forcefield disappeared. "Whatever you say, boss." As he marched out of the room, he turned and winked at Niall. "See you, shrimp."

Danny turned to Colin. "I don't need you to fight my battles for me!"

"I was trying to..."

But Danny just turned his back and walked away.

Colin looked over at Niall, who was now standing next to Renata, holding her hand. "What did he mean about my dad being evil?" Niall asked.

❀

Dioxin woke as the car slowed to a crawl; it was approaching a pair of gates set into a four-metre-high steel fence. "Where are we, Laurie?"

"North-east Wyoming."

The unmanned gates swung open and they drove

through, the car ploughing furrows in the snow. They drove along a short tree-lined road and into a small town square. "There's no people," Dioxin said. "Stop the car a minute."

Laurie pulled the car over to the side and Dioxin got out. He took a deep breath, the ragged remains of his nostrils flaring. "Fresh-cut timber. Drying plaster. These buildings are all brand new." He leaned back into the car. "You built this place?"

"We did. Right now, there's only a handful of people here. We're expecting the first citizens to arrive in the next couple of months. This will be your base of operations while you're dealing with the Paragon situation."

Dioxin looked around, his breath misting in the air. "I was expecting an underground lair at the very least. Man, this is one creepy little town..." He pointed towards the roof of a nearby store. "Hidden camera... Another one over there... High-tech alarms on all the buildings. Unpickable locks on the doors." He walked to the nearest store window and pressed his hand against the glass. "Shatter-proof glass." He peered through the window into the empty store, then walked a little further along the street, knelt and scraped the snow from a square metre of the pavement. *Reinforced concrete slabs, probably six inches thick or more.*

Dioxin brushed the snow from his hands and returned

to the car. "You've built this place to last and you've thought of almost everything. Phone lines, TV points and Internet connections in all the stores. Solar panels on all the roofs. Wheelchair access everywhere. Street signs all perfectly clear and legible. You even have smaller signs on every corner with the street names in Braille. Except... You know what's missing?"

"What's that?"

"You don't have many traffic signs. You know, parking restrictions and all that."

"We won't need them. The citizens won't park illegally."

"A town this size must have cost a couple of billion dollars. Who's behind it?"

"Get in. I'm taking you to him."

Dioxin climbed back into the car and they drove off once again. "So... You've built yourself a perfect, private town surrounded by an unscalable fence. You trying to keep people in or out? Or both?"

"We're just providing a nice place for the people to live."

"Why?"

Laurie steered the car along a wide, pedestrianised street. "Because if we give them what they want, they won't leave. This town is just the first of many."

"Trutopians," Dioxin said and laughed. "I thought you guys were just another dumb cult, but you've really got something here."

"There are over seventeen million Trutopians throughout the world," Laurie said. "That's a larger population than many countries. There's almost a million Trutopians in the US alone, and we're growing at a rate of about seven per cent a month. By the end of next year we'll have enough people to directly influence Congress. Four years, maybe five, and we'll have enough political strength to elect any candidate of our choice to the presidency."

"It's not possible to eliminate the criminal class: if the Trutopians don't allow criminals or undesirables to join, then the world will be seriously divided. On one side, the peace-loving Trutopians in their perfect, impenetrable communities. On the other side, the rest of the world in their polluted, crime-ridden cities. That won't sit well with a lot of people. It's basically apartheid."

"No, it's not. Anyone can join the Trutopians."

"But those who don't fit in are expelled. Trust me on this: you can't save the world by turning all the criminals against you. You could be looking at civil war on a global scale."

"There's no progress without conflict," Laurie said.

He drove the car down into the empty underground car park of a large apartment block and stopped close to a set of doors.

Dioxin grabbed his bag and climbed out. "No welcoming committee?"

"*I'm* the welcoming committee. Follow me."

127

Laurie led Dioxin through the doors, along a short corridor and into an elevator. He slipped a key-card into a hidden slot, then the elevator began to rise.

The elevator doors opened on to a bright, well-decorated lobby. Laurie and Dioxin stepped out. "We have the top three floors," Laurie said.

"And who is 'we'?"

Laurie didn't reply. He led Dioxin through the lobby, their footsteps echoing across the marble floor. They stopped outside a door that had a red light above it. "He's recording," Laurie said. Seconds later, the light blinked out. "All right." Laurie opened the door and ushered Dioxin inside.

It looked to Dioxin like a small television studio. One wall was covered in monitors, all showing different television channels. Against another wall was a podium, backed by a set of dark blue curtains and the Trutopian banner. Two video cameras were pointed at the podium.

In the centre of the room, at a large cluttered desk, an overweight, bearded man sat typing on a computer keyboard. Without stopping what he was doing, or even looking up, the bearded man said, "Dioxin. The legendary poisonous supervillain. Took us a long time to track you down."

"Reginald Kinsella. The Trutopians' new leader."

"That's me," the man said, still typing. "But I want to

know more about you. As far as anyone in the government knows, you died ten years ago, dissolved into soup by your own acids. What really happened?"

"I feigned unconsciousness, slipped away when I was sure no one was watching. There was enough of my skin and blood left behind that they assumed I'd just broken down into nothing."

"As simple as that?"

"No. Every nerve in my body was in agony. My skin was peeling away. I lost a *lot* of blood. It took me months to recover."

"After Ragnarök's last battle, the first report we have of you is when you helped assassinate a certain US senator. You did a good job, made it look like an accident. Even today no one suspects. You spent the next few years in Europe, Asia and Africa, moving from one country to another. You left a trail of dead plastic surgeons in your wake – I'm assuming that you forced each one to do some repair work on your skin – but they were so far apart that no one realised there was a serial killer on the loose."

Dioxin moved around to stand in front of the desk. "Look, just stop typing – it's distracting!"

"Not to me," Kinsella said. Nevertheless, he pushed the keyboard away and looked at Dioxin. "I'm going to rule the world, Mr Dioxin."

"I kinda picked up on that."

"And you are going to help me. I want the new heroes out of the way. But they're strong: we can't easily fight them on a physical level. So we have to fight them politically."

Dioxin nodded. "You want to discredit them, strip them of the people's support."

"Exactly. Though if you *can* kill them, then by all means do so. Except one. I want one of them by my side. To guard against future superhuman threats."

"Discredit them, kill them, divide them. I can do that. But I want Paragon." Dioxin held up his hands. "He did this to me."

Kinsella raised an eyebrow. "Really? I thought your own acids did that."

"As soon as I realised that I was no longer immune to the acid, I knew I had to get it off my skin. There was a fountain nearby. Water dilutes acid. I could have washed the acid off and got away with only minor burns, if Paragon hadn't slowed me down."

"I don't have much love for Paragon myself. You'll get him. Not at first though. First, we've got something *really* special planned for him. Trust me: you're going to love it."

"So now you tell me about yourself," Dioxin said. "I don't like working for people I don't know. If I don't know someone, I can't trust him."

The bearded man stood up and moved around the desk. He pulled off his jacket and tossed it to Dioxin.

"Padded," Dioxin said.

"Right." Kinsella unbuttoned his shirt and slapped the fake latex beer belly that had been strapped around his waist. "The beard is fake, too. I'd prove it, only it takes half an hour to get the damn thing off." As he buttoned his shirt up once more, he said, "The old guy who set up the Trutopians was pretty smart, but he didn't have the vision it takes to make the organisation really work."

"How did you get the job?"

"It wasn't hard. I persuaded him to take me on and hand over control. He wanted someone intelligent and absolutely honest." Kinsella smiled. "I'm intelligent enough to be able to fake the honesty."

"And the reason for the disguise?"

"I've encountered the new heroes before and I don't want them to know that I'm running the Trutopians."

He reached out his hand to Dioxin. "My real name is Victor Cross."

11

AT SAKKARA, LATE in the afternoon, Colin sat in the machine room chatting to Razor.

"Right," Razor said, switching on a computer monitor. "Your first real training session is tonight. So here's what you'll all be wearing." The monitor showed a rotating three-dimensional image of a black, tight-fitting costume.

"Aw! You mean I'm not going to be wearing my Titan costume any more?"

"Josh wants everyone wearing matching outfits. A leftover from his days with The High Command, I suppose. Anyway, these things are knife-proof, bullet-proof and fire-proof. They're a matt-black finish, so they don't reflect much light, which will make it easier to hide in the dark. And they're insulated, too, which is just as well because it's going to be absolutely freezing out there tonight."

"That's not a problem for me," Colin said. "I don't seem to feel the cold much these days."

"Well, not everyone is as lucky as you are." Razor reached into a drawer and pulled out a lump of something that looked like a cross between leather and rubber. "This is what it's made of," he said, handing it to Colin.

Colin twisted the material around in his hands. "Oops. Tears easily."

"For you maybe. *I* need a hacksaw to get through it! Your helmets will be made of this stuff, too."

"Helmets?"

"Yeah." He tapped at the keyboard and another screen appeared, this one showing a rotating head wearing a one-piece cowl. "Covers most of your face, so that'll help keep your anonymity. Not that there's any point with you because I doubt there's a person on the planet who doesn't know what Kid Titan really looks like."

"It's Titan, not *Kid* Titan."

Razor grinned. "Whatever you say." He tapped at the monitor with the end of his pen. "The helmets have a two-way radio built in, so that you can communicate with the others or with us here."

"No cape?" Colin asked. "I want a cape! Capes are cool!"

"Colin, each one of these suits costs about half a million dollars. It'd cost nearly that much again for a cape. So. No capes."

"But we're all going to look the same! Can't we all have a different symbol on the chest? I could have the 'T' from the Titan costume. Renata could have a diamond."

"You'll have to talk to Josh about that. He's very into the whole image thing."

"What about weapons?"

"You don't need any weapons. But I'll show you some of the cool stuff we're working on for the new Paragon armour."

Razor led Colin over to another workbench, this one covered in odd-looking equipment. "We're trying to fit most of the weapons right *into* the suit. That's one of the things that's been slowing us down." He pointed to some of the items in turn. "Gas-powered grappling gun, with a fifty-metre line. The line can hold about half a tonne. It'll fit into the suit's left wrist. The right wrist will have a Taser. Let's see..." He picked up a bundle of pebble-sized black objects. "Knockout-gas pellets. We're building a launcher for them that'll go on the suit's right forearm. Oh and there's *this* beauty!" He grunted as he lifted up a football-sized object. "We call it a blackout bomb. It's way too big at the moment – we're trying to get it down to about the size of an apple."

"What's it do?"

"It's basically a smoke-bomb, but instead of smoke it pumps out billions of tiny black particles that just drift about in the air. The cool part is that the labcoats here have come up with a way to generate a small electrical field that'll prevent the particles from dispersing too far."

"Which means?"

"If you activate one of these, you get a sphere of solid darkness that'll fill a large room. It only lasts a few minutes, but even your enhanced night-vision probably wouldn't be able to see through it. And then there's the hushbomb. We don't have a working one yet. The idea is that it takes in all the sound waves around it, and broadcasts them back inverted, cancelling out the real sound waves. Throw one of them at someone and he'll be temporarily deaf. It should be very effective if we can combine it with the blackout bomb."

Looking around the workbench, Colin spotted a device that looked like a complex hand-gun. "What's this?" He grabbed it and started aiming it at various objects around the room.

"That's a glue gun," Razor replied.

"Wow! How's it work?"

"It's not a *weapon*, Col. We use it to glue things to other things."

"Oh." Colin squeezed the trigger and a long stream of glue squirted out, landing all over a large spanner that was resting on the bench.

"Damn!" Razor said. "Grab it quick before the glue sets!"

Colin took hold of the spanner and picked it up. The heavy steel bench rose in the air, its contents crashing on to the floor. "Strong stuff."

Razor looked at him. "You or the glue?"

Colin bent down and began picking up the fallen items. "Sorry about that. Hope I didn't break anything."

As he replaced everything on the bench, he noticed that one of the items looked like a steel glove. "Part of the new Paragon suit?"

"Yeah. Here, let me show you how it works..." Razor pressed something on the inside of the glove and it split open along the palm. "See these little pads? They're pressure switches. They can sense how much pressure the wearer is applying. There will be hundreds of these all over the suit."

"What for?"

"The suit's too heavy for someone to move around in it as it is. These switches read the wearer's movements and send that data to the computer, which uses the information to decide how to control the motors and miniature hydraulic pumps."

Colin nodded. "Clever. Sol said that the suit will be like a robot that you wear."

"Exactly."

"That gives me an idea..."

❂

At that moment, Colin's parents and Solomon Cord were in Sakkara's Operations Room – called Ops – to plan the coming night's training session.

Joshua Dalton had spread a map of Topeka over the

large table. "On a night like this I'm not expecting them to run into any trouble, so they won't be out long. It'll be a test of their new uniforms and equipment as much as anything else."

He pointed out various locations on the map. "We'll drop them off here, get them to move to here, here and here, then back to their starting point where Renata can do her thing." He glanced up at Caroline. "You talked to her about that?"

Caroline nodded. "She's OK with it."

"Good. Let's hope it works." Looking back at the map, he said, "If everything goes well tonight, I'm going to put Colin, Yvonne and Butler on the Alpha team. Sol will lead Renata and Mina on the Beta team."

"Colin and Renata have only been here for a day," Warren said. "I'm not sure they're ready to go out yet. They've never even *seen* the city."

Cord said, "The world knows they exist now. It won't be long before they're called to help out in some crisis. We need them ready as soon as possible. And I'm not just talking about the superhumans: I want to fully train my daughters. And Razor."

"No," Josh said. "They'll be a liability."

"I'm with Sol on this one," Caroline said. "What if someone else figures out a way to strip their superhuman powers? After Ragnarök's machine was

137

used a lot of us would have died if Sol hadn't been there. We need ordinary humans as much as we need superhumans."

"Right now," Cord said to Josh, "your people are working round the clock on the new Paragon armour. It's still months away from completion, but once the prototype is up and running we will be able to replicate it. We could have more than just *one* Paragon."

Josh said, "I seem to remember Max making that same suggestion to you about sixteen years ago. You refused. What's changed since then?"

"With his mind-control powers, Max was one of the most powerful superhumans. I didn't trust him. And I was right not to."

"But you trust me?"

Solomon Cord shook his head. "Not yet. But then *you're* not the most powerful. Of these new heroes... Butler's self-obsessed and dangerous. Renata's got a lot of baggage because of the ten years she lost. Danny... even leaving aside the fact that he doesn't have any powers, we all remember what happened to his father. Let's just hope that he only inherited Quantum's speed and not his instability. Mina's too self-conscious and Yvonne is too flighty. Colin is the only one of them we can fully trust."

Warren grinned. "He takes after his old man."

"Colin's reliable, pretty calm in a crisis, incredibly resourceful... Let's be honest, Warren, when *you* were his age, would you have been able to do what he did in Jacksonville? He was completely alone, in a country he knew nothing about, no money, no food... The only thing he had was my name, but he managed to get all the way to Virginia and track me down. And he even picked up an ally along the way."

Josh said, "Actually, I've got serious reservations about Razor."

"I know you do," Cord said. "But the point is this: of these six new heroes, Colin is the only who has definitely got what it takes. It's not superpowers that make someone a hero. It's an instinctive knowledge of right and wrong, and the courage to always – *always* – stick to what you know is right, no matter what the consequences might be."

As Solomon Cord flew the StratoTruck towards the heart of Topeka, Colin looked around at the other teenagers. They were all wearing their new black uniforms. Yvonne and Mina were so close in height and build that with their masks on the others were having trouble telling them apart.

"We definitely need some sort of symbols!" Colin said. "Yvonne, what's your superhero name?"

"I'm Mina."

"Oh, right. Sorry. So what name are you using?"

The girl shrugged.

Yvonne said, "She doesn't have one. We've never been able to come up with a good name for either of us. I want a name that sounds cool and describes what I can do."

"Yeah, but what *can* you do?" Butler asked, then quickly added, "What I mean is, Renata can turn herself into a diamond-hard substance, so Diamond is a good name for her. But what about the rest of us? We need names that are relevant to something that makes us different from each other. I was thinking of calling myself Forcefield, but... It sounds kinda lame."

Renata said, "Your forcefield appears like a giant bubble, right? So that's what you call yourself: Bubble."

The others laughed.

Yvonne said, "He's right about me though. I can't go calling myself Brainy or something like that. And Thalamus has already been used. I want a name like Sage, but people would just think of herbs."

"Maybe you and Mina could be Sage and Onion?" Butler suggested, laughing.

"I don't think we need *your* help to solve this one, Bubble."

Butler looked disgusted. "Yeah, very funny. Joke's over."

"Are you still going to call yourself Kid Titan?" Yvonne asked Colin.

"It's Titan, not *Kid* Titan!" he replied. "No one can ever get that right!" He sighed. "You know, maybe I *will* change it. Yeah, I will. From now on, I'm not Titan any more. I'm going to pick a new name!"

"One minute!" Cord called. "Prepare yourselves!"

"We're ready," Colin said, pulling on his mask.

"You know the route. It shouldn't take you more than an hour. Caroline's back in Ops; she'll be monitoring your positions and keeping you up-to-date over the radio."

Cord manoeuvred the StratoTruck until it was hovering four metres over the roof of a tall building. "Here's your first surprise: I'm not going to land. You'll have to jump." As he spoke, the hatch opened and freezing air rushed into the vehicle.

Renata went first. She stepped out and turned herself solid, crashed to the snow-covered roof below and turned human again.

Butler followed her, his transparent, flexible forcefield appearing around him as he dropped.

As Yvonne, Mina and Colin jumped down, the StratoTruck rose into the night sky and vanished.

"All right," Colin said. "I have absolutely no idea where we are. Anyone?"

His mother's voice came over the radio. "You need to go north from your position, Colin."

"Yeah, but which way *is* north?"

"Look around: there should be a tall building with twin spires. That's directly to your east. You can work out the rest from there."

"Thanks, Mum."

"You're welcome. Now we expect you to be able to do the rest of this patrol without any help from us. You're on your own, in other words."

Colin walked to the edge of the building's roof and pointed across the street. "We have to get over there. Any ideas?"

Yvonne said, "We climb down the fire escape, cross the street and climb back up the other fire escape."

Renata turned to Butler. "How big can you make your forcefield?"

"Pretty big. I've never really tested it for size."

"And does it have to be round?"

"Any shape I want, but I have to be on the inside."

"Here's what we'll do then. You turn on your forcefield to cover all of us, extend it across the street to the other building and we'll walk across."

"Then how do *I* get over?"

"You walk across on the inside of the forcefield."

"But when I move, the forcefield moves with me! To

142

keep it in the one place I'd have to move it backwards at the same speed as I move forwards..." Butler peered down over the edge. "We're about fourteen floors up. If it fails... No, I can do this." He frowned in concentration.

Colin noticed that the wind suddenly stopped. He looked around and saw that they were all now inside what appeared to be a giant, flexible glass shell. As they watched, one side of the shell stretched out over the street and on to the roof opposite.

"Someone want to test it?" Butler asked, his voice strained.

Renata said, "I'll do it. I've got the best chance of surviving the drop." She crouched at the edge of the roof and reached down with her hand. "Seems solid enough." Taking a deep breath, Renata stepped out. The forcefield gave slightly under her weight. It felt like walking on a thick rubber mat. "It's working!"

She quickly ran across to the opposite roof and the others followed. Colin looked back at Butler and flipped the switch on his radio. "You OK for this?"

"I can do it."

The forcefield shimmered and shifted as Butler began to move, but it held. As he stepped on to the roof next to the others, he allowed the forcefield to drop. "That was pretty cool," Butler said.

"Nice work, Bubble," Yvonne said, grinning.

"Do *not* call me that!"

Most of the new heroes were freezing by the time they had made their way back to their starting point. Colin was the only one who didn't seem to be affected by the cold.

The snow started falling again as they waited for the StratoTruck to return. Butler sheltered them with his forcefield, opening it briefly every couple of minutes to replace the stale air.

When the StratoTruck arrived and the others were climbing on board, Renata held Colin back. "I've got something to show you," she said, as she led him to the edge of the roof. She put her right hand on his shoulder as she pointed down to the ground with her left. "Look."

Colin looked. He always felt a little uncomfortable being so far from the ground. "What?"

Renata pushed.

Colin barely had time to see the look of anticipation on her face before he was suddenly tumbling down through the air. *Oh crap! I'm going to die!*

"Fly, Colin!" Renata shouted. "Fly!"

You can do it! His mind screamed. *Fly! Fly! Fly! FLY!*

Colin hit the ground face first.

12

God, that hurts! Colin said to himself. *Am I alive? Must be if it hurts.*

His father's voice said, "Didn't work, huh?"

Colin painfully raised his head to see Warren standing in front of him, wearing a heavy overcoat and a woollen hat. He pulled his hands out of his pockets, then reached down and helped Colin to his feet.

From behind them came a resounding *crash*. They turned to see Diamond – in statue form – topple over on to the street. A second later, she glistened and turned back to her normal self, then stood up.

"What the hell were you *thinking*?" Colin shouted at Renata.

She shrugged. "We thought it would be a good idea."

"A good idea? Look!" Colin pointed up. "That's where we were! Fourteen floors up! And you *pushed* me!"

"I see it didn't do any damage to your complaining glands," his father said.

"Dad, I could have broken my neck!"

"But you didn't."

"The two of you, listen to me very carefully: I. Cannot. Fly."

145

"Well, we know that *now*," Renata said.

"You think I haven't tried? I try every day! I do it the clever way, by trying to take off from the ground."

"Is your headset still intact?" Warren asked. "Caroline, can you hear him?"

Caroline's voice said, "There's a sort of high-pitched squealing coming through. So yes, it's working fine."

"Great," Colin said sulkily. "You're all against me."

"Hold the chatter," Caroline said. "I'm getting a report of a disturbance three blocks east of your position. Go and check it out."

Renata looked around. "Which way is east?"

"That way," Colin said, pointing.

"Make it fast," his mother said.

Leaving Warren behind, Colin and Renata started to run along the deserted street. *This is why we need Danny with us*, Colin said to himself. *He'd be there and back by now, if he had his powers.*

"What's the situation, Mrs Wagner?" Renata asked as she ran.

"It's a domestic disturbance. A known wife-beater. A lot of shouting, glass breaking."

"Do we have the right to enter someone's house?"

Colin said, "Let's just make sure that everyone is safe. *Then* we can worry about whether we're trespassing."

They rounded the last corner on to a quiet, dark

146

street. Six-storey-tall tenement buildings loomed over them. "We're here. What's the address?"

"Number three-seventeen, second-floor apartment, at the front."

"I see it," Colin said. "I'll take care of it."

Colin dashed across the street. *I might not be able to fly*, he said to himself, *but I'm strong enough to jump!* He leaped on to the iron railings in front of the building. The window above his head was open and a light was on. As he was about to leap, Renata shouted, "Wait!"

At that moment, another scream echoed through the street. *Don't have* time *to wait*, Colin thought. He crouched and jumped – diving straight through the open window. His hands hit the rough, bare floorboards and he flipped over on to his feet.

Right in front of him, a large heavy-set man had his arms wrapped around a scared-looking woman.

Without a word, Colin grabbed the man, lifted him off his feet and threw him to the floor. "How does *that* feel?" Colin asked. "You like being on the *receiving* end of a beating for a change?"

Something bounced off Colin's head, but he barely noticed it. "You think it's OK for someone who's strong to pick on someone who's weak? Because from where *I'm* standing, *you're* the weak one. You ever lay a hand on this woman again and you're going to have a hell of a time trying to pick up your teeth with broken fingers!"

"Leave him alone!" the woman screamed. He turned to see that she was hitting him across the head with a ceramic lamp.

"Please stop that," Colin said. *God, I've read about how abused wives sometimes stand up for their husbands, but this is crazy!* She kept hitting him. "Stop, please." The lamp finally shattered across Colin's face. "I promise that you're safe now. He won't hurt you again."

"He has *never* hurt me!"

"Um... Are you sure?"

"What do you mean, am I sure? We've been married for twenty-six years! He's never so much as raised his voice to me!"

Colin cringed. "But... There was a police report. About a domestic disturbance."

"Yes! Next door! We're the ones who called the cops!"

"Your light was on..." Colin said, realising that it was a very weak argument.

"Sure it was. The noise next door woke us up."

Caroline's voice came over the radio. "You got the wrong apartment, Colin!"

"Aw crap!" He looked sheepishly at the couple. "Sorry about that."

"Renata's already taken care of it!" his mother said.

"OK. Thanks."

The woman was helping her husband into a chair. "Who are you talking to?"

"My mo..." Colin paused. "Er... Headquarters. Sorry about the mistake."

"No harm done," the man said. "And you meant well. What's your name, son?"

"Wait a second," the woman said. She stepped up to Colin – she was a little taller than him – and looked closely at his face. "It's hard to be sure with your mask on, but it's you, isn't it? Rube, this is the new Titan!"

Great, Colin thought. *I decide I'm going to change my superhero name and then someone finally gets it right!* "Uh, no, I'm not Titan. I'm new at this. As you can tell. Sorry again about the mistake."

There was a screech of tyres from outside and the room was filled with flashing blue and red lights. Colin looked out the window to see Renata pushing a scrawny, wild-looking man out to a waiting squad car.

Rube stood next to Colin, looking out. He rested his hand on Colin's shoulder. "So you got the wrong apartment. At least you tried. You did more than most people do."

"What *is* your name, anyway?" the woman asked.

Colin shrugged. "I haven't decided yet."

The helicopter swooped so low over the trees that Dioxin was sure he'd be able to hear the branches hitting the landing struts any second now. Far ahead, he could see the lights of the small airport.

He glanced around. The copter was filled with mercenaries, a hand-picked team. Dioxin had worked with all of them before at various different times. He knew all their strengths and weaknesses.

The pilot said, "Three minutes! Hold tight." The copter swerved to the left and began to drop.

"All right, people!" Dioxin shouted. "You know the job. We go in hard and fast. I want a high rate of property damage and casualties. In and out as fast as possible. Got me?"

As one, the soldiers nodded an affirmative.

"You've been briefed on the two targets. Find them first; separate them from the others. Shoot them if necessary but do *not* kill them! Anyone else is fair game. Remember, this is a PR exercise. We *want* them to know what hit them."

The pilot's voice said, "We've got their attention. ATC is ordering us to back off."

"Ignore them!" Dioxin shouted. "Continue as planned!"

"Wilco."

The copter touched down right outside the passenger terminal. "Go!" Dioxin shouted.

He watched as the soldiers leaped from the copter and burst into the terminal, guns firing. Even over the roar of the rotors, he could hear screams from inside the building. He counted to twenty, then followed them.

Even though only seconds had passed, the terminal was almost completely gutted. There were bodies everywhere. Dioxin looked around. "No one left for me?"

"No, sir," one of the mercenaries replied, "just the two targets." He gestured towards a middle-aged man and woman lying on the floor. "Unconscious. Non-lethal wounds."

"Good work." Dioxin strode through the wreckage, stepping over the bodies, occasionally prodding one with his foot. Satisfied, he turned to the nearest mercenary. "Make the mark."

The man looked around and spotted a blank wall that was relatively undamaged and free of blood-splatters. He unclipped a can of spray paint from his belt and began to scrawl a message.

"If you don't want to be Titan any more, Col, I've got a good name for you," Razor said over breakfast the next morning. "Pancake!"

"Let it go, Razor," Colin said, spooning up the last of his cereal.

"How about... The Apologiser!"

Danny laughed. "Gravity Boy!"

Stephanie said, "I've got it... Downfall!"

This sparked another round of laughter from the group. Despite his embarrassment, Colin couldn't help smiling at that one.

Yvonne said, "Forget about it, Colin. I'm sure that every superhero has a night like that when they're starting out."

"Thanks."

"No problem. Roadkill."

Everyone erupted again.

"God, you lot are so immature!" Colin said. He looked at Razor. "Especially *you*. Garland."

Razor almost dropped his coffee cup. "What did you just say?"

"Nothing. Garland."

The older boy's eyes blazed. "Who told you?"

"Who told me what, Garland?"

"Oh, for the love of... It was Sol, wasn't it? I begged him not to say anything!"

Grinning, Colin said, "So what's your middle name, Mr Lighthouse?"

Razor slumped forward and put his head in his hands. "I can't believe he told you *that,* too!"

To the others, Colin said, "The first time I met Mr Garland Lighthouse here he refused to tell me his real name. Now we know why."

They all jumped when an alarm rang out.

"What the hell is that?" Butler asked.

Josh's voice boomed out of some hidden speakers. "This is a priority-one alert! All senior members to Ops immediately!"

"This is *not* a drill! All non-essential personnel will be evacuated immediately following this meeting," Josh said.

On one side of the briefing room, Colin stood with Danny, Renata, Yvonne, Mina, Razor and Butler. On the other side were Josh and Solomon, wearing his Paragon armour.

"Until further notice," Josh continued, "we run with a skeleton-crew only. I'll be honest: we don't know exactly what we're facing. We don't know when it's going to happen, but we do know that it's not going to be good. What bothers me most is that outside of this building, only a handful of people know where we are. I would trust each one of them with my life. They will never talk. No one else even knows that this place *exists*. As far as the rest of the world is concerned, you're all currently somewhere in Manhattan. But somehow our security has been breached. It can't be by someone on the inside because we monitor all communications in and out."

"So how do you know that there *is* a breach?" Danny asked.

"Because of this…" Josh hit a switch on his console and a large screen lowered from the ceiling. "Last night, a small airport in Nevada…" The screen showed security camera footage of eight well-armed men bursting into the airport. They fired indiscriminately and continuously. Then a ninth man entered, looked around and seemed pleased with the results.

"Two survivors. Almost one hundred fatalities," Josh said.

"My God… That's… Who *are* they?"

"We don't know, Renata. They came out of nowhere. Whoever they are, they knew exactly what they were doing. This was not a random strike; from the security camera footage it's clear that they knew the layout of the place and where all the staff would be. The man with the serious facial scarring appears to be the leader, but we don't know anything else. The National Security Agency and the Department of Homeland Security are at the scene now, but it's doubtful they'll turn up anything useful."

Renata said, "If these people were professionals, why did they leave all the security cameras running?"

"They wanted us to know," Solomon said coldly. "They did it because they wanted us to know that they *could* do something like this, that they were willing to do it and that they know about us."

The screen showed a large white wall, with a single word spray-painted on it: *SAKKARA*.

13

JOSH LEFT THE room to prepare everyone for the evacuation, but Solomon remained behind to talk to the teenagers. "They know where we are. We don't even know *who* they are. Façade believes that the attack was a deliberate attempt to provoke us and I'm inclined to agree with him."

"So if these killers know about us," Renata said, "then that might mean that someone on the inside told them."

Razor said, "Sol, this might sound dumb, but... Couldn't it be a coincidence? For all we know there could be an old rock band called Sakkara."

"Think about that for a minute, Razor... A team of ruthlessly efficient, highly-trained soldiers attacks an airport and murders almost a hundred people just so that they can spray-paint the name of their favourite band on the wall. I really don't think so."

"They're going to come here," Danny said. "We have to prepare for war."

Colin – who had remained silent throughout the meeting – said, "We have to assume that they know everything about us. *Everything.* I don't think that it's a

155

good idea to evacuate. That only means that we'd have to protect our people somewhere else. They're better off here, for now."

"So what do you think we should do?" Butler asked angrily. "This is a textbook terrorist strike: they come out of the blue, hit a random target and disappear."

Solomon held up his hands to halt the discussion. "This is not a *debate*, people! We don't know where – or if – they're going to strike next. We've got the NSA and the FBI feeding us everything they have about the airport strike, but the chances are that we are only going to hear about further attacks when it's too late to do anything about it. I want you guys training around the clock. Razor, get back to the workshop. We're going to double-shift on the armour. Mina? I've been reading about these bursts of strength you've had. I want you working with Warren and Caroline on that. We need to find a way for you to trigger your strength whenever you want. Danny... I don't care what problems you and Façade have had in the past: he knew more about Quantum than anyone else, so you're working with him. We're going to see if it's possible to get your speed back. Renata? You're with me for now. The rest of you: hit the gym."

As the others filed out of the room, Renata asked, "What do you need me for?"

Solomon hesitated before answering. "There's been a... development. Some of the others didn't want you to know about this, but we knew you'd find out sooner or later." He reactivated the screen. "This message appeared on the Trutopians' cable channel about an hour ago."

The screen showed Reginald Kinsella standing in his office, talking to the camera. He looked exhausted and was shaking slightly. "Last night's horrendous attack on the airfield in Nevada was an unforgivable act. It's my sad duty to confirm that seven Trutopians lost their lives. Their names are being withheld until all their relatives have been contacted. The only positive news I have to report is that the two survivors – Trutopians – are responding well to treatment. They were seriously wounded but are expected to recover. They've been transferred to the Trutopian hospital in their home town of Breckin Falls, Cleveland. They are..." Kinsella glanced down at a sheet of paper, "Maria and Julius Soliz."

Renata's face turned pale. "Oh my God! That's my mom and dad!"

❄

Colin and Danny were in Danny's room, standing still. Colin had his eyes closed, frowning in concentration, using his highly-developed hearing to listen to what was being said in the Ops room. "She says she *has* to go to them." A pause. "Josh is refusing to let her go. He says it's too dangerous."

"How does she sound?" Danny asked.

"A bit scared... Actually, so does Josh... Now Sol's sticking up for her. He's offered to take her to see her family. Josh says that we can't spare him. My dad agrees with Josh."

"Damn."

"All right, now Façade has said *he'll* take her."

Danny nodded. "Good idea."

Colin opened his eyes and looked at his friend. "You trust him?"

"I guess. What are they saying now?"

"OK... Josh is trying to argue that there's no point in Renata going to see her parents because she'd never be allowed into the hospital." Colin smiled. "Renata's just said, 'Allowed? Like they could stop me!' Now my mother's whispering something... Oh." Colin's face fell.

"What is it?"

"She's just whispered, 'Colin, you'd better not be listening in to this'."

"Doesn't matter. Listen anyway. You can always lie about it later."

"Hold on, someone's coming," Colin said.

There was a knock on the door. Danny opened it, to see Stephanie Cord standing there. "Is Colin with...? He is. Colin, can I talk to you for a minute? Uh, alone?"

Danny said, "I've got to say goodbye to my mother and Niall anyway." He left the room.

Stephanie closed the door behind him and stepped up to Colin. "I don't know where they're taking us. Somewhere safe, Josh says."

"I'm sure everything will be fine."

"Promise me something, OK?"

"Anything," Colin said.

"Promise me that you'll keep my dad safe."

"I will, of course," Colin said. After a pause, he added, "Was... Um... Was there anything else?"

"Like what?"

"I don't know."

She smiled. "I want you to keep yourself safe, too. Is *that* what you wanted to hear?"

Colin looked away. "I guess."

"If anything happened to you, I'd probably miss you a bit. For a while. But don't worry on my account; I wouldn't dwell on it. I'm sure I'd get over it pretty quickly."

"Well... that's good."

Stephanie smiled again, winked at him and moved towards the door. "Look after yourself, Colin. I'd hate to have to find someone else to pick on."

14

IN THE EARLY hours of Christmas Eve, the helicopter carrying Dioxin's strike team touched down in the football field of a high school in the small town of Morgan in Utah.

Dioxin himself broke into the school and planted the explosives, while his mercenaries emptied drums of kerosene in a precise pattern over the field.

They moved on to a second school, then a third and a fourth.

The explosives all detonated at the same time, destroying the buildings and igniting the kerosene patterns on the football fields.

In each case, letters of fire spelled out the same seven-letter word: *SAKKARA*.

❖

Nine hours later, in a large shopping mall a few miles south of Fort Collins, Colorado, cheerful families and panicking last-minute shoppers bustled about to the tinny sound of *Jingle Bells* and other holiday songs.

A bag slung over his shoulder, Dioxin walked in through the mall's main entrance, not caring that people were staring at his scarred face, that parents were herding their children away.

The crowds parting ahead of him, he walked up to the enormous Christmas tree, where a fat man dressed as an elf was unloading brightly-wrapped presents from a sack.

"Hi," Dioxin said.

The elf turned around and gasped when he saw Dioxin's face. He quickly regained his composure. "Sorry, I didn't mean anything by that."

Dioxin smiled. "I get it all the time. Listen, all us guys down at the fire station made a collection: we got some more presents for you to hand out." He passed over the bag. "Yeah, this guy whose house we saved last year made a huge donation, so we thought we'd spread the happiness around. Just hand 'em out to any little kids you see. No charge! And tell them they're not to open the presents until tomorrow morning!"

"Will do. That's real good of you, thanks."

"It's our pleasure," Dioxin said. He smiled and walked away.

He hung around the mall for the next few minutes, keeping one eye on the elf as he began handing out the small presents to eager children.

As Dioxin had expected, it wasn't long before one little boy was too eager to wait for Christmas morning. He tore into the wrapping on the present and pulled out a white plastic cube with a large red button on the top. The boy pressed the button.

Dioxin immediately held his breath. He covered what remained of his nose and walked out into the parking lot.

Through the doors, he could see the little boy lying on the ground. Within seconds, everyone around him had also collapsed. Dioxin turned and walked slowly towards his car.

The invisible gas contained in the boxes wasn't fatal, but it caused temporary blackouts, headaches and extreme nausea that would last for days.

In eight other shopping malls throughout the state of Colorado, the same thing was happening.

In each case, Dioxin's mercenaries made certain to leave the bags behind. At the bottom of each bag was a simple note: 'A gift from SAKKARA.'

In Sakkara's Ops room, Solomon Cord stared at the large video screen. Warren and Caroline Wagner sat either side of him. Josh Dalton hit the video's 'Play' button.

Reginald Kinsella appeared on the screen. "The destruction of the four schools in Utah by this 'Sakkara' group is a deliberate attack on this country's young people! Thousands of students are now without schools and hundreds of faculty members may lose theirs jobs! But this morning's attacks on nine different shopping malls – *all* of them within Trutopian communities – was nothing short of an act of *terrorism* against our organisation!"

Joshua Dalton's cellphone rang. He hit a key to pause the video, then answered the phone. "Dalton... Yes, I'll hold..." A couple of seconds later, he said, "No, General. No warning whatsoever. There was no way we could have anticipated... Yes, I understand. We'll keep your people informed." Josh put his phone away and looked around the Ops room at the others. "That was General Piers, our liaison with the military. He has ordered us to stop these terrorists by any means necessary. He stopped short of blaming us for the attacks, but only just." Josh sighed. "Unfortunately, we have absolutely no leads. These people could strike again, any time, any where. Someone give me *something* to work on!"

Caroline Wagner said, "Kinsella's becoming quite a powerful man. It seems to me that whoever is behind these attacks wants to set him against us."

Her husband nodded. "Our enemy is making more enemies for us."

"Either that," Solomon said, "or someone is trying to elicit sympathy for the Trutopians."

Josh continued: "Luckily, all of those schools were empty, but the cost of repairs is going to cripple their communities. As for the attacks on the malls, the latest report is that *hundreds* of people – most of them children – have been hospitalised. No fatalities, thank God, but what if these attackers had used a lethal gas?"

"What else does Kinsella have to say?" Caroline asked.

"Just the usual stuff about how great his organisation is. No crime, everyone lives without fear. Until now."

"No word on how these perpetrators managed to get inside their gated communities?"

"Not as such, but he went to great lengths to explain that the attacks were the work of outside forces." Josh dropped into a chair and buried his face in his hands for a moment. "All right," he said, looking up. "That's bad enough, but the really bad news is that somehow the name Sakkara has been directly connected with us. It's out there on the Internet. There's nothing we can do about it, short of shutting down the entire Internet. And believe me, if we could do that, we *would*." He began tapping at a keyboard and the television picture was replaced with a website. "Conspiracy theories for beginners, this one. It's a very simple site, run by a fifteen-year-old kid in Devon, England. Look at this..." He clicked on one of the page's links.

The screen showed the words, "Sakkara – the New Heroes' Headquarters!" complete with a rough drawing of the building.

"Thankfully, it doesn't give our location," Josh said, "but it's got a lot of the facts right." He looked around the table. "I have absolutely no doubt now that someone connected to this organisation is a traitor."

Everyone looked around at each other.

"Any ideas who?" Warren asked.

"Yes. All this started to happen after you arrived," Josh said.

"You're not saying that it's me, are you?"

"No. But it could be someone else who arrived at the same time: Façade."

❊

Later, sitting on the edge of the roof of Sakkara and looking west towards the city lights of Topeka, Danny and Renata listened to Colin as he related the highlights of the discussion that took place in the Operations Room.

"We know the traitor isn't one of us three," Renata said, scooping up a pile of snow into a ball. "And Josh is sure that it's not one of his people. *Could* it be Façade?"

"No, I don't think so," Danny said. "Even when he was working with Max, he believed he was doing the right thing."

"He was a criminal before Max recruited him," she reminded him.

"True, but that was a long time ago." Danny looked at Colin. "How well do you know Razor?"

"Well enough to know that he's happier here than he ever was before. He's not the traitor. He'd never betray Sol."

"Butler then," Danny said. "He's always swaggering about like he's better than the rest of us."

"Just because he's a scumbag doesn't mean he's a traitor," Renata said. She got to her feet, then stepped back and threw the snowball as hard as she could. It disappeared into the darkness. "How's that?"

"The farthest one yet," Colin replied. "Got to be half a mile, at least."

Renata sat back down again. "What about Mina or Yvonne?"

"Not likely," Danny replied. "They've been here all their lives. They wouldn't throw that away."

"They might if they hated the place. They're both a bit weird anyway. Mina's only said about four words in the whole time we've been here, and all the stuff about her being able to see people's auras? Give me a break!"

"You don't believe it?"

"Not for a minute. And you know what else is weird about her? This super-strength she's supposed to have from time to time. Well, I know we haven't been here that long, but I haven't seen any evidence of it. Have you?"

Danny and Colin shook their heads.

"So, since we don't know for certain that she's got *any* powers, how do we know she's a superhuman at all?"

"That's a good point," Colin said.

"Yeah," Danny said. "And here's another thing... Why have they been here all their lives if superhuman powers don't kick in until you hit puberty?"

Colin said, "Maybe they were just more likely to develop powers. Maybe one of their parents was a superhero."

"Or a supervillain," Renata said. "Ragnarök, maybe, or Slaughter."

"Y'know, that could be why Butler is afraid of Yvonne," Colin said.

The others looked at him.

"You didn't notice that? When he's around her he's always very careful not to upset her and he does whatever she says."

"Maybe he's in love with her," Renata said.

Danny nodded. "Could be. She's certainly good-looking."

Renata raised an eyebrow. "Is she really?"

"Um..."

"Look, I'm not saying that Yvonne or Mina *is* the traitor, but if I was them, I'd be anxious to get away from Sakkara. I mean, they're practically prisoners. We've only been here a couple of days and I'm going stir-crazy already."

Colin said, "You're going to go and see your family, aren't you? Even though Josh doesn't want you to."

"God, let me tell you, Josh was a lot more fun ten years ago. I used to think he was so cool. Now there are times when it's all I can do to stop myself from punching him."

"Don't change the subject!" Danny said.

"Look," Renata said. "My parents are still in hospital – back home in Breckin Falls – but at least they're out of danger. And whether Josh likes it or not, I'm going to see them again. How, exactly, is someone supposed to be able to stop me? Col, you're the only one who might be strong enough and I know you won't try. Will you?"

Colin shook his head. "No. But if you're going to do it, then do it. Go, see them and get back here."

They fell silent as Solomon Cord approached, wearing his Paragon armour. "What are you kids up to?"

"Nothing."

"I've been making some modifications to the jetpack. Thought I'd take it out for a spin." In the half-darkness, he gave Renata a significant look. "I'm heading south-west. Probably get twenty miles or so, maybe as far as the airport. Could get a lot further than that, of course, if I wasn't carrying anything. But twenty is about the best I can do."

Colin got to his feet. "It's getting cold. I'm going in." He glanced back at Renata and nodded, then walked towards the stairwell.

Solomon put on his helmet and spoke into the microphone. "Caroline? Sol. I'm on the roof. About to test the mods to the pack. Warming up the systems and will be departing in about a minute." He looked at Danny and Renata. "Say your goodbyes or whatever it is that you need to do." He walked away.

"Ready?" Danny asked, helping Renata to her feet.

"No... I don't have my helmet... But this is the best chance I'll get. If there *is* a traitor, I don't want him to know I've gone."

Danny hesitated. "You... uh... You *will* come back, right?"

She nodded. There was an awkward moment between them, then they heard the sound of Paragon's jetpack starting up.

The moment lost, Renata stepped away from Danny. "I'll

come back." She turned and ran towards Solomon, who scooped her up in his arms and zoomed off into the sky.

Danny watched the point of light shrink and vanish. "Damn."

15

THE NEXT MORNING after breakfast, Joshua Dalton gathered the teenagers in the Ops Room. "Where's Renata?" he asked, looking at Danny.

Danny looked around. "She could be still in bed."

"She's not. We logged her going out on to the roof last night with you, but she never logged back in. What happened, Danny?"

"I've no idea. Maybe she's still up there?"

Josh sighed and walked right up to Danny. "Where is she?"

"I honestly don't know." *He's not going to let this go*, Danny thought. "Josh, if Renata's missing then maybe we should be out there looking for her!"

Josh stared at him. *He wants to see if I'll look away.* Danny had once read that people who are lying tend to glance down or touch their face. He kept his eyes fixed on Josh's.

"All right," Josh said, stepping back. He looked at the others. "There's strong evidence to indicate that someone in Sakkara has been leaking information to our enemy. Renata's disappearance suggests that either *she* is the traitor or she has been taken."

"She could have just left on her own," Razor said.

"How? The grounds are monitored by motion detectors. The only person who'd be fast enough to get through undetected is Danny and his powers have gone." He glanced again at Danny. "You holding something back?"

"No!"

"You are all confined to your rooms. You are stripped of your television privileges. And until we learn otherwise, we're going to treat Renata as hostile."

"That's crazy!" Colin said.

"No, it's just wise."

In a cold voice, Yvonne said, "Josh?"

"What?"

"Look at me... *Let it go,* Josh."

The man sighed. "All right, all right. Carry on as normal. But... Keep vigilant! We still don't know what we're up against!"

Josh dismissed them and as they made their way along the corridor, Danny turned to Yvonne. "Thanks. It's bad enough being stuck here over Christmas without being grounded as well."

❀

An hour later, Mina approached Razor in the machine room. He was hunched over the workbench, soldering iron in one hand and a complex mechanical device in the other.

Without looking up, he asked, "What can I do for you, Mina?"

"You knew."

"Knew what?"

"Renata."

Razor put down the soldering iron. "All right, Mina. I know you're not big on conversation, but if you want people to know what you're talking about, you have to actually *tell* them."

Mina hesitated for a moment, then said, "You knew Renata was gone, didn't you?"

"No."

"Your aura tells me you're lying. Just like you were in Ops."

Damn it, Razor said to himself. *Didn't know she could do that!* He knew he had to change the subject. "Are you really serious about this aura stuff?"

She nodded.

"You're the only superhuman I've ever heard of who can do that. What's *my* aura like?"

Hesitantly, Mina said, "Your aura is tainted."

"What does that mean?"

173

"The future. It's bad."

Razor shuddered. "OK, now you're starting to freak me out! Mina, do you know how crazy that sounds?"

"I am *not* crazy!"

"I'm not saying that *you* are crazy, just what you're saying." He pushed his chair back from the bench and leaned back, arms folded. "All right then. Tell me about the auras. What do they look like? Do they come in different colours and shapes, is that it?"

"Different colours, shapes, tones, patterns, emotions, time, weight... Every aura is different, but there are patterns. People from the same family usually have similar auras."

"Would you be able to know if someone was a superhuman just by looking at their aura?"

Mina thought about this, then nodded. "Yes, now that there's more than just me, Yvonne and Josh."

"Josh has a superhuman aura, too? So the aura doesn't change when they lose their powers..." Razor said thoughtfully. "So how does it work? When you look at me, what exactly can you see?"

"There's a glow. Bright and dark patches drifting through it. It changes with your mood."

"How close does someone have to be before you can see their aura? Would you be able to see it from, say, a hundred yards away?"

174

"If I know what someone's aura looks like, I can always find them. If they're within about eight miles."

Razor bit his lip as he thought. "Where's Colin right now?"

"In his room."

"Butler?"

"The gym."

"And your friend Danny? Where's he?"

"In the gym with Butler. They're not talking to each other."

"I'm not surprised. So what is it between you and Danny? You like him, don't you?"

Mina blushed, but didn't reply.

"Colin said that back home all the girls liked Danny. Until he lost his arm."

"Danny's got a pure aura. Not a *completely* pure one, but the closest I've ever seen."

"Oh God, you didn't tell him that, did you?"

Mina shook her head violently. "No! Of course not!"

"Good. So are you telling me you know where everyone is, all the time?"

"Not automatically. But I can find them if I look hard enough."

"All right then... Here's an important one: what makes a superhuman aura different from everyone else's?"

175

"There's an extra twist. It's hard to explain... There's *more* to a superhuman aura."

"Are there any people here who don't have powers but they do have that twist to their aura?"

"Yes. Mr and Mrs Wagner, Façade, Josh and Niall."

"So when Niall reaches puberty he's going to be a superhuman?"

Mina nodded.

"Can you tell whether Danny's lost his powers forever?"

She looked away. "I can tell that he's holding something back. It could be that he's just not *letting* himself use his powers. But it might be something else. If someone's hiding a big secret it shows up in their aura. Like Josh and Mr Wagner."

"Who else?"

"People keep secrets for a reason."

"Who else?" Razor repeated, more firmly.

"Yvonne. She's had the same thing for a long time now. I think she might have found out something about our parents, but she's not telling me. *You* have a secret, too. Not just about Renata. Something else."

Razor glanced down at the mechanical device on his bench. "Yeah, I do. But you can't tell *what* those secrets are, right? Just that we have them?"

"That's right."

"Good. I promise you that this secret isn't a bad thing. Do you believe me?"

Mina looked at him carefully, then nodded.

Dioxin sat on a chair in front of the wall of television screens. Each screen showed a different channel, but all of them were reporting the same story.

"I've got to hand it to you, Cross," Dioxin said. "You're a lot more fun to work with than Ragnarök was."

Victor Cross smiled. "And it's going to be even more fun after tonight." He turned up the volume on one of the channels. It showed recent footage of Paragon in flight. The reporter's voice said, "Government officials are refusing to comment, but it's widely accepted that Paragon, Diamond, Kid Titan and possibly three other teenage superhumans are currently operating from a base somewhere in Kansas."

The screen switched to footage of the destruction of the schools and the airport, plus body counts and costs in millions of dollars, then cut to an interview with a grime-covered, exhausted-looking fire chief. "If these new heroes ain't gonna stop the terrorists, the least they could do is come here and help us search for the survivors. What's the use of superhumans if they're just gonna sit around on their butts at a time like this?"

"Time for my own broadcast," Cross said, reaching for his keyboard. He tapped away at the keys for a few seconds, then slipped a DVD into his computer. "Took me three takes to get this right."

A large screen in the centre of the wall blanked out, then showed the Trutopians' logo, with the words, 'Stand By'. A voice said, "We interrupt this programme for a message from Reginald Kinsella."

A second later, Cross's disguised face appeared on the screen. "My friends... This was supposed to be my Christmas – or, if you prefer, winter holiday – message. I was going to talk about the great strides our community has made over the past year, how successful we have been at drastically cutting down crime. But... my conscience will not allow me to do that, not while people in the outside world are hurting.

"This is not a time for panic. I am certain that the Sakkara terrorists will be brought to justice, if not by the new heroes then by the regular authorities. There is no reason to assume that the superhumans have abandoned us: I'm sure that they're doing everything they can to help. However... we relied on the protection of superhumans for a long time, then they seemingly disappeared and we had to learn to fend for ourselves. Who can say whether this time they are here to stay?

We cannot assume that they will always be here for us. More importantly, this new generation of superhumans has only been active for a short time. Perhaps the question that we should be asking is not 'Why don't they do anything?' but '*Can* they do anything?'"

A pause. "In light of these attacks, I'm asking that every member of the Trutopian community be extra vigilant over the holiday season. This should be a time for peace, not destruction. It saddens me to have to do this, but... for the safety of us all, I've just given the order that security on our communities be doubled from now until the foreseeable future. All public areas are to be closed immediately. They will be checked and double-checked for explosive devices, and will not open until we are absolutely certain that they are safe. All stores, restaurants, bars, entertainment establishments, churches and schools are hereby closed. A dusk to dawn curfew is in place."

Dioxin turned to Cross. "You're cancelling *Christmas*?"

Victor grinned. "Yeah."

"Nice."

On screen, Kinsella continued. "Anyone who has business outside their own Trutopian community will unfortunately not be able to go to work. From now until further notice, the gates are closed. I promise you that this will only be a temporary situation. My friends, I don't make these decisions lightly. This is for our own safety. If the superhumans can't protect us, we have to protect ourselves. Thank you for listening."

The phone on Cross's desk rang. "Victor Cross. Speak to me." He listened for a moment. "That's good... At what time? Got it." He hung up.

"So now what?" Dioxin asked.

"Now *I* sit back and deal with the fallout of that announcement and *you* get your men ready. You're going to Topeka. That was our little puppet in Sakkara on the phone. He's just given me Paragon's schedule."

16

Colin and Danny were in Sakkara's gym, taking turns to half-heartedly toss a basketball through a loop Colin had tied in one of the ropes.

Colin knew that he could make every shot, but he deliberately missed a few: Danny was finding it difficult enough to even pick up the ball.

"This is the worst Christmas Day *ever*!" Danny said. "My mum and Niall are in some safe house God-knows-where, there are no presents, no decorations and no nice food. *And* Renata's gone. I hope she's going to be OK."

The ball bounced back to Colin and he caught it left-handed. "I'm sure she will be. She's able to look after herself." *Go on*, Colin urged himself. *Say it!* "So, um, you and her are... Well, what's happening there? Are you going out together or what?" He threw the ball at the loop.

"Close one... No, we're not," Danny said. "But... I get the feeling that something *might* happen."

"Doesn't it bother you that she's really twenty-four?"

"No she's not! She was frozen for ten years! Physically and mentally she's only fourteen!" He sighed. "She likes me, I know that much."

"So does Mina." Colin sighed. "Just once I wish some girl would show some interest in *me*!"

"What about Stephanie? She's always teasing you. And it's pretty clear that you're crazy about her."

Colin hesitated. "Clear to you or clear to everyone?"

"Everyone." Danny trapped the basketball with his foot, then leaned over to slip his hand under it: it was the only way he could pick up the ball.

"There's just no way a girl like her would go for someone like me," Colin said.

"Well, you know how to find out, don't you? When they all get back from the safe house, you could *ask* her."

"I can't do that! What if she said no?"

"What if she said yes?"

"She wouldn't say yes."

"Then forget about her."

"I don't think I can."

Danny raised his eyes. "God, that's pathetic, Col!" He spun the ball on one finger. "Hey, I can still do this!"

"Suppose I do ask her out," Colin said, "and she says no and then tells everyone and laughs about it?"

"Would you go out with the sort of person who would do something like that?"

"Well, no."

"Do you think Stephanie is that sort of person?"

"Maybe. I don't know. Probably not."

"There you are, then. Just *ask* her!"

"Or I could get Renata to ask her," Colin said thoughtfully.

"Yeah, but—"

The alarm sounded. They jumped to their feet and ran towards Ops. As they rushed into the room, Caroline was speaking into the communicator, "No way to tell whether it's the same people. A large black copter, coming out of nowhere... Strafing the railway carriages."

Paragon's voice replied, "Doesn't matter whether it's them or not. Whoever it is has got to be stopped."

Josh turned to Colin. "Get to the roof! Now!"

Façade was running towards the StratoTruck as Colin emerged on to the roof. "What's going on?" Colin asked.

They climbed into the vehicle and Façade began the start-up sequence. "Strap yourself in. We've just got a report of an unmarked black helicopter attacking the industrial railway station five miles north of here. By sheer luck Paragon was already in the air; he's gone to investigate. Now sit down!"

"What about Danny and the others?"

"We don't have time to wait for them."

Warren reached the jet's ramp. "Let's go."

Colin put out his hand to stop his father. "You won't be any good to us, Dad! They need you more here!"

Warren hesitated. "Colin..."

"Dad, get back inside and make sure all the doors are sealed!"

"No, I'm coming with you."

"You're not!" Colin put his hand on his father's chest and pushed. Warren tumbled backwards down the ramp and on to the roof. "Take it up, Façade!" Colin shouted. "Go! And don't close the hatch!"

"You're the boss. Hold tight."

The force of the sudden vertical take-off almost knocked Colin off his feet. When the StratoTruck was clear of the roof, it spun about until it was facing north, then surged forward.

Colin looked out at the lights of the city streaming by below, and felt the familiar queasiness and dizziness of vertigo. *What am I going to do?* he wondered. *Jump? What if I miss?*

Seconds later, Façade said, "There they are. Dead ahead, moving away from us."

"Where's Sol?"

"I don't see him..."

"Match their speed and course! Get as close as possible to that copter!"

Paragon soared through the night sky, straight towards the large helicopter. As he neared, the copter ceased its attack and banked away.

Have they seen me? Or have they just finished what they came here to do? He increased his speed, then flipped over on to his back and grabbed one of the copter's landing struts.

He clawed his way across the underside towards the starboard hatch, then pulled himself up. *This is why I need the new armour! I'd be able to just tear the hatch off!* Holding on with one hand, he removed a small magnetic grenade from his belt and attached it to the door. He set the timer for three seconds and then let go, allowing himself to drop.

Paragon activated his jetpack just as the grenade exploded, ripping the helicopter's door from its frame. He increased his speed, angled himself correctly, then flew straight through the open doorway.

He collided with a large man, knocking him to the floor. Instantly – and with no care for their colleague's safety – two other men opened fire.

The bullets ricocheted off Paragon's armour. "Cease fire!" A rough voice yelled.

Paragon leaped at the nearest mercenary and

smashed him against the bulkhead. "Drop your weapons and set this thing down!"

Dioxin stepped out of the shadows and yelled to the pilot: "Move it! We've got what we came for!"

"Who are you? What do you want with me?" Paragon demanded, advancing on him.

Dioxin laughed and held up a small black device. He pressed a button on it...

...and Paragon's armour instantly powered down.

"We don't want *you*, Paragon. We want your armour." He pressed another button and the armour began to unseal itself.

Paragon darted for the doorway, but two of the men grabbed hold of him. He lashed out, hitting one of them in the face with his steel-gloved fist. He jabbed his elbow at the second man's solar plexus, but the man side-stepped and the blow did little damage.

As Paragon struggled, two more men jumped on him and began to remove his armour. "Who *are* you people?"

"Isn't it obvious? We're the bad guys," the scarred man said. "But you know who *I* am, don't you, Paragon? After all, you're the one who did *this* to me!" He indicated the extensive scarring on his face and hands. "You turned me into a monster. Children *scream* when they see me. Children like Alia and Stephanie."

Solomon Cord stared at the scarred man. "Oh God."

"God won't save you now, Cord! I had a chance for a normal life and you *ruined* that! You destroyed my future. Now I'm going to destroy something you value just as much!"

"You're a goddamned psycho!" Cord yelled. "I've never seen you before!"

Through gritted teeth, the scarred man said, "Ten years ago... I could have washed the acid off my skin. You slowed me down! I had third-degree burns over eighty per cent of my body. It's taken *nineteen* skin-grafts for me to look even this good. *You* did this! You stopped me from getting to that fountain!"

"Dioxin. We... Everyone thought you were dead. Dissolved by your own acid."

For a moment, Dioxin's snarl vanished. "There were times when I wished I *was* dead. But... there were many more times when I wished *you* were dead. And guess what, Cord? Sometimes, if you believe in them strongly enough, wishes come true." He nodded towards the doorway. "Throw him out. Let's see if this superhero can fly without his damned jetpack."

❖

"I see him!" Colin yelled. "He's falling!"

"At this height, he'll hit the ground in about thirty seconds!" Façade said.

Colin gripped the back of Façade's seat. "Get after him! We can catch him!"

"But…"

"Quiet!" Colin concentrated.

Faintly, he could hear Solomon saying, "Colin, wherever you are I hope you can hear me. It's Dioxin! He was after the armour! Tell Razor he has to find a way to disable it!"

The StratoTruck pitched and staggered as Façade manipulated the controls, attempting to match the speed at which Cord was falling.

Colin stood in the hatchway, one hand gripping so hard it was biting into the metal frame. "Closer… Closer!"

❖

As he fell, Solomon Cord saw the StratoTruck approaching and realised what they were trying to do.

He stretched his arms and legs out, trying to slow his descent as much as possible.

The ground rushed towards him.

The StratoTruck was pointing straight down now, inching closer and closer to him. He could see Colin in the doorway, his hand outstretched.

Come on, come on! Solomon said to himself. He took

another look at the ground. *Too late! They're not going to make it!* "Pull up!" He shouted to Colin. "You'll be killed!"

His fingertips brushed against Colin's for a brief moment.

"Pull up!" he yelled.

Below, he could clearly see the lights of cars on the busy highway. *Oh God, I hope it's painless!* He closed his eyes. "Vienna…"

Then he felt a strong hand grip his and roughly pull him on board the StratoTruck.

17

VICTOR CROSS, EVAN Laurie and Dioxin examined the disassembled Paragon armour, spread out on a workbench in front of them.

"We're trying to reverse-engineer the armour's control systems," Laurie said, "but it's not going to be easy... not even counting the unique alloys it's made of, this thing is an absolute masterpiece. You're sure that Cord doesn't have any superhuman abilities?"

"He doesn't," Cross said. "But he has a tremendous aptitude for mechanics. Plus they have a hell of a lot of resources and experts at Sakkara."

Dioxin asked, "How long will it take to get it working?"

"A few weeks, maybe a month," Laurie said. He indicated the circuitry on the inside of the armour's chest plate. "If they'd used off-the-shelf components it would be a lot simpler, but this is all custom-built, right down to the microprocessors. I've never even *seen* anything like this before. It's got a lot of sensors and technical data-streams, all feeding into the helmet where the information is projected on to the inside of the visor. Infra-red, enhanced night-vision, audio pick-ups, targeting, fuel optimisation..."

Dioxin interrupted him. "Forget all that crap. Just make the damn rocket-pack fly."

"It's a *jetpack*, not a rocket-pack," Laurie said, looking almost offended that Dioxin didn't know the difference. "A jet engine mixes its fuel with the air. A rocket uses only the fuel it can carry."

"So what?"

"So if you want to increase the range of either of them, you have to add more fuel. Obviously. But doubling the fuel of a rocket wouldn't get you double the range because the heavier something is, the more fuel it needs to fly, and the fuel itself adds weight, whereas—"

"Did I ask for a science lesson?" Dioxin snarled. "Make it fly! You *can* do that, can't you?"

"The fastest way to get it all up and running would be to rebuild the circuitry from the ground up."

Cross said, "I want to know exactly how they built it as much as you do, Laurie, but we don't have time for that. Strip out everything you can't get working immediately and concentrate on the jetpack. And I want weapons. This armour... it's a flying computer. And we don't need a flying computer. We need a flying gun."

As Cross turned to leave, he added, "Commandeer any personnel or equipment you need, Laurie. I want this armour ready for action by tomorrow morning. Dioxin is going to war."

Laurie muttered, "Thought we already *were* at war."

Dioxin laughed at that. "You mean all that destruction, all those deaths? Laurie, that was a light rain compared to the storm that's about to hit them."

Renata Soliz let go of the underside of the speeding truck and crashed to the ground. She tucked herself into a ball, rolled and landed on her feet.

She walked to the edge of the freeway, then dropped the five metres to the road below and walked towards her home town of Breckin Falls.

It had been a tough journey. Paragon had flown her to the airport south of Topeka, twenty miles away from Sakkara. Booking a flight would have been impossible, so Renata had sneaked through the airport's access corridors until she was able to make her way through to the runways, then hid in the undercarriage of the first plane she could find that was going to Cleveland.

Now, at almost two o'clock in the morning, she was walking down Thorndale Hill for the first time in over ten years. Fresh snow had begun to fall and Renata couldn't help thinking of a huge snowball fight she'd had with her sister the previous winter. *No, it wasn't last winter*, she corrected herself, *that was eleven years ago.*

Solomon Cord had told her that her parents had only recently joined the Trutopians. "They just signed their house over to them," Cord had said. "In exchange, they were given a small apartment inside the gated community. Your mother now works for the organisation, tending the grounds. Your father still has his office-cleaning job, but he's had to abandon his clients outside the community. They pay fifteen per cent of their earnings to the organisation. That's on top of the usual income taxes they pay to the government."

The Trutopian section of the town was not hard to find. A high fence ran the entire length of Mull Avenue, cutting right across what had once been a busy road. Now, recently-erected signposts pointed to alternative routes.

Keeping to the shadows, Renata made her way along the undergrowth next to the fence until she reached the main gate. Two uniformed men stood outside the closed gates, occasionally stamping their feet to keep warm. *Private police force*, Renata said to herself. *No easy way past them.*

She briefly considered walking up to the guards and just telling them who she was, then demanding to see her family, but dismissed that idea: her family didn't know that she was still alive, and the last thing the new heroes needed was their enemy finding out anything else about them.

She looked up at the fence. *Probably electrified. The current won't hurt me but it might set off an alarm.* She quietly made her way back along the fence until she found a spot out of sight of the guards. The fence was about three metres high. *I can't jump that high without a run-up, and I can't take a run-up because then the guards would see me.*

Renata looked around: further back, right next to the fence, there was a high ridge of packed snow, created by a snow-plough that had recently cleared the road.

She ran for the ridge, leaped on to it and vaulted over the fence, clearing it by only a couple of centimetres.

Landing quietly in a snowdrift, Renata looked around. She was on the edge of a narrow road. *This wasn't here ten years ago. Looks like it circles the whole community.* As quietly as she could Renata darted through the streets, hoping to find a signpost directing her towards the hospital.

The whole place was eerily silent. In a wide pedestrianised street, a few stores had their Christmas lights on, turning the snow alternately green and red. *Why is it so quiet? Surely* someone *should be out at this hour?*

As she made her way towards what was once the town square, Renata heard footsteps crunching through the snow. She looked about for cover, but couldn't see anything.

Then she spotted a podium that supported a life-sized

ice sculpture of Santa and his elves, and ran over to it, hoping that the falling snow would cover her tracks. She jumped on to the podium and turned herself solid just as two of the private police officers rounded the corner. They looked cold and miserable. One of them glanced at Renata as they passed. "Nice sculpture," he said to his colleague.

When she was sure they were gone, Renata turned herself back to normal and continued her search for something – anything – that would point the way to the hospital.

As she passed an apartment block, she almost walked right into another guard, this one on his own.

The guard had just enough time to say, "Curfew violation!" before Renata jabbed a sharp punch at his jaw. The man keeled over into the snow.

"Sorry," Renata muttered as she checked his breathing. *He's OK, but I can't just leave him here. He might freeze to death.* Then she heard more footsteps approaching and she looked around desperately. *There's nowhere to hide!*

Thinking quickly, she called out, "Is someone there? Help me!"

A second security guard came charging around the corner.

"Oh thank God!" Renata said, "I looked out the window and saw him just lying here! He must have slipped on the ice!"

The policeman examined his colleague. "You should have called it in, Miss. You're breaking curfew."

"I know. Sorry. I panicked."

"You go on back inside and I'll forget about the violation."

"Thanks. I hope he's going to be all right." She ran towards the apartment block's entrance, then, making sure that the policeman wasn't watching, she ducked down under a bush and waited.

A few minutes later an ambulance pulled up. Two paramedics checked the unconscious guard, then lifted him on to a stretcher and loaded him into the vehicle. The fallen man's colleague climbed into the back and closed the door.

As the ambulance began to move away, Renata darted after it. She dived to the ground head-first, skidded on the packed snow until she was right under the vehicle, then flipped over on to her back, gripped the undercarriage and allowed herself to be dragged along.

18

SOLOMON CORD – BATTERED, bruised and aching, but still alive and intact – climbed painfully out of bed and made his way to the machine room, where the labcoats had been working around the clock on the new Paragon armour.

Razor looked up when he saw Cord approaching. "You were advised to take it easy."

"I'm not known for my tendency to follow advice." Cord stood on the far side of the bench, looking down at the device on which Razor was working. "What are you doing? This isn't part of the system."

"Yeah, this is just a little side-project I'm playing around with." He pushed the device aside.

"Razor, we don't have *time* for side-projects!"

"If you say so, boss. So what was it like? Scary?"

"Terrifying," Solomon said.

"Good thing Colin was there."

"Yeah. You know what I'm thinking?"

"That we should build jetpacks for *all* of the new heroes?"

"No, but I like that idea. I was thinking that maybe the

197

new armour is too complex. Maybe we should abandon it for now and just go back to the old design."

"What does Josh think of that?"

"I haven't approached him about it yet."

Razor ran his hands through his long hair. "Between you and me, Sol, I don't entirely trust him."

"Nor do I. Not after what happened with Max."

A voice from behind them said, "I don't blame you."

They turned to see Joshua Dalton standing in the doorway. He walked over to them. "But I'm not my brother." Josh dragged over a stool and sat down. "Believe me, there aren't many things worse than finding out that your own brother almost condemned thousands of people to death."

"Have you seen him since his arrest?" Solomon asked.

"No. Neither has Roz. We don't want anything to do with him."

"What happened to all his money?" Razor asked. "Isn't he, like, a multi-billionaire?"

"All of his personal assets were seized by the Justice Department. They're the ones who gave us the StratoTruck. His companies were taken over by their boards of directors. Most of them are still operating as normal. Though their stock took a pretty big hit when the news broke that he was being indicted for tax evasion. The shareholders lost a lot of money."

Razor shrugged. "No big deal. It's not like it's real money."

"Josh," Solomon said. "Dioxin knows where we are. We have to do something about that."

"When we're back up to strength, we'll go after him. In the mean time all we can do is sit and wait."

Razor said, "Back up to strength... Josh, that's asking a lot. We have no Paragon armour, and Yvonne and Butler and Mina have almost no experience. The only functional superhuman we have left is Colin. We can't put everything on his shoulders!"

"There's also Renata."

"I thought you were saying that she might be the traitor."

Josh shrugged. "You sure you have no idea where she is?"

Solomon said, "Give her time. She'll let us know when she wants to come back."

⚙

Renata hid in a storeroom on the hospital's ground floor. Only a couple of nurses were on duty, and from what Renata could tell, there were very few patients.

She pushed open the door a fraction and peered out. *OK, the coast is clear!* She ran silently to the nurses' station and quickly flipped through the clipboards, checking the patients' names. Her heart almost missed a beat when she found what she was looking for: "Maria Soliz, Room 418."

She put the clipboard back and looked around at the signs suspended from the ceiling. *418 – has to be the fourth floor... Can't risk taking the elevator.* Renata ran towards the stairway and quietly raced up the stairs.

The door leading to the fourth floor had a small glass panel, and through it she could see one of the private security guards sitting outside room number 418.

There's no way I'm going to be able to get past him.

Steeling herself, Renata stepped out into the corridor.

The officer noticed her immediately and got to his feet. "Stop right there, missy! Restricted area."

Renata kept walking.

"Did you hear me?"

She ignored him.

"I said stop!" The man put his hand on his gun. "This is your last warning!"

Renata lunged forward, grabbed him and slammed him against the wall. She let him drop unconscious to the floor, then pushed open the door to her mother's room.

Inside, a middle-aged woman was lying on the bed. Her face and arms were covered in bandages, and she was hooked up to a heart monitor and an oxygen tube.

That can't be her, Renata thought. *She looks so...* *old.*

Then she glanced at the woman's left hand and saw her wedding ring. She sat on the edge of the bed and whispered, "Mom? Mom, can you hear me?"

Maria Soliz stirred and moaned a little. Her eyes briefly flickered open.

"Mom?"

"Dreaming... My little girl..." She opened her eyes. "I know it's a dream, Renata. You vanished. Ten years ago. I miss you. I dream about you a lot."

Renata reached out and took her mother's hand and squeezed gently. "This isn't a dream, Mom. I'm really here."

"No..."

Renata brushed her hand across her face, wiping away her tears.

Then Maria Soliz suddenly sat up and grabbed her daughter's arms. "Oh my God! *Oh my God!* Is it really you?"

"Yes, Mom, it's me!"

Renata's mother wrapped her arms around her. "We thought you were... How? How is this possible?" She let go and pressed her hand to her mouth. "They brought you back to me! Oh my God! Your father said that I was crazy to even think it. Everyone said that you were dead!

201

But I knew – I *knew* – that you were still alive!"

Renata smiled. "I'm alive! But... you have to keep your voice down! I'm not supposed to be here! I kinda had to sneak in."

"Who knows? Did you talk to your father yet?"

"No, not yet. Mom, I can't stay long, but I wanted you to know that I'm all right."

"Renata, it's been ten years! Where have you *been*?" She peered closely at her daughter. "You haven't changed."

"I know, I—"

"No, you haven't aged at all! That's not possible! You still look like a fourteen-year-old!"

"I'm a superhuman," Renata said. "I was with Energy, Titan, Thalamus and the others ten years ago, on the first Mystery Day. I got frozen..."

"My daughter was *not* a superhuman!"

"I am, Mom. The morning I went missing... It was my first real mission. I didn't have a costume, so I borrowed Bobby's Zorro mask. I took Dad's old leather gloves as well, the ones he used to use in the garden. I can turn myself solid. Watch!" Renata's skin rippled and glistened. She became transparent and unmoving. After a few seconds, she turned back.

"That was *you* on the news! You're Diamond?"

"That's me, Mom. I don't really have time to go

through the whole story, but basically I got frozen for ten years. When I woke up, they wouldn't let me come home. They didn't say it, but I think they were worried that being frozen for so long might have affected me mentally. After a couple of weeks, they sent me to live with the Wagners. You'd like them a lot. It was the best place for me."

"The Wagners? You mean Energy and Titan?"

"That's them."

"Then whoever made that decision was right. It *was* the best place. Energy and Titan... if their son is as strong as the papers say he is, then there was probably no safer place in the world."

Renata smiled. "True. Except that I'm stronger than he is. Mom... what are you *doing* here? With the Trutopians I mean."

"They're good people, Renata. It's the only way forward. The world has to be saved and if the governments won't do it, then it has to be done by a private organisation."

"That's Reginald Kinsella talking, Mom. Not you."

"Don't you remember what it was like back in the old neighbourhood? We lived in fear! Practically every day there was a mugging, or a burglary, or worse. Two years ago a man was shot dead on the road, right outside our house. The police never caught the killer. Since we joined the Trutopians we've never had to worry about anything like that."

"What about Samantha and Bobby? Did they join too?"

"No. No, they didn't and they said we were wrong to do it. But now look! You've come back to us!"

"That doesn't have anything to do with the Trutopians," Renata said. "The organisation is only one step away from a dictatorship. Do you *know* what's happening right now? Kinsella has ordered the communities to be closed! No one is allowed in or out!"

"What we've lost in freedom we've more than gained in security!"

"That's Kinsella's words again! Mom, I don't want to get into this with you now! I'm going to contact my friends. We'll arrange for you and Dad to be transferred to our headquarters. You'll be safer there."

Maria Soliz shook her head. "No. We're staying here. The Trutopians have been very good to us! We have full medical coverage here! That's something we *never* had in the outside world. And now you're back with us! The apartment's not big enough for three, but we'll ask them to move us to a bigger one. I'm sure they won't mind, not with you being a superhuman. They'll be delighted to have you in the organisation! Maybe they'll even give us a house. And they'll probably reduce our taxes, too because now we have a dependant."

"Mom, stop! I'm not joining the Trutopians!"

"But... No, you have to!" Mrs Soliz paused. "If you were frozen all this time, then technically you're still only fourteen. You have to do what we say! You'll have to go back to school, too. You'd like the school here. It's a friendly place. There's never any bullying or any sort of peer pressure."

"Mom..."

"Your father and I will be released in a couple of days, then you can come home with us and we can see in the New Year together!"

Renata stood up. "No. You and Dad should come back with me. I don't like the way these people operate, Mom."

"You might think that this is a dictatorship, Renata, but they look after their own."

"Yeah, that's one of the things that bothers me. I—"

The door behind Renata was pushed open. She turned to see a stern-looking policewoman standing in the doorway. "Renata Soliz, I'm arresting you on charges of trespassing on Trutopian property, unlawful entry and assaulting a police officer. You have the right to remain silent..."

Renata interrupted her. "You *really* think that you can take me in?"

Her mother said, "Renata, please... We don't want

any trouble. Just do whatever she says. Everything will be fine."

"Mom, I'll be in touch as soon as I can. Give the others my love." Renata moved towards the door, but the policewoman grabbed her arm to stop her.

"You're to come with me, Miss Soliz."

Renata stared at her. "You're either very brave or very stupid. Now let go of my arm."

"I *know* who you are. You might be a superhuman, but that doesn't mean that you're above the law."

"True. But it *does* mean that you can't stop me." She pulled herself free and walked out of the room.

The policewoman's radio crackled. "Captain, we've just got a call from Mr Kinsella. He's on his way here. He wants to talk to the girl in person."

19

IN THE DINING hall at Sakkara, the rest of the new heroes were sitting up late, discussing the attack and Colin's rescue of Solomon Cord.

"We can't go on like this," Butler Redmond said. "We're just waiting here for another attack! We should be out there *looking* for this Dioxin guy. That helicopter didn't just vanish! Someone must have seen it."

"What do *you* think, Yvonne?" Colin asked. "You're the one with the enormous IQ. How would you find that helicopter?"

The dark-haired girl said, "That model has a range of about twelve hundred and sixty miles on a full tank of fuel. Divide that distance by two, under the assumption that it went back to where it came from. So the initial search radius is six hundred and thirty miles. That gives us a search area of almost four thousand square miles."

Danny whistled. "And for all we know it could have refuelled somewhere along the way. So that's no good. What about the DNA evidence left on Solomon's skin by Dioxin's men?"

"My dad said they ran the DNA samples through their

207

computers," Colin said. "They can't find any matches."

"Well, I say we start closer to home," Butler said. "Pick the person most likely to be the traitor and interrogate them." He glanced at Danny. "Starting with Façade."

"He's not the traitor!" Danny said.

"He worked for Max Dalton and he betrayed him to help you guys. That means he has a history of betraying people."

Colin said, "Façade risked his life to save Solomon. If the StratoTruck had crashed *I* might have survived it, but there was no way Façade would have. As far as I'm concerned the man is on our side."

"Well, all I'm saying is that he's proven that he can't be trusted. And he keeps to himself, you notice that? He never talks to anyone else."

"That's because no one will talk to *him*," Danny replied.

"Yeah, but—" Butler stopped talking.

Razor had entered the room, carrying a large object wrapped in a strip of thick canvas. He stopped in front of Danny and dropped the package on the table. It landed with a heavy thump.

"What's this?" Danny asked.

"Christmas present," Razor said. "Open it."

Danny unwrapped the canvas, then jumped back as though he'd just had an electric shock. He scrambled out

of his chair and backed away. He stared at the object –
a complex mechanical arm – as though it was the most
terrifying thing he'd ever seen.

Razor picked up the arm and flexed its joints. "You
can thank Colin for the idea. It's a long way from being
finished, but when it is it should be pretty useful. A hell
of a lot stronger than your original arm, too. It's based
on the new Paragon armour, but instead of pressure
switches to control the motors, we'll rig it so that it
reads your nerve signals. It'll take some practice, but you
should eventually be able to use it like it was your own."

Danny swallowed. "No." He backed away even further,
shaking his head. "No. No *way*, Razor! You should have
asked me first!"

"Oh c'mon, Dan! What's the problem? We spent *ages*
putting it together!"

Danny turned and ran from the room.

Razor sighed and turned to Mina. "Now you know my
big secret. What's he so upset about?"

Mina said. "He's afraid of something. I've never seen
someone so afraid."

Colin said, "Mina... I've just had a thought... Razor
was telling me what you told him about superhuman
auras. Can you sense all of the superhumans in this
building?"

She nodded.

"What about Renata? Can you sense where she is?"

"No, she's too far away. After a few miles everything gets too fuzzy."

"When Sol was on the copter, that was only about five miles from here. Could you sense him there?"

Again, Mina nodded.

"How many people were on board, not counting Sol?"

"Nine or ten."

"Now think back: what were their auras like?"

Mina closed her eyes, frowning in concentration. "Excited, nervous... Running on adrenaline. They were... Wait... There was one that was different." She opened her eyes and stared at Colin. "Dioxin. He has a superhuman aura."

"Would you recognise his aura if you saw it again?"

"I think so."

Colin grinned. "Mina, you've just made our lives a hell of a lot easier!"

❄

The policewoman escorted Renata to a small hotel in Breckin Falls, just inside the gates of the Trutopian community. As they walked, Renata asked, "How did you even know I was here?"

"The guard you knocked unconscious woke up."

"And Kinsella is coming all this way just to see me?"

"*Mr* Kinsella. Yes, he is."

"What's he like in person?"

"I don't know," the woman said. "I've never met him before."

A blast of warm air rushed out as the policewoman pushed open the hotel's doors.

The hotel receptionists watched them approach, and Renata felt a little conspicuous wearing her black one-piece uniform.

"This way," the policewoman said and led Renata along a short corridor. At the far end of the corridor, two black-suited men stood either side of a set of double doors. One of them was tall and completely bald. The other was about Renata's height and had a mean, dangerous look on his face.

"We'll take her from here, Captain," the short one said. To his colleague, he said, "Frisk her."

Renata stepped back. "Either of you lay one hand on me and you'll spend the rest of your lives pining after your missing teeth."

The policewoman said, "I'll do it. Arms out, Ms Soliz."

"Why? I mean, you know what I can do. If I wanted to hurt someone I wouldn't need a weapon."

The two guards exchanged a glance, then the short one said, "All right. You will stay ten feet away from Mr

Kinsella at all times. Do not attempt to touch him or pick up anything that might be used as a weapon. If we even suspect that he is in any danger, we will act accordingly. Do you understand?"

Renata raised her eyes. "Whatever."

"Do you understand?" the man repeated.

"Yes, I understand."

To the policewoman, the taller man said, "Leave."

Obediently, the woman turned and walked away.

The doors were unlocked and the two bodyguards escorted Renata into the room.

It was completely empty, except for two uncomfortable-looking plastic chairs, set facing each other, about ten feet apart. The shorter man pointed to the chair farthest from the door. "Sit."

Renata sat. The bodyguards went back outside, closing and locking the door behind them.

Now what? Do I just wait here until Kinsella shows up?

She began wondering how she was going to persuade Kinsella to let her parents go, then caught herself. *No, they can leave the Trutopians any time they want to. I have to make them want to leave. But... why? Mom seems happy here, and I'm sure Dad is, too. Maybe it isn't so bad.*

But there was still something about the organisation that bothered her. Something she couldn't quite pin down.

The doors opened again and Reginald Kinsella strode into the room, smiling. He looked to be in his mid-twenties and carried himself well despite being rather overweight. Kinsella was wearing the same neatly-pressed dark blue suit he always wore on television.

"Renata Soliz?" He stretched out his hand. "Reginald Kinsella. Good to meet you!"

Renata stood and shook his hand. *Strong grip. Confident.*

"Sit, please. Now, Renata... May I call you Renata or would you prefer Diamond? Or Ms Soliz?"

"Renata is fine." She peered at him. "Don't I know you from somewhere, Mr Kinsella? I don't mean from seeing you on television. I've just got this feeling that I've met you before."

He grinned. "I get that all the time. I suppose I just have one of those faces!"

Renata paused. "I know I've seen you before."

For a moment, Kinsella's smile slipped. "I can't imagine how. Before you disappeared I was only eleven years old!"

"So that means you're only twenty-one now, but you're in charge of the entire Trutopian movement."

"That's right. But we're not a movement. We're just people who want to live in peace. Look, I can see that you're pretty tired, so I'll jump to the point. You're a

213

superhuman. We need you. No doubt you've heard about these attacks... Whoever or whatever this group Sakkara is, they're extremely dangerous."

"Sakkara is *not* the name of the terrorists," Renata said.

Kinsella frowned and scratched at his beard. "How could you know that? Do your people know something about the terrorists that the rest of us don't?"

Uh oh, Renata said to herself. *I shouldn't have said that*. "No. Look, what is it you think I can do for you?"

"It's mostly a publicity thing. We want people to know that the Trutopians have the protection of you new heroes. You, your friend Colin Wagner and whoever else might be with you. We want to promote the idea that our way of life is safer for their families."

"It wasn't safer for my parents."

"No, that's true. I'm truly sorry that such a terrible thing happened. But they're in good hands now, I assure you. And now they have their daughter back! Remarkable, truly remarkable. Can I ask what happened? How did you manage to reappear after a decade without ageing a day?"

"I'd rather not say, Mr Kinsella. Look, I don't mean to be rude, but I *am* exhausted. I need to find somewhere to sleep."

"I've taken the liberty of booking you into a suite here for the night, at our expense. So feel free to indulge yourself. But in the mean time, do please consider my offer. For hundreds of years the ordinary man has been downtrodden by incompetent governments, by the rich, by the criminal class, by oppressive religious dogma. We've dispensed with all of that. No Trutopian ever goes hungry; there is no crime. Our people are free to follow any political or religious beliefs; they can come and go as they please. All we ask is that they don't harm anyone, they pay their taxes and they obey the rules of the community."

"But they're not free to come and go as they please right now, are they, Mr Kinsella? You've sealed off the communities."

"That's necessary, but unavoidable. It's only until the current crisis has ended."

"So they aren't allowed outside the gates, but *you* are? One rule for them, another for you."

Kinsella paused. "That's one way to look at it, but you could also think of it as me putting myself at risk in order to help ensure the safety of the rest of the community. Think about the future, Renata. It's not set in stone. *We* shape the future, every one of us. Unfortunately, we can't always see what that shape will be."

"What's your point?" Renata asked.

"The Earth is overpopulated, overpolluted, its resources dwindling. Many – if not most – of its countries are run by incompetent or corrupt governments. Left in their hands, the situation is not going to improve. Can you honestly picture any of the world's most powerful countries suddenly deciding to abandon nuclear arms? Can you picture them cutting pollution levels? I don't mean *agreeing* to cut pollution – they do that all the time – I mean actually *doing* it? In many countries the people are starving to death while the rest of the world throws out bread that's more than a day old. The surface of the planet is eighty per cent water, but every day thousands of people die of thirst. Pharmaceutical companies charge hundreds of dollars for vital medicines that cost only cents to produce. All of the world's religions have the same basic rules, yet the people clash over their religious differences instead of celebrating their similarities...

"But if there is *one* lesson we have to learn from history, it is that governments do not last forever. Every empire falls and they always fall for the same reason: they look at the Earth and they see boundaries. Different countries, religions, societies. But in reality there *are* no boundaries. There are no Americans, or Spanish, or Japanese, or any other nationality. Those are just labels we apply to ourselves. The truth is that we are all the same species and we *all* have the same simple goal: to live in peace."

He's right, Renata said to herself. *He's absolutely right. But...* There was still something wrong, something she couldn't quite place.

Kinsella continued. "And that is the Trutopian goal, too. To live in peace." He leaned forward, hands clasped together, resting his elbows on his knees. "You new heroes... You hold the future of this planet in your hands. All young people do, of course, but you in particular. You have a responsibility to the children who have yet to be born. You may have children of your own one day: wouldn't you rather they were born into a world without fear, without violence? You can help make that happen, Renata. You and your friends."

He stood up and stretched. "I'll leave you to sleep on those thoughts. As I said, there's a suite booked under your name. Stay for as long as you like. If you need me, if you need anything at all..." He handed her a business card. "Just call." He started to move away, then looked back. "I believe in you, Renata Soliz. I know that it's a big decision, but I trust you to make the right choice.

"The future is in your hands."

❖

As the helicopter touched down in the desert, Evan Laurie clipped the jetpack to Dioxin's back.

"It's done?" Dioxin asked, twisting about to look.

"Hold still! All right. It's done. You know how to control it?"

"Yeah, yeah." Dioxin turned to face Laurie and spread his hands, palms up. "Switches on the palms of the gloves. Left hand controls the vertical thrust; right hand controls the forward thrust."

"And steering?"

"Lean left or right as required."

Laurie nodded. "That's it. Just don't lean too far in any one direction until you get the hang of it."

"I don't get how Paragon was able to, you know, fight and everything while he was flying."

"He had years of experience. Plus his systems had an automatic balance feature. We didn't have enough time to get something like that working. Now... your weapon."

Dioxin turned his right arm over to show the small missile launcher.

"There are fourteen missiles in the cartridge. Because of their small size, the missiles only have a range of about a hundred yards. They're not particularly accurate, but they should do the job. The payload is a combination of nitric acid and nitrobenzene."

"Which means?"

"Point and shoot. Makes big bang." Laurie stepped back. "I think you're as ready as you'll ever be."

Moving slowly, Dioxin climbed down from the copter.

He hit the radio switch on his helmet. "OK so far. Armour's kinda heavy though. It's harder to walk than I expected."

"Get clear of the copter and start up the jetpack," Laurie said.

Dioxin walked out a little further. "Here goes…" He briefly touched the control on his left hand. The jetpack whined, but nothing happened.

"It's pressure-sensitive," Laurie's voice said. "Try it again."

Dioxin pressed harder on the control and could feel the jetpack pulling at his back. He increased the pressure a tiny amount and suddenly he was being lifted off the ground. "Yes!" He touched the control on his right palm and found himself drifting forward.

After an hour of practice, Dioxin had mastered the jetpack. He flew back to the copter and landed right inside the doorway. "When all this is over, I'm keeping this thing!"

Laurie said, "No, we'll need it back. We haven't had time to disassemble it yet. We're not sure how it works."

"How's the fuel level?"

Laurie checked. "About half-empty. You're at least thirty pounds lighter than Solomon Cord, and with most of the armour's circuits stripped out, the jetpack should have a much greater range."

"Not bad… All right, top me up and then we're going to have a little fun in the city of broken dreams."

Even at seven o'clock in the morning, the streets of Las Vegas were busy. Late-night gamblers returning to their hotels waved bleary greetings to early-morning gamblers eager to get started.

Almost unnoticed among the millions of lights, a bright dot streaked out of the sky, slowing as it approached the famous Las Vegas Strip, the street on which the world's most famous casinos stood.

A trio of drunken, middle-aged men – all dressed in fishing gear because they'd told their wives they were spending a few days "on the lakes" – were the first to see the armoured man descend from the sky and land heavily on the Strip.

"Hey! Hey, it's Paragon! All right!" One of the men rushed over to the armoured figure. "Hey, man! You're my kid's hero!"

Dioxin looked at the man, then at the other people who were now running towards him.

"Hey, how about an autograph, Paragon?" the man asked.

Dioxin swung his steel-clad fist, smashing it into the man's grinning face.

Without a word, he raised his right arm, pointing it upwards, and fired. A miniature rocket streaked out, crashing into the elaborate electronic display that covered the Strip.

The display shattered, showering everyone with millions of shards of glass. As the screams echoed around the Strip, the armoured man aimed at the lobby of the nearest casino and fired again. Another massive explosion. He fired again and again.

20

AT SAKKARA, THE adults were discussing the discovery of their new early-warning system: Mina's aura-detecting ability. They had gathered in the computer room, where, surrounded by the massive Cray XD4 supercomputers, Josh had been overseeing the accumulation of data regarding Dioxin's attacks.

"We've shut down all but the most essential processes," Josh said. "We're analysing *every* piece of data regarding the attacks, even down to the stores that sell the brand of spray paint they used at the airport. If there's a pattern there, we'll find it. Right now," Josh said, "Mina's on the lookout for any unknown superhuman auras. If Dioxin gets within about eight miles of here, she'll know."

Warren said, "That's not good enough. We need to take her out, see if we can track him down."

"He could be *anywhere*, Warren. At least if Mina's here then we'll be prepared for an attack."

"We can't just sit here and wait for him! What if he doesn't come this way? Hundreds more people could die. We have to go looking for him!"

"No! Warren, I'm in charge here. *I* make the decisions."

Warren was about to reply when he was interrupted by Façade's voice over the intercom. "Guys, I've got bad news." There was panic in his voice. "My God... Josh, turn on the TV!"

Josh switched the monitor to a television channel. It showed a shaky, grainy aerial view of complete devastation. Millions of tonnes of rubble, half-destroyed buildings. Dozens of emergency workers were milling about, coordinating the removal of the rubble.

Warren swore. "That... that's Las Vegas! What the hell happened to it?"

Josh turned up the volume and a reporter's shaken voice boomed out. "...less than an hour ago. The famous Sands Hotel has been completely destroyed. There are walking wounded everywhere. First estimates from the emergency services indicate that the fatalities could be in the hundreds. If you've just joined us, you're looking at the shocking remains of one of the world's best-loved cities: Las Vegas, Nevada. Yesterday, the city was packed with holidaymakers. Now, the Las Vegas Strip has been reduced to rubble..."

The scene changed to a hand-held camera on the ground, pointed towards a grime-covered man who was stumbling over the wreckage. The man's face was streaked with blood and tears. "Help us!" the man shouted, his voice cracking. "Put down that damn camera and *help* us!" Then, behind him, one side of a fifteen-storey hotel suddenly collapsed. A thick grey cloud of concrete dust rushed towards the camera, enveloping the man. The camera bobbed and weaved as its operator ran for cover.

A reporter's voice – out of breath – said, "Good God, that hotel... Unbelievable! I'm told that the hotel had *not* been fully evacuated."

The cameraman ran back to the scene as the dust began to settle. The whole street was covered in rubble and fragments of brick. Then the camera zoomed in on a dust-covered shape in the middle of the street. The man was not moving.

Josh switched over to another channel. It showed the same scene.

A third channel showed more footage from the air. The reporter said, "...former superhero known as Paragon, who recently resurfaced after ten years."

Solomon Cord stared at the screen. "What the hell...?"

"Eye-witnesses claim – I'm sorry, I've just been told that we have Reginald Kinsella, leader of the Trutopian movement, on the line right now. Mr Kinsella, what's your take on all this?"

A photo of Kinsella appeared in the corner of the

screen. Kinsella's voice said, "Well, I'm shocked, David. Just shocked. To think that someone of Paragon's reputation would – for whatever reason – stoop to such a callous, barbaric act is, frankly, beyond belief."

Solomon roared: "No!"

Kinsella's voice continued. "If the eye-witnesses are correct, then there is no doubt that the attacker was indeed Paragon. His armour is unique. It couldn't be anyone else. It's inconceivable to think that this... this *murderer*... has been operating with the full support of this country's government and the United Nations."

Then the reporter cut in. "Sorry to interrupt, Mr Kinsella... we're getting reports of a *second* attack by Paragon, this one just north-west of Spring Valley. According to the reports, the former hero has just targeted a mile-long section of state highway 159. Mr Kinsella, could these incidents be in any way connected to the recent Sakkara attacks?"

"I don't know, David, I really don't. I *can* tell you that just a few hours ago one of the new heroes – Diamond – personally told me that Sakkara is *not* the name of the terrorist group. This suggested to me that they know more about the attacks than we do. But now we find out that Paragon himself could well be the one behind the attacks." Kinsella hesitated for a second. "David, you of course will be aware that the Trutopians have for some time been following the activities of the new heroes, and we've also been investigating the *former* superheroes. In the past few days we've uncovered some facts that we chose not to make public, but in light of this morning's events... I can tell you that Paragon's real name is Solomon Cord."

❂

Despite the luxury of the hotel suite that Reginald Kinsella had booked for her, Renata had had a restless night. The meeting with her mother, and the later meeting with Kinsella, had rattled her. Kinsella's arguments had been very convincing; the world was not going to get better on its own. It needed a push. *But who is he to decide what's right for everyone else?*

Then again, the thought had occurred to Renata that the average person was more concerned with his or her own happiness than with investing in the future of the planet. *Maybe it* will *take someone like Kinsella to change things. Someone with a strong, clear vision of how the future should be and the resources to make that future happen.*

When she finally drifted off to sleep, these thoughts ran through her head and infected her dreams. She dreamed of a good world, a clean world. A utopia where every human being lived in peace and without fear. Then her dreams were shattered by an all-too-familiar sound... police sirens.

Renata sat up, instantly awake, and realised that the sirens were coming from a television set in the room next door.

She had a quick shower and returned to the bedroom. As she was pulling on her uniform, she noticed that the noise from the adjoining room was still continuing. She turned on her own television set, switched it to the news channel. "What...?" She turned up the volume.

On screen, a terrified, shaking woman was saying, "He had these rockets that came out of his arms and he just started blasting everything around him! He didn't care that there were *people* in those places!"

A bloodied and bruised man pushed his way in front of the woman. "Somethin' oughta be done about those superheroes! They're supposed to be the good guys! They're supposed to protect us, not destroy the places where we live and work!"

Renata could feel her blood running cold. "Oh God..."

The screen cut to a TV studio, where a slim, well-dressed man was being interviewed. "Las Vegas was a city of sin and vice," the man said calmly. "A modern-day Gomorrah. Some would say that its destruction is long overdue."

Off-screen, the interviewer asked, "Would *you* say that, Reverend?"

The Reverend smiled slightly. "The actions of this man, this Paragon – the very name is a contradiction – are certainly questionable."

Renata gasped.

"Questionable?" the interview said. "Paragon has quite possibly killed hundreds of people! What's your take on that?"

"I would never condone the wilful destruction of property, nor the injuring of *innocent* people. I don't need to remind you that the wages of sin are death."

Renata turned off the television set and grabbed for the telephone. She dialled a number. After four rings, it was answered. "Milton's Stapler Services, how may I help you?"

"This is Renata Soliz."

"Putting you through now, Miss Soliz."

A few seconds later, Danny Cooper's voice said, "Renata? Where are you?"

"Cleveland. Danny, tell Josh to pick me up. I've just seen the news... Is it true?"

"It wasn't Sol. They stole his armour. He's freaking out, Renata. They're working like crazy to get the new armour up and running, but Razor reckons they're still weeks away. We have no leads. We don't know where to start. But we do have..." He paused. "Look, I'll tell you when you get here. How far away is Cleveland?"

"About eight hundred miles."

"We'll send someone to pick you up, but it's a long way. Can you start heading in this direction?"

"How? I don't have any way to get there!"

"OK. Well, we'll think of something. You just keep in touch. And look after yourself, all right?"

"I will. You too." Renata said goodbye and hung up the phone. *What am I going to do? It'll take ages to get back to Sakkara.* Then she glanced at the business card on the bedside table and picked up the phone again.

She dialled the number on the card, and seconds later a voice said, "Reginald Kinsella. Talk to me."

"Mr Kinsella, this is Renata."

"Renata, this isn't a good time... Have you been watching the news?"

"Yes. You said I was to call you if I needed anything. Well, I do need something. I need transport. *Fast* transport."

"To where?"

"Sorry, I can't tell you that."

"I understand. But if you can at least give me some idea of the distance, then I'll know whether you need a car or a helicopter."

"A helicopter."

"You're still in the hotel in Breckin Falls?"

"Yes."

"Be outside in five minutes."

"And I need a cellphone, too."

"That's not a problem. The pilot will have one."

"Thank you, Mr Kinsella. I promise I'll make it up to you!"

He chuckled. "Oh, you shouldn't say something like that to me, Renata! I have a tendency to hold people to their promises."

※

The new heroes were assembled in Ops as Joshua Dalton spoke on the phone to the US president. Colin stood leaning against the wall, watching Josh and listening to the voice on the other end of the phone. Colin had heard the president's voice many times before, but that had always been on television, when he was calm and everything was under control.

"We can't *find* him!" Joshua Dalton roared. "If *your* people can't, how the hell are *we* supposed to?"

"I'm told that the most recent sighting of Paragon was—" the president said.

"I'm telling you for the last time! That was *not* Paragon! That was Dioxin! He stole the Paragon armour!"

A pause, then the president said, "Mr Dalton, do not

speak to me in that manner. I can cut your funding at a stroke. I can have your organisation investigated, dismantled and everyone involved prosecuted. Is that what you want?"

Through gritted teeth, Josh said, "No."

"Then you will find this man – I don't care whether he's Paragon, Dioxin or Clint Eastwood – and you will bring him to justice. Alive. Do you understand me?"

"We don't have the resources to track him and your people are stalling me at every turn. We need full access to all of your telemetry and satellite data, and we need..." Josh hesitated for a moment. "We're going to need you to stand down the Air Force, cancel all commercial and industrial flights. If Dioxin is the only thing in the air it'll be a lot easier to spot him."

"If I call off the Air Force then he'll have free reign to do whatever he wants."

"Mr President, he pretty much has that anyway," Josh said.

"We would have to declare a national state of emergency."

"I'm surprised you haven't done that already."

"Do not try to tell me my job, Mr Dalton!" The man sighed. "Arguing isn't getting us anywhere. Can you promise me that you *will* find this psychopath if I agree to your requests?"

"No, I can't promise that. But it would make the job a lot easier."

"Then consider it done. You have six hours, Dalton. Any later than that and you're under investigation, regardless of the outcome."

"I understand. We'll do our best, Mr President."

"Yes. You will. Or I'll see to it that everything about your organisation becomes public knowledge. Then you will have to answer not only to me, but to the people of the United States of America." The call was disconnected.

Josh looked around the room. "That went better than I expected. All right, people... this is where we start to fight back. With every unnecessary aircraft grounded, the satellite images should have a much easier time picking out Dioxin's location."

"He'll need to refuel every couple of hours," Solomon Cord said. "That tells me he's got a chopper on stand-by."

"Good. That increases our chances of finding him. In the mean time, we have to pick up Renata. Reginald Kinsella's people are taking her to an airfield just outside Cedar Rapids, Iowa. We'll meet her there. Once she's back here, we can take the StratoTruck out with Mina on board and try to find Dioxin. The president has given the order to stop him whatever the cost. Do you all understand that? The president has told me he wants Dioxin dead."

Colin jumped at that. "What? No he didn't! He definitely said that he wants him alive!"

"You were *listening*? Colin, that's a federal offence."

"What are you doing, Josh? You can't order us to *kill* someone!"

Josh frowned. "What...? Something's... Did I say dead? I meant alive. Dead is no good to us: we need to know who Dioxin is working with." He dropped into a chair and rubbed the back of his head. "I haven't slept in almost forty-eight hours."

Warren said, "Then *get* some sleep. We're going to need you in top condition for this."

"Right. I will, once we're ready." He took a deep breath, then said, "Warren, take the StratoTruck and pick up Renata. The rest of you, get something to eat and prepare yourselves for battle."

Danny said, "Josh, we need the StratoTruck here: if we find Dioxin we'll need to be able to get to him as quickly as possible. Send a copter for Renata instead."

Josh considered that. "Good point. Façade can do it; he can fly a helicopter. As soon as we find Dioxin, Warren will take Mina, Colin and Yvonne in the StratoTruck. Butler? You're staying here – we'll need your forcefield if they launch an attack on us."

Then Yvonne said, "No. I'm not going."

"Yvonne..."

Her voice cold and flat, Yvonne said, *"Do not ask me again."*

"I understand. You all know what you have to do. So do it."

As they left the room, Danny said to Colin, "Once again I'm left on the substitute bench."

Façade said, "You can come with me for Renata, Danny. We've never really had a chance to talk. And it could be a while before we get another chance."

Then Colin heard his father whispering, "Colin? Get to the machine room, right now. Keep it quiet." He glanced over to Warren and Solomon, who were standing next to Mina.

Colin slipped away from the others and down to the machine room.

Razor looked up when Colin approached. "How did it go?"

"Not well. We've got the president's backing – for now – but we're still no closer to finding Dioxin."

The doors opened on the platform above them and Solomon came rushing down three steps at a time. Without a word, he picked up a hand-held device from Razor's workbench and flipped a switch on it. "If anyone has this room bugged, they won't be able to hear us. Colin... the only people I completely trust in this place are you, your parents and Razor. Someone has been feeding information to the enemy and I have a bad feeling that

Josh is somehow involved. Warren is going to take you and Mina to look for Dioxin."

"I know," Colin said.

"I mean, right *now*. Josh is stalling. We should have been out there hours ago."

"Yeah, but—"

Solomon interrupted him. "We know that Dioxin has to be somewhere in Nevada or one of the neighbouring states. The StratoTruck is the fastest way to get there. You're going to scout around until either the satellite data gives us an exact position or Mina can sense him. It's a risk; the StratoTruck still has no armour or weapons. It was supposed to have been upgraded, but for some reason Josh kept putting it off."

"How could he be the traitor?"

"We don't know. He might *not* be, but he's definitely getting in the way more than he's helping. We have to go it alone. Now get going. Your dad and Mina are waiting on the roof."

Razor slapped Colin on the shoulder. "Good luck."

"Thanks."

"You're going to need it," Razor added, with a smile.

As Colin reached the door, Solomon said, "Colin?"

"Yeah?"

"Come back alive. If you don't, Stephanie will really give me a hard time over it."

21

AS THE COPTER roared through the sky towards the city of Cedar Rapids, Danny sat in the co-pilot's seat and watched the landscape stream by below.

"I don't know anything about you," Danny said to Façade. "Nothing real. Every time I've tried to talk to you, either you didn't want to know, or Mum or Niall were there, or I just couldn't think of what to say."

"Danny, I can only apologise so many times for what I did! But I genuinely thought—"

"That you were doing the right thing. I know. And I also know that if you hadn't agreed to take Quantum's place, Max Dalton would have had me killed. Façade, I'm not blaming you for anything. Not any more. It's just... Like I said, I don't know anything about you. I never knew you could fly a helicopter. I don't even know your real name!"

"My name is Hector Thomas Millar. I was in the US Air Force for twenty-three years," Façade said. "I don't think there's an aircraft that I *can't* fly."

"But... you took over from Quantum eleven years ago. So that means that you joined the Air Force more than thirty-four years ago! And you have to be eighteen to join, right? That would make you at *least* fifty-two years old!"

Façade nodded. "At least."

"But… You don't look any older than Colin's dad!"

Façade smiled. "Quantum was a lot younger than me when I changed my appearance to match his. Since then I've aged at the usual rate."

"How old are you really?"

"I'm sixty-one."

"Sixty-one! But you have a nine-year-old son!"

"So? Men can father children at any age. Charlie Chaplin was in his seventies when his youngest son was born."

"Razor said that Mina told him Niall has a superhuman aura. He might inherit your shape-changing ability."

"For his sake, I hope he doesn't. The only good things that ever came out of my powers were meeting you and your mother, and having Niall."

Cautiously, Danny said, "I've been thinking about that sort of thing a lot… Do you have any other children?"

"No. Niall's the only one."

"Were you married before?"

"I was, back about twenty-five years ago."

"What happened?"

"She died."

"Oh."

Danny was about to ask how it happened when Façade said, "I don't want to talk about it. Someday, but not now."

"OK. Sorry."

"Danny, this is a serious situation, you do understand that, don't you? This isn't like what happened in California. Max Dalton wasn't evil, he was just wrong. But Dioxin is a murderer, plain and simple. If we don't stop him he will just go on killing."

"I know that."

"There's a chance that not all of us will survive." Façade glanced at Danny. "I'm telling you this: if your powers really are gone, I want you to stay out of the line of fire. Do not try to be a hero!"

"I'll give my friends whatever help I can," Danny said.

"No. You have to think of your mother and Niall. They need you more than Colin and Renata do."

"Mum and Niall are safe. The others aren't."

"If Sakkara falls, *no one* is safe!" Façade said angrily. "Danny, you have the potential to be the most powerful superhuman this world has ever seen. Even more powerful than your father. Quantum was practically unbeatable, but, well… he was also unstable. He had visions."

"I know that."

After a moment's pause, Façade said, "I heard about

your reaction when Razor showed you the artificial arm. You freaked out."

"I didn't exactly freak out. I was just surprised, that's all."

"Danny, I know you better than you think I do. Your reaction was more than just surprise." Façade stared at him. "You've seen something, haven't you? You inherited more than just Quantum's speed. You inherited his visions."

Danny's mouth dried up. "I..."

"What have you seen?"

"Nothing."

"Don't lie to me, Danny! I spent years disguising myself as other people and that was more than just changing my face to match theirs. I learned everything there was to know about body language. I know when someone is lying. What did you see?"

"I've never told anyone. Not even Colin... It only happened once. I saw myself. Older than I am now, but not much. I was leading people – I couldn't really see who they were – and we were being chased by an army. I think it was the war my father predicted. My right arm was gone, replaced with something mechanical."

"So you're thinking that if you never take an artificial arm, you'll be able to avoid that future?"

"Yeah."

239

"That doesn't mean that the war itself won't happen."

"I know that," Danny said quietly. "But... Sometimes I can't help thinking that maybe Max Dalton was right."

"When Quantum spoke about his vision of the war, he never said anything about you having an artificial arm. I'm sure that if he had seen that, he would have mentioned it. It could be that back in California you *did* change the future he predicted."

"Then what future was *I* seeing?"

"I wish I knew the answer to that."

The StratoTruck raced at full speed over the Rocky Mountains. As Warren Wagner piloted it, Colin and Mina sat in the back.

Colin pulled on the gloves of his uniform and flexed his hands. "This is not the most comfortable thing I've ever worn," he said. He turned to Mina. "How are you doing?"

"OK."

Colin picked up his helmet and put it on. "Nervous?"

"A little. I've never been on a mission before."

Warren said, "Don't worry, Mina. All you'll have to do is find Dioxin and Colin will take over from there." He glanced over his shoulder. "You feel up to the challenge, Colin?"

"Do we have a choice?"

"Not really. You're absolutely certain that you can't fly?"

"It's never worked so far. But you and Mum could, so I *should* be able to."

"Yeah, but our flight worked in different ways. Mine was more like some sort of anti-gravity thing. I just had to concentrate on it and it happened. But your mother was able to fly by manipulating energy. I'm not really sure how that worked."

"Well, either way it *doesn't* work for me. And I don't think I'm as invulnerable as you are, Dad. I nearly sprained my ankle yesterday in the gym."

"You're still the best weapon we've got, Colin. Maybe we should have taken Butler with us. He'd have been able to trap Dioxin in his forcefield."

Colin said, "He would have been trapped in there with him though. He has to be on the inside of it."

"I still don't know why we didn't bring Yvonne," Warren said. "She's strong, too, right? Not as strong as either of you, but she's also smart. It would have made tracking Dioxin a lot easier."

"We didn't bring her because Josh said no," Colin said.

Mina made a tutting noise.

"What's that mean?" Colin asked her.

"She has him wrapped around her little finger! Josh *always* does what she says!"

Warren said, "Regardless of how we might feel about Josh, he's not stupid. He knows how to get the most out of people. Comes from years of being in his brother's shadow, I guess. He—"

Mina interrupted him. "He's there!" She pointed off to the left. "For a second I was sure... Go that way, Mr Wagner! I might be able to pick him up again!"

⁂

As Dioxin marched through the small town, people scattered in panic. "Ah, now this takes me back!" he said into his communicator.

"You've got company," Victor Cross's voice said. "The new heroes are coming in from the south."

Dioxin immediately fired up his jetpack at full power, heading north. "I'm on the move... What's going on?"

"They have a way to locate you," Cross said.

"How? We scanned the armour for tracking devices. Didn't find anything."

"They're not tracking the armour, Dioxin. They're tracking *you*. Mina has some kind of power that allows her to spot superhumans, even from miles away. They're bearing down on you right now."

"Damn it! OK, I'm heading back to base!"

"No," Victor said firmly. "You cannot come back here. If this girl can spot superhumans, she'll find *me.* That girl is now your top priority... When you find her, I want you to tear her head from her shoulders. Got that? We cannot allow her to survive."

"Got it. How much time do I have?"

"Minutes, at best... There should be a forest to your east. Their craft won't be able to follow you in there."

"I see it. On my way," Dioxin said. He slowed, angled slightly to his right, then increased his speed and zoomed straight for the dense forest. "Cross... This armour is fireproof, right?"

"Yes. Why?"

"Just had an idea."

"Mina?" Warren asked.

"Very close... He's in that forest dead ahead! He's not moving any more."

"He's waiting for us," Colin said. "How close can you get, Dad?"

"Not close enough. We can set down at the edge of the forest. You'll have to run from there."

That would take too long. Colin unbuckled his

seatbelt. "Unseal the hatch! Hover directly over him, Dad!"

"What are you going to do?" Warren asked.

"I'm going to jump."

"Are you *crazy*?"

"Probably." Colin opened the hatchway and looked down. "Mina?"

"He's right below us!"

"Drop us down, Dad! Close as you can!" *I survived a fourteen-storey fall on to solid concrete. I can do this!*

"He's starting to move again, Colin!" Mina said.

"Damn it!" Colin put one hand on each side of the hatchway, took a deep breath and flung himself out.

He didn't know what kind of trees they were, but they hurt: he was hit in the face and body as he smashed down through branches and was glad of the tough material of his uniform.

There! Directly below him, he could see Dioxin, wearing Paragon's armour.

The scarred man looked up at the noise of the breaking branches, but was too late: Colin landed right on top of him, sending him sprawling to the ground.

Colin tucked his legs under him and rolled on to his feet. Dioxin had landed on his back and was starting to get up.

Colin charged at him, smashing into Dioxin's chest.

He clung on, forcing the armoured man to stagger backwards. He dug his fingers into the armour's back-plate and tried to tear it apart.

Dioxin swung his fist at Colin. The blow caught him above the left ear, knocking his helmet off and sending him reeling backwards. Dioxin sneered. "That hurt? Good!" He aimed his wrist's rocket launcher at Colin. "This'll hurt a hell of a lot more!"

He fired.

Colin saw the rocket coming and jumped to the side. The missile exploded somewhere behind him. Dioxin fired again and again.

Colin ducked and rolled, planted his feet against the stump of a tree and leaped forward.

Dioxin activated his jetpack and soared out of reach. Floating three metres above Colin, he said, "Thanks for walking into my trap, kid!" He laughed. "Look around you!"

Colin risked a quick glance. The trees behind him were ablaze.

Dioxin spun around, launching another volley of rockets. Within seconds, Colin was surrounded by a ring of fire.

"Don't play with the big boys, Wagner, unless you want to get hurt!" He aimed his rocket launcher at Colin. "Where are you going to run to *now*?" He fired.

The missile hit Colin point-blank in the chest, the explosion knocking him backwards. He smashed against a burning tree and collapsed.

"You're a tough little kid," Dioxin roared. "But *nothing* is tough enough to survive *this*!" He pulled the spare cartridge of missiles from his belt and threw it down at Colin. He launched another stream of missiles.

The last thing Colin saw was a blinding flash as all the missiles exploded at the same time.

❁

The StratoTruck was rocked by the force of the explosion. As Warren struggled with the controls, Mina watched Dioxin soar out of the smoke and flames and disappear into the sky.

The StratoTruck now steadied once more Warren stared at the inferno. "Colin…"

The entire forest was engulfed in flame. As they watched, several of the largest trees in the centre of the forest collapsed and disintegrated under the extreme heat.

"Colin!"

Mina put her hand on his shoulder. "I… I can't sense him any more, Mr Wagner. He's gone. Colin's gone."

22

"**WE CAN'T STAY** here, Mr Wagner," Mina said. "Dioxin might come back!"

"No! Colin could still be alive in there!" He switched on the radio. "Colin? Colin? Respond!"

Silence.

"Colin! Come on, son! Say something!"

Mina said, "Mr Wagner, I can't sense *anything* down there! I was focussed on Colin right up to the explosion – his aura just vanished! He's gone!"

"He is *not* gone!" Warren roared. "Can you sense Dioxin's aura now?"

"No."

"Then if he's out of your range, we still have some time."

"Even if by some miracle Colin is still alive down there, there's no way we can get to him! We have to leave!"

Numbly, Warren shook his head. He stared at the StratoTruck's screens. "Come on, come on! Damn it, the heat is too much! It's screwing up the sensors! Maybe if we focus on the centre of the explosion... There." He pointed at one of the screens. It showed that almost all

247

of the trees in a thirty-metre radius had been destroyed.

Mina leaned over his shoulder. "Can you see anything?"

"No, but... maybe he was able to run before the explosion happened."

Mina paused. "No. He was right in the middle of it. I'm sorry, Mr Wagner, but I can't detect anything at all down there."

"He could be unconscious!"

"I'd still be able to sense him."

Warren swallowed. "My son..."

Mina suddenly grabbed Warren's arm. "Dioxin! He's coming back!"

Warren glanced out through the windscreen: a dark object was approaching fast. There was a sudden flare, then a second.

"He's firing at us!" Mina screamed.

As Warren spun the StratoTruck about, the first missile streaked past, missing them by less than a metre. The second exploded against one of the StratoTruck's short wings, knocking Mina to the floor.

"Hold on to something!" Warren shouted. He pushed forward on the StratoTruck's joystick, then yanked it to the left, sending the craft into a spinning dive. A third missile shot past them, heading towards the ground.

Warren pulled the joystick up, then hit full power as

the craft soared into the sky. The sudden surge of acceleration bore down on him like a great weight and he eased off the power. "OK, OK... We're well out of his range now. We were lucky – that missile didn't do any serious damage." He called over his shoulder. "You all right, Mina?"

She grabbed the back of his seat and pulled herself up. "Yeah. I think so."

"We're going back to Sakkara."

"You have to tell the others," Mina said. "About Colin."

Warren pulled off his headset and handed it to Mina. "I can't do it. Caroline... Someone has to tell my wife that our son is dead."

"I'll do it. You get us back to Sakkara as fast as you can."

❀

Even before the helicopter touched down on the airfield outside Cedar Rapids, Renata was running towards it. She jumped in and it immediately took off again.

"You OK?" Danny asked.

"I'm fine. A bit stunned at what's been going on with Paragon's armour though. Who's doing it?"

"Someone from your past," Façade said. "Dioxin."

"No... He died ten years ago!"

"I wish that were true, Renata. Warren, Colin and Mina are out there looking for him now."

Danny quickly explained the situation, then added, "The only chance we have is that Dioxin is leaving a trail of destruction. Every time he stops to do some damage, it increases the odds that we'll find him."

"How's Sol taking this?"

"He's furious," Façade said. "The labcoats are working like crazy to get the new armour ready, but they're nowhere near close enough. Even if – hold it! Message coming through from Sakkara..." Façade listened. "Yes, Josh, we've just picked her up. We're heading back to base now... *What*? Say again, Josh... Oh Lord... You're certain? Yes, I'll tell them. And tell Warren and Caroline I'm sorry."

Danny felt his blood run cold. "What is it?"

Façade glanced around at them. "Just... sit tight, OK?"

Danny swallowed. "Why should you tell Warren and Caroline that you're sorry?" *Please God, don't let this be what I think it is!*

Renata whispered, "Colin..."

Façade nodded. "They found Dioxin. He attacked... Colin's dead."

"No!" Danny screamed. "No, that's not right! He can't die! Colin is the one! He's the bravest of all of us! *He's* the hero!"

"I'm sorry, son. I truly am."

Her eyes filled with tears, Renata wrapped her arms around Danny and hugged him close, as much to comfort herself as him. To Façade she said, "We're not going back to Sakkara yet. Take us to where it happened. I want to see for myself."

"But we—"

"Take us to Colin!"

"The Wagner kid is dead, Cross," Dioxin said. "The whole forest is burning. It's got to be hotter than hell back there!"

"You're *sure* he's dead?"

"I'm sure that I'm not going back to check! He's one vicious little fighter. His old man was never that bad. I hit him point-blank with a full cartridge of missiles. You should have seen the explosion! It ripped the whole forest apart like it was made of paper."

"What about Mina?"

"No luck there. They took off before I could get to them. That machine of theirs is fast."

"I'm sending your team to pick you up," Victor said. "Until we are absolutely certain that their little superhuman-detector is dead, you are not to come back here. Do you understand me?"

"I understand. But I'm going back anyway. If you don't want them to know we're working together, then maybe *you* should leave the base."

"Dioxin," Cross said, his voice calm and deliberate. "I'm not telling you again. You are not to come back here while that girl is still alive. When we modified Paragon's armour to fit you, we planted a very powerful charge inside it. If you come within fifty miles of this base, I will detonate that charge. *Now* do you understand me?"

Dioxin swore. "All right."

"Good. I'm tracking your path. Turn ten degrees to starboard and keep on that course. The copter will rendezvous with you in about fifty minutes and take you to Sakkara. Our man on the inside will make sure that their automated defences are down by the time you get there."

In the forest, lying in a bed of white-hot cinders, the body of Colin Wagner suddenly spasmed and opened its eyes.

Colin sat up, oblivious to the intense heat. He looked down and saw that his uniform was damaged, but mostly still intact. *Good thing they made it fireproof!*

He opened the uniform at the neck and checked

himself: there was a large bruise on his chest where the missile had struck him.

Is that it? he wondered. *Is that the only injury I've got?* He ran his hands over his face and head. *Aw no! All my hair has burned off! I'm bald!*

He pushed himself to his feet and looked around. The trees all around him had been destroyed by the explosion, but he was almost completely unharmed.

Back in the toy store, when my Titan costume caught fire... I didn't even notice. And this heat... Colin pulled off his gloves and tentatively reached down and pushed one hand into the cinders. He could feel some heat, but not nearly as much as he'd expected. *I'm fireproof!*

The night of our first patrol in Topeka, everyone except me was freezing. I don't really feel the cold any more, and heat doesn't affect me.

Looking around once more, Colin realised that he didn't know which way he should go. He couldn't even judge by the position of the sun; the sky was blocked out by a thick column of smoke. He chose a direction at random and started walking.

Something indistinct slowly drifted across his path; a thin wisp of blue light. *What on earth is that?*

He reached his hand out towards the light and it instantly faded. *Never seen anything like that before.* He remembered the video of Quantum they'd watched, the first night they arrived at Sakkara. Quantum had said, "The blue lights. They drift about, cluster around certain people, and enhance our abilities." *Is that the stuff that makes us superhuman?*

I'm not as tough as Dad was or as fast. I can't fly.

I chose the name Titan because I thought – because everyone thought – that I was going to inherit all of my dad's powers.

It never occurred to anyone that I might inherit my mother's powers instead.

He stood still, allowed the heat of the fire to soak into his body. He could feel the energy surging through him. He held out his hand, palm up, and concentrated, shaping the energy into a small ball of flame that briefly danced and flickered in his hand before fading away.

That is just too cool! What about lightning? Mum could make lightning... He concentrated again, tried to visualise the energy turning into electricity. There was a brief spark between his thumb and index finger. *When I get back to Sakkara, I'll have to ask her how to do that properly.*

Colin Wagner, the thirteen-year-old son of the legendary superhero known as Energy, walked out of the inferno.

23

THE COPTER TOUCHED down on the edge of the burning forest. Façade left the cockpit and followed Renata and Danny out of the copter. "Renata, this is pointless. Nothing could survive in there."

"Do you have any fire-fighting equipment on board?"

"Extinguisher and flame-retardant blankets."

"Get them."

"And the first-aid kit," Danny said.

As Façade returned to the copter, Renata said to Danny, "Do you think...?"

"That he could still be alive? I don't know. He's not as strong as you are, or as fast as I am. But he's tough and brave."

She smiled. "Colin's afraid of heights, did you know that?"

"No."

"He wouldn't admit it though. He always got nervous when we were on a high building."

"I didn't know that. I thought the only thing he was afraid of was homework. And when we were little kids he used to be terrified of Mr Blobby."

Renata laughed for a moment, then covered her mouth with her hand. "We shouldn't talk about him in the past tense."

Façade came up behind them. "Flame-proof blankets, first-aid kit, fire extinguisher... but they won't do any good."

Then a large burning tree at the edge of the forest was suddenly torn apart, showering them with sparks.

Smiling, Colin pushed his way through the flaming debris and marched towards his friends.

Renata's mouth dropped open in shock.

Danny said, "*Colin*? I don't believe it!"

Colin ran his hands over his scalp. "Oh great. I just *knew* you were going to give me a hard time over this! My hair *will* grow back, you know!"

"We were told you were dead," Façade said. "Mina said your aura disappeared; she couldn't sense you any more. Colin, your mother and father think you're dead."

Colin swallowed. "We have to tell them!"

"Wait," Renata said. "This is a terrible thing to do to your parents, Col, but if no one knows you're alive then that gives us an advantage. We know that someone in Sakkara is a traitor. If they think you're dead, we'll have a better chance of flushing them out."

Colin thought about this for a moment. "All right. All right, that's what we'll do. Let's go."

They ran back towards the copter and jumped in. "How *did* you survive?" Danny asked.

"Turns out I'm fireproof. I get that from my mother's side of the family." He looked past Danny's shoulder. "Look, there's another one!"

Danny turned around. "Another what?"

"You can't see it? It's sort of a pale blue light. It's right in front of you!"

"I can't see anything," Danny said. "Renata?"

"Nope. Sure you're not imagining it, Colin?"

"No, it's definitely there. Danny, put your hand out, see if you can feel anything."

Danny raised his hand, then shrugged.

"It's gone," Colin said. "Disappeared when you pushed your hand through it."

"All right," Renata said. "We need to get you back to Sakkara. Get you checked out." She reached out and ran her fingers over Colin's head. "Perfectly smooth! So your skin is fireproof but your hair isn't."

"You're just lucky it wasn't the other way around," Danny said.

"You sure you don't want us to tell your folks that you're still alive?" Façade asked as the copter ascended once more.

"Positive," Colin said. "If there is a traitor, this is the best way to find him. And Façade... I *really* won't be

257

happy if I find out that it's you. Understand me?"

Façade smiled. "Perfectly."

"Set a course for Sakkara, fast as you can!"

Dioxin flew straight up to the copter's open hatch and shut off his jets as he touched down. Inside, his team of mercenaries were running a weapons check.

"You still tracking the new heroes' craft?" Dioxin asked the pilot.

The man nodded. "They're heading right back to Topeka."

"Can we overtake them?"

"Not a chance. That thing has got five times our speed. At least."

"Got to get me one of those, too." Dioxin turned to the nearest man. "What's the status?"

"All locked and loaded, sir."

"You all know what you have to do?"

"Cross briefed us. With Titan's kid dead and Diamond out looking for his body, the only one we have to worry about is Redmond, and according to the reports he's far from being ready to fight."

"What about the girl who can detect superhumans? Cross said something about her occasionally showing incredible strength."

"She'll be taken out of the picture before we get there."

"Good. The building's defences?"

"In theory they can seal the whole place tighter than a duck's ass, but our inside man will have disabled the doors. There are no human guards. We should be able to get in and out without any real resistance."

"And the target?"

"Everything's arranged. Check the map..." The man passed Dioxin a hand-held computer. "There's a small storeroom off the machine room. Only one door, no windows. That's the rendezvous point."

Dioxin manipulated the computer's controls. The three-dimensional image rotated, showing him a complete plan of Sakkara. He smiled. "Then we're ready." He reached around and unclipped the jetpack from his back, then refuelled it from the spare tank. He loaded a fresh cartridge of missiles into the launcher on his wrist and attached another two cartridges to his belt. "All right, men... Don't go thinking that this will be a walk in the park. There are still four ex-superheroes in that place. They might not have their powers any more, but they're going to fight like wildcats to defend it. Expect strong resistance. Assume that everyone you meet but our target will be hostile and treat them accordingly. I do not want *any* of them walking out of that place, you got me?"

As one, the men nodded.

"I promised Solomon Cord that in exchange for him stealing my future, I would steal something he valued just as much. And I've done that: I've taken his reputation. No matter how this turns out, no one will remember Paragon as a hero. Now... now we're going to go a step further. We're going to steal *his* future."

On the roof of Sakkara, Solomon Cord stood beside Caroline Wagner as they watched the StratoTruck approaching.

Behind them, Razor, Butler and Yvonne were waiting in silence.

Joshua Dalton said, "We shouldn't be out here. We're too exposed."

"Shut up," Cord said, without looking at him.

The StratoTruck touched down and Caroline ran towards it. Then the hatch opened and her husband was standing there, his face pale and drawn.

"What happened?" Caroline asked, sobbing. "How did he die?"

Warren walked down the ramp, brushed the tears from his eyes and wrapped his arms around her. "He was incredible... He just jumped out, straight down through the trees. Absolutely fearless. You would have been so proud of him. And then... and then there was a huge explosion. Dioxin set the entire forest on fire. We couldn't get close enough. We waited, but he... he didn't get out. Mina said his aura disappeared."

As the Wagners walked towards the stairway, Josh approached them, but was stopped by Razor who pulled him aside.

"Don't you say a word, Dalton!" Razor hissed. "You say one thing about how you told them not to go and I swear to *God* I will put you in the ground!"

"I would never do something like that," Josh said. "Colin was... He was a good kid. He deserved a better fate than that."

His face pale and grim, Razor went over to Mina. They stared at each other for a few seconds, then Mina turned and walked away.

Yvonne said, "Mina?"

"Leave me alone!"

"But..." Yvonne stopped when Butler put his hand on her arm.

"She needs time," Butler said. "She'll be OK."

Solomon Cord waited until Caroline and Warren were gone, then said, "Everyone, prepare for an attack! Mina, I know you're in shock, but we need you to stay alert – you're our only early-warning system. Razor, get on to

261

the chopper; I want Renata back here ASAP. And I want all of our defences on-line! Now *move*, people! We're going to lock this place down."

As everyone rushed back inside to prepare, Solomon walked to the edge of the roof and looked out over the city.

"Colin..." he said aloud. "You were a great kid. I'm going to miss you. I don't know how I'm going to tell Stephanie. I know she always gave you a hard time, but that was just her way. She would never admit it, of course, but I think she was a little bit in love with you." He looked down at his hands: they were shaking. "Goodbye, my friend. Now... now I'm going to kill the man who betrayed us."

24

JOSHUA DALTON SAT in his office, speaking into the phone. "Colin Wagner is dead." He listened for a moment. "Mina wasn't able to pick up any trace of him... Daniel Cooper and Renata Soliz haven't returned yet." He listened again. "The remainder of my funds will be transferred to your account first thing in the morning... Yes. I will." He hung up the phone and began typing furiously on his computer.

Josh gasped and jumped to his feet when something cold and metal pressed into the back of his neck.

"Before I kill you," Solomon Cord said, "I want you to tell me who you were talking to. If you won't talk, I'll kill you and find out the hard way. Now turn around slowly and keep your hands where I can see them."

Josh raised his hands and turned around. "What are you doing, Sol?"

"Who were you just talking to?"

"When?"

"Just now! On the phone!"

Josh frowned. "You're losing it, Sol. I wasn't on the phone."

"I saw you. I heard you." He pressed the muzzle of the gun against Josh's forehead. "You have three seconds."

"Sol, I *wasn't* using the phone!"

"Three."

"Are you crazy? I just came in here because... because..."

"Two."

Joshua Dalton looked around wildly. "What *am* I doing in here?"

"Don't try to play that game with me, Dalton! One!"

"No! Don't! I swear to *God*, Sol! I don't know what you're talking about!"

Solomon Cord frowned. "Look at your monitor."

"Why?"

"Just look."

Josh glanced at the computer screen. "What the hell is this?"

"That's what you were doing when I stopped you."

"These are the instructions to erase a phone call from the system log! Sol, I don't even remember coming in here!"

"Have the instructions been executed yet?"

"No, not yet."

"Good. Find the last number called from that phone. And don't try anything stupid."

Josh tapped away at the keyboard. "It's a cellphone."

"Call it."

Josh dialled the number, then Solomon pulled the phone away from him. The phone rang once, then was answered. "Victor Cross. Talk to me."

Solomon paused for a second then slammed the phone down.

"This is impossible," Joshua Dalton said. "I don't have any memory of this! Who *was* that?"

"Victor Cross."

Josh frowned. "I know that name from somewhere…"

"He was one of your brother's top scientists," Solomon Cord said.

"Yes…" Josh said, nodding. "Yes, Victor Cross. He disappeared. We couldn't find him. Then we stopped looking." Again, he frowned. "Why did we stop? We forgot all about him! How is that even *possible*?"

Then Josh went pale and collapsed back into his chair. "Oh God. Cord, I don't think this was the first time. I thought I was just overworked – I mean, I haven't slept properly in *weeks*. I keep finding these gaps in my memory. Usually it happens only every couple of months, but lately it's been more and more often."

"How long has this been going on?"

"When I was a kid, it used to happen all the time, but that was Max, using his mind-control powers to make me do things and not remember."

"When did the lapses start again?"

"I'm not sure. That's the thing about memory; you can't remember what you can't remember. I started noticing it a couple of years ago, shortly after I came here."

"Either you're lying to me or someone has been controlling your mind."

"Mind-control..." Josh shook his head. "Impossible. Max was the only superhuman we ever heard of who could do that... What if *he's* doing this? What if my brother never lost his powers? No, no. That can't be it. If he could still control people then he'd never have allowed himself to be arrested. It has to be someone else. One of the kids. Butler. We don't know all of his abilities yet. It has to be him."

"No," Cord said. "He's only been here a few months. It has to be either Mina or Yvonne."

"Well, it's not Yvonne. It must be Mina."

"Why not Yvonne?"

"Because it's not."

"Why are you so sure it's not her?"

"Because it isn't."

Solomon Cord swore. "If she can control minds, how the hell are we going to stop her?"

"She *can't* control people's minds!"

Cord said, "Josh... Listen to me, OK? Yvonne has used her mind-control power to convince you that she

266

hasn't *got* mind-control power! She's the traitor!"

"She can't be the traitor. She told me she wasn't."

"Damn it! Josh, stay right there! Touch nothing! I've got to find her!"

He ran from the room.

❊

"Mina? Are you there?"

Mina was lying on her bed. She glanced up to see Yvonne standing in the doorway. "Go away!"

"I just want to know that you're all right." Yvonne walked into the room and sat on the edge of the bed. She reached out and stroked her sister's hair. "Everything will be OK."

Mina sobbed. "Colin... He was younger than us and he's *dead*! And I didn't do anything! I should have been able to help him!"

"You're certain that he's dead?"

She nodded. "His aura vanished when everything exploded. It was like... closing your eyes. All of a sudden it was gone." She shuddered as she remembered the sensation. One second she was reading Colin's aura – bright and strong, burning with anger and determination – and Dioxin's aura, which was also bright, but sharp, flecked with evil. Then the forest erupted and there was nothing. Not even Dioxin's aura. *Dioxin's aura vanished too*, she realised. *And Mr Wagner's. Even my own! The heat from the explosion! It must have been masking their auras! Colin could still be alive!* She sat up suddenly. "I have to tell them!"

Then Yvonne, her voice cold and hard, said, "*Sleep.*"

Instantly, Mina felt drained of energy. "Got to…" Her eyes closed momentarily and she forced them open. "I have to tell them…"

Again, Yvonne said, "*Sleep.*"

Mina closed her eyes.

"*Sleep and don't wake up.*"

25

SOLOMON CORD RACED through the corridors of Sakkara. He found Yvonne's bedroom and kicked open the door. *Not here... Mina's room!*

He stepped back out into the corridor and found himself face to face with Yvonne. The dark-haired girl was staring at him, eyes blazing. *"Drop the gun."*

Solomon opened his hand and the pistol fell to the floor.

"I knew it would be you," Yvonne said. "And I knew you'd come this way. You people keep forgetting how smart I am."

"What have you *done*, Yvonne?"

"You can't talk any more."

Solomon tried to speak, but no words came out.

Yvonne smiled. "I wasn't sure whether that would work on you. It doesn't work on everyone."

He leaped forward, his hands grabbing for her throat. Yvonne stepped aside and smashed him in the head with her fist, knocking him to the floor. "And you seem to have forgotten that I'm strong, too."

Solomon rolled away from her, scrambled to his feet and pressed his fingers into his ears.

269

"Clever," Yvonne said. "If you can't hear me, I can't give you orders." She smiled again. "But then if you can't hear me, why am I telling you any of this?"

She suddenly charged at him and ploughed her left fist into his stomach.

Solomon instinctively dropped his arms to block the punch and Yvonne yelled, *"Stop!"*

He froze.

"You will not harm me. You will not seek help. You will obey my commands."

Yvonne stepped around him and walked in the direction of the machine room. "*Follow me.*"

Unable to do anything but obey, Solomon followed the girl. She entered the machine room and looked down from the platform to the people working below. "Everyone!" she shouted. "Can I have your attention please?"

The labcoats below looked up.

"Sleep."

One by one, they all dropped to the floor.

Yvonne led Cord down the stairway and into a small storage room. She closed the door behind her. "Now we wait."

Dioxin leaned out of the copter's open doorway, looking towards the pyramid ahead.

"Sixty seconds!" the pilot called.

Behind Dioxin, the eight mercenaries stood waiting, ready to jump into action.

"What's the status from our man on the inside?" Dioxin said into the radio.

"No word," Victor Cross replied. "But..."

"But what?"

"He may have been compromised. Someone else called the number a few minutes ago."

"Damn. You want to abort?"

"No!" Cross said. "We still have to get the girl out of there! Proceed as planned!"

"Copy that." Dioxin switched off the radio. "We've got a green light, men! Make me proud!" He jumped from the copter and immediately activated his jetpack.

As the copter hovered over Sakkara, the eight men clipped their descent-ropes on to the rails and jumped out, sliding quickly and silently down to the roof. Dioxin touched down next to them.

"Good... no alarms," Dioxin said. He pointed to the StratoTruck. "Destroy their craft!"

One of the men unclipped a hand grenade from his belt. "Take cover!" He pulled the pin and threw the grenade into the StratoTruck's open hatch. The explosion shook the entire roof.

Dioxin followed his men down the stairway to the heavy steel door.

"Locked!" one of them said. "I don't think we can by-pass it!"

"Damn it... these doors should have been open! Everyone get back!"

As the mercenaries raced for cover, Dioxin raised his arm and fired two missiles at the doors.

When the smoke cleared, the doors were still intact.

Dioxin swore. "There's no other way in!"

Razor lay on the floor of the machine room. He opened his eyes and risked a quick glance. Around him, his colleagues appeared to be fast asleep.

What was all that about? he asked himself. He had been testing the prototype of the hushbomb and hadn't heard anything. It was only when everyone else in the room had started to fall to the ground that he'd glanced up towards the door, to see Yvonne standing there, with Solomon behind her.

Unseen by Yvonne, Solomon had mouthed the words, "Lie down!" and gestured with his hands that Razor was to fake being asleep.

Razor hadn't known what was going on, but he

trusted Solomon Cord with his life: he'd dropped to the ground and lain still.

Now the door to the storeroom opened again and Yvonne led Cord out. She was talking on a cellphone. "Cord interrupted him before he could give the order to disable the defences," Yvonne was saying. "We're going to the roof. Anyone tries to stop us and I'll order Cord to deal with them."

Razor waited until they had left, then he jumped to his feet. *So she's the traitor... working with Josh maybe.*

"Anyone else awake?" Razor asked quietly.

One of the labcoats, a middle-aged woman, raised her head. "What's going on, Razor?"

"You tell me! What did she do?"

"She ordered everyone to sleep, and... they all did! When I saw Solomon signalling to you, I figured I'd better lie down with the others."

"I think we're about to be invaded," Razor said. He looked around. "Start dragging the others towards the back of the room. We'll need to set up a barricade."

Moving quickly, Razor began to gather up some of the equipment from his workbench, then he ran over to the wall, to a red alarm button. He hesitated for a moment, then slammed his fist on to the button.

❁

Dioxin stepped back as sirens suddenly began to wail through the building. "Aw hell... They just can't make it easy for us, can they?"

Then the huge steel doors unlocked and slid open. He looked at the dark-haired girl. "You Yvonne?"

"I am. Tell your pilot to land and take me out of here! I'll get Cross to send another helicopter for you."

"What about him?" Dioxin asked, looking towards Solomon Cord.

"I could order him to die... But no. I'm taking him with me. He could be useful."

As the copter descended once more, Dioxin led his men through the doors.

Yvonne called, "Dioxin? I don't want my sister to die. *Do not let any harm come to her!*"

Dioxin nodded, then turned to his men. "You three get to the computer lab and start downloading the data. The rest of you work your way down to the basement. I want every room checked. Shoot to kill. Just because they look like kids doesn't mean that they're not dangerous. And you'd better make *damn* sure they're dead!" He pointed to Cord. "That man somehow survived a ten-thousand-foot drop from the copter – and he's not even a superhuman."

Consulting the map on the hand-held computer, Dioxin made his way towards the living quarters.

In his office, Joshua Dalton was racked with fear and guilt: the revelation that Yvonne had been controlling him had broken through the barriers she had imposed on his memory.

He reached under his desk. There was a nine-millimetre automatic hidden there, for just this sort of emergency. He pulled the gun loose and checked that it was loaded.

They played me. Victor Cross... The one outstanding link to Max's operation. We never even looked for him, damn it! Why not?

Then he remembered. *She told me not to look for him.*

Josh felt his skin begin to crawl. *What else did she make me do?*

The memories started to come back. Phone calls and e-mails to Victor Cross, sending him detailed plans of the building, telling him about Paragon's armour and how to disable it. Telling Cross how to find Colin Wagner and Danny Cooper. Leaking information on the real identities of Titan, Energy and Quantum to the press.

And he remembered, finally, where Yvonne and Mina came from.

My God, how could I have forgotten that? Every one of us who knew; we all forgot! How many minds has she altered?

He jumped at a noise outside in the corridor and crouched low, gun at the ready.

Cross knows everything about us. He knows where the safe houses are!

And my money! She made me give him almost all of my money and I didn't even realise. I've been funding our enemy's operation and giving him all the help he needs!

The door to Josh's office was kicked open and an armed man burst in. Without pausing, Josh aimed the gun at the man's head and pulled the trigger.

The man staggered backwards and collapsed.

Josh reached out and pulled the machine-gun from the dead soldier's hands, dragged the body into the room and quickly searched it. *My brother did what he thought he had to do, to save the world. He believed that superhumans were a threat.*

He was right.

Josh pulled the clip from the machine-gun and examined the bullets. They were black, with a slight shine. *Teflon-coated ceramic shells. The only bullets that can penetrate the kids' new uniforms.* His stomach churned.

Josh checked that the corridor was clear and ran, talking into his head-set. "This is Dalton, coming down from level six. Caroline, the building has been breached! Took out one member of their advance party. Looks like a merc. No ID, no insignia. What's the ETA on the Air Force?"

Caroline Wagner replied, "Nothing, Josh. No response yet."

"Damn. They've got to be jamming our signals somehow!" Josh charged down a flight of stairs. "Warren? You there?"

"I'm here, Josh. No sign of Yvonne. Mina's asleep... we can't seem to wake her."

"Take her with you and get to the machine room. There's a better chance of holding them off there until help arrives!"

"Help?" Warren said. "Josh, we're on our own here! There's no one left who *can* help us!"

As Josh reached the door to the machine room he was spotted by two of the mercenaries, who immediately opened fire. He dived through the door and raced backwards down the stairs, keeping his machine-gun trained on the door.

"Over here!" a voice called.

Josh turned to see Razor and Butler in one corner of the room. They'd erected a makeshift barricade from the heavy steel workbenches. Some of Sakkara's other technicians were with them, quickly dragging the labcoats behind the barriers.

Josh ran over. "My God... You do a body count?"

"They're not dead," Razor said. "Yvonne ordered them to sleep and they did. How she did that, I don't know.

Josh, the only way into this room is through those doors. We should be safe here for a while. But... there's a few people missing, including Mina and the Wagners."

"I know. Butler? How's that forcefield of yours? You think you can protect this room?"

"I don't know, I—"

At that moment, the doors above were blasted apart. Everyone ducked down behind the benches just as four of the mercenaries charged into the room, guns firing.

Josh checked the cartridge on the machine-gun, then passed his hand-gun to Razor. "You know how to use that?"

"I've seen a few movies," Razor said. "I know the principle."

"You need to conserve your fire!" Butler said. "And just *squeeze* the trigger: don't pull it!"

Razor said, "When I need the advice of a military-school dropout, I'll ask for it!"

"They won't keep this up for long," Josh whispered. "They'll just lob a grenade at us."

"Not if they can't see us." Razor held up one of the blackout bombs. He handed it to Butler. "You'll have to do it. It's way too heavy for me to throw far enough."

Butler shook his head. "No, they'll see me!"

"Use that forcefield of yours. It's bullet-proof, right?"

"I don't know."

"Only one way to find out."

Again, Butler shook his head. "No. If I have the forcefield up, I won't be able to throw the bomb out through it!"

"To hell with you then," Razor muttered. He pulled on a pair of thick, odd-looking goggles, then looked around on the floor. He spotted something and grabbed it. "Josh, cover me."

Josh popped up from behind the bench and began firing. Keeping low, Razor dashed across the room. When he found a clear area on the floor, he activated the heavy blackout bomb and rolled it towards the doorway.

The bomb burst, instantly covering the soldiers with a thick, black cloud. There were shouts of surprise, then they begin firing indiscriminately.

Razor flipped a switch on the side of the infra-red goggles; he could just about make out the mercenaries' blurry images.

Keeping as low as possible, Razor squirmed forward and aimed the glue-gun at the mercenaries, spraying its entire contents over their faces, hands and feet. Within seconds, they had stopped moving.

Grinning, Razor turned back to the others, then Butler called, "Razor! It's Josh! He's been hit!"

Consulting the map on his computer, Dioxin made his way to Sakkara's living quarters. He smashed open the first door. The room was clearly unused.

The next room was empty, too. According to the map, the third room was Mina's. He kicked open the door and walked in. Immediately, something slammed into the side of his helmet. Dioxin staggered and whirled around. Warren Wagner stood in front of him, brandishing a fire-axe.

Dioxin laughed and stood in place, allowing Warren to take another swing. The axe clanged off the armour. "Not even a scratch!" Dioxin said. "That the best you can do?"

He threw a punch at Warren, who ducked just as Dioxin's metal-clad fist ploughed into the wall.

Warren rolled to his feet and swung again with the axe, this time hitting Dioxin in the back of the knee. The armoured man stumbled, but didn't fall.

Warren backed up. "Come on then, murderer! Fight me man to man!"

"So *you're* Titan," Dioxin said, marching further into the room. He spotted Caroline crouched down against the wall, holding on to the comatose Mina. "And you even brought your wife along for the show."

Dioxin rushed at Warren, ploughed right into him. He put his armoured hand on Warren's face and slammed his head against the wall. Warren dropped to the floor, unconscious.

Dioxin reached down to take Mina, but Caroline pulled her away. Dioxin laughed at this futile act of defiance. He raised his wrist, aiming the rocket launcher at Warren. "Put the girl down or your husband is dead."

"You're probably going to kill us anyway," Caroline said. "What do you want with her?"

"Nothing. But her sister doesn't want me to hurt her." Seeing Caroline's reaction to this, he smiled. "You didn't know, of course. Yvonne can control people's minds. She's been using Dalton to feed us everything we needed to know about this place. Now hand her over or your husband will burn. Like your son did."

Caroline said, "You fire that missile and the blast will hurt Mina."

Dioxin sneered. "Like I could give a crap!" He tried to fire the missile, but somehow he couldn't do it. "Damn it! Why can't I fire?"

"Because if Yvonne's mind-control is anything like Max Dalton's was, then you have no choice but to follow her orders," Caroline said. "If you don't, it'll cause a feedback loop in your brain that could trigger an aneurism. What were Yvonne's words exactly?"

"Do not let any harm come to her." He reached out and grabbed Mina's arm.

"Stop!" Caroline shouted. "Look closely, Dioxin! I've got my thumb pressed on Mina's carotid artery. If you don't back down, I'm going to tear her throat out. You know what'll happen then, don't you? You'll have allowed harm to come to Mina, directly violating Yvonne's order! You'll be dead within seconds."

"You're bluffing!"

"Am I?"

"You'd never harm her!"

"You're really willing to take that chance?" Caroline glanced around, desperate for something that would help. Then something caught her attention; looking past Dioxin, through the window, she could see that a helicopter was approaching fast.

26

NIGHT WAS FALLING as the copter approached the roof of Sakkara. Renata said, "The StratoTruck... It's been destroyed!"

"At least that means we know they made it back," Façade said. "Hold on. I'm setting her down!"

"No, it's too dangerous for you!" Renata said. "Me and Colin will jump out. You two need to go and get help from somewhere!"

"I'm coming with you," Danny said.

Colin said, "You're not. Sorry, Dan, but we can't put you at risk." He glanced at the doorway: Renata had already jumped. Without another word, Colin followed her.

Danny looked at Façade. "We should—"

"No. We shouldn't! Renata's right. We'd be more of a liability than a help. We're going to the safe house."

"Façade, I can't just sit around the safe house doing nothing! Not while all this is going on!"

"We won't be doing nothing – we're going to get your mother and Niall and everyone else out of there. If Sakkara has been compromised, then there's a good chance that Dioxin's people know the location of the safe house. Let's just hope they haven't already found it!"

"You don't need me for that! I think… I think I *can* help, Dad!"

Façade stared at him. "Are you saying what I think you're saying?"

"I'm not absolutely certain… but if there's even the slightest chance that I can help, I have to take it!"

Façade nodded, then angled the helicopter back towards Sakkara.

As quietly and quickly as possible, Renata and Colin ran through the corridors. There was debris everywhere, broken glass, shattered computers, scorch marks on the walls.

They made their way to Josh's office and stopped when they saw the mercenary's body.

"Right between the eyes," Colin said. "Good shot."

"Better check him for weapons," Renata said.

"*You* check him! I'm not touching a dead guy!"

"Being dead isn't contagious, Colin."

Colin was about to respond, then froze. "Danny's coming! I should have known he wouldn't listen."

Renata peeked out into the corridor and spotted

Danny approaching. She waved him over. "Nice going," she whispered. "So who's going to watch *you* when all hell breaks loose?"

Danny looked down at the dead man. "Looks like all hell has broken loose already."

Colin said, "Not yet it hasn't."

"We should get to the machine room," Danny said. "They were building weapons for the new Paragon armour."

Colin paused, listening. "I can hear Dioxin, talking to my mother... Mina's room!"

"You two go," Danny said. "I'll be OK."

As Colin and Renata ran off, Danny cautiously made his way to the entrance to the machine room.

He silently stepped through the ruins of the door and looked down. Most of the workbenches had been piled up against one wall and directly below, through a strange, thinning black mist, he could see four of the mercenaries lying on the ground. They were in very awkward positions and appeared to be unconscious. His heart beating like crazy, Danny crept down the stairs and approached the men from behind. This close, he could see that they'd been glued to the floor.

Moving quickly but quietly, Danny reached in and took hold of one of the mercenaries' guns, then instantly jumped back as a bullet whizzed past.

A voice called out, "Danny?"

"Razor?"

"Get over here!"

Danny stepped around the unconscious mercenaries and ran over to the barricade of workbenches.

"Anyone out there?" Razor asked.

"No, it's all clear. What's the situation here?"

"It's not good," Razor said. "We don't know how many of them there are. They had us pinned down in here. Josh took a bullet in the chest. He's still alive, but only just." He gave Butler a look of disgust. "This guy's a dud. But *you*..."

"What about me?"

Razor grinned. "You've got your powers back!"

"No I haven't."

"He's right," Butler said. "You dodged that bullet."

"No I didn't. On the way here I got the feeling that I could do it, that I could move fast again, but it's no good. The power is gone. There's nothing there any more."

"It's all in your head, Danny," Razor said. "Look, I know you went through a tough time after the mine, but you are not responsible for what happened to Quantum!"

"I realise that," Danny replied. "But there's..." Out of the corner of his eye, he caught sight of the mechanical arm. "There's something else."

Shaking his head, Razor walked up to Danny and

looked him square in the eye. "Something else. Is that so? Well... *Get over it!* People are dying here, Danny! Butler has the power to save them, but he hasn't got the guts. You've got an even greater power and it's looking like *you* don't have the guts either!"

Danny yelled back. "Shut up, Razor! The power is gone!"

Razor suddenly punched Danny in the face, knocking him backwards.

"What was *that* for?"

"That was for being too scared of yourself to save your friends. You want another one?" He started pushing Danny in the chest. "You don't kick-start that super-speed of yours and we are *all* dead. I might as well have a little fun before I go!"

Another punch. Danny dodged it, but only barely.

"They're going to kill us and then they're going to find your mother and your little brother. You think Dioxin will let *any* of them live? He's going to hunt them down and murder them, just like he murdered your best friend!"

Razor swung another punch at Danny and this one he dodged easily. "Colin's not dead, Razor. He survived the fire. We brought him back with us."

Razor stopped and stared. "What?"

"Colin's alive."

❖

"Gunfire," Colin said. "Coming from the computer room, I think... No, the firing has stopped." He listened more carefully. "Sounds like there's a couple of our people pinned down."

"Go help your parents," Renata said. "I'll take care of this."

As Renata ran towards the computer room, she tried to remember the room's layout. *Most of the giant supercomputers are lined up against the walls, but there are a few in the middle of the floor.*

Closer to the room, she could hear shouting: "Give it up!" a man roared. "You are outgunned! Throw out your weapons and surrender!"

A woman shouted back, "Exactly how dumb do you think we are?"

Renata crept forward. Through the open doorway she could see four of the labcoats crouched behind the nearest supercomputer. The woman was holding a small hand-gun. Behind her, two of her colleagues were frantically tending to an older man, who was covered in blood. There was only a narrow gap between the enormous Cray computer and the doorway.

As Renata watched, the woman pushed her gun around the supercomputer and let off a couple of deafening shots.

Renata realised that the woman was using the reflective side of a compact disc to see the positions of the gunmen. *That's clever*. She moved a little closer and then the woman spotted her.

The woman held up three fingers, then pointed towards the other side of the room. Renata nodded.

Three of them. One or two I might be able to tackle myself, but not three. She knew what she had to do and it was risky. She waited until the woman let off another couple of shots, then jumped through the doorway, landed directly in front of the gap between the supercomputer and the door, and immediately turned herself solid.

Bullets ricocheted off Renata's crystalline form as, behind her, the labcoats dashed out to safety.

Now what do I do? Renata wondered. In solid form, she couldn't hear anything, but could still just about see. The three gunmen stopped shooting and one of them approached her while the others kept their guns trained on her.

The mercenary tentatively poked Renata in the stomach with the muzzle of his gun. He turned to his colleagues and said something, then started to move past her, towards the door.

Instantly, Renata unfroze herself, locked her arms around the man's neck, holding him in front of her. "You shoot and you'll hit your friend!" Renata shouted.

Blam!

The soldier's head was thrown backwards and then he slumped down.

The man who had fired said, "What was that you were saying?"

Still holding on to the dead man, Renata froze herself. *They killed him! They just…What can I do? They know I can't move like this!* As she watched, one of the remaining men moved towards the door, acting as a lookout while his colleague attached a device to one of the supercomputers. *So that's what they're doing here; they're trying to steal information!*

I can't move fast enough to stop them and if I stay like this long enough they'll just escape past me.

Renata waited for her moment: when she was certain that the mercenaries' attention was elsewhere, she turned back to her human form and threw the dead man's body at his colleagues. She knew she had only seconds to act: she spun around, grabbed the nearest supercomputer and lifted it off the ground. *I hope these things aren't too expensive!* Power cables and data lines snapped as she wedged the huge computer in the doorway. *They'll never get out past this!*

One of the men recovered and fired a short burst from his gun just as Renata was turning solid again. Her body jolted suddenly and there was a brief flash of pain in her stomach.

They shot me! Oh my God! Renata was unable to look away from the spray of blood that had erupted from her stomach and been frozen in mid-air.

The bullet is still inside me! If I turn human again, it could kill me!

The man who had shot her walked over and examined the crystalline blood with curiosity, then turned his attention to the supercomputer wedged in the doorway.

At least I've got them trapped here, Renata thought. *They won't be able to harm anyone else.*

❀

Slumped against the wall of Mina's bedroom, Warren Wagner groaned and his eyes began to flicker.

Without looking at him, Dioxin said, "Your husband's waking up, Mrs Wagner. I think we both know him well enough to guess that he's going to try something heroic. Something that will definitely get you both killed. Make it easy on yourself. Let go of the girl."

"No."

"So it's a stalemate?" Dioxin asked. "I hurt you, or try to take Mina away from you, and you'll hurt her. I don't really think you'd do that, Energy! You were a superhero! I know you'd never harm an innocent person."

"To save my life and my husband's life? Yes, I would

do it. And if I do, you'll be allowing it, going against Yvonne's order. I'm telling you, you'll die if you do that. With her sort of mind-control your brain has been reprogrammed at its most basic level. You cannot disobey the order!"

"You could be bluffing..." Dioxin thought for a moment, then a slow smile crept across his scarred face. "But there's a solution." He activated his helmet's radio. "This is Dioxin! Put me in contact with Yvonne immediately!"

Seconds later, Yvonne's voice came over the radio. "What is it?"

"You ordered me not to hurt Mina. Because of that, I'm stuck here. I need you to reverse your order!"

"I don't want my sister hurt!"

"*I* won't hurt her, but Energy here is threatening to kill her if I try to separate them. Your order prevents me from allowing Mina to come to harm. I promise that I will do my best to keep her safe!"

A brief pause, then Yvonne said, *"Do whatever you feel is necessary."*

Laughing, Dioxin reached down and pulled Mina away from Caroline. He threw the girl on the bed, then locked his hand around Caroline's throat and hauled her to her feet. He pressed the muzzle of his rocket launcher into her face. "No more games, Energy."

Then a voice from the doorway said, "Dioxin. Let her go. Now."

Dioxin whipped around to see a dark figure glowering at him.

Caroline didn't immediately recognise the young man. His eyes burned with anger and confidence and for a brief moment she thought she saw a small electrical spark crackle around his right fist. "Colin!"

27

HIS ROCKET LAUNCHER still aimed at Caroline, Dioxin said, "Oh for crying out *loud*! Why aren't you dead?"

"That's one of my powers, Dioxin. I cannot die. I cannot be stopped." *I wish*, Colin added to himself. "Now let her go. That's your last warning."

"Kid, I swear to you that if you take one more step I'll blow your mother's head off."

Then Colin heard his father's voice whispering, "Get ready..." Warren's hand crept out towards the fire-axe.

Warren leaped up from the floor, swinging the axe into Dioxin's visor. The armoured man staggered as Warren pulled Caroline from his grasp.

Colin charged. He smashed into Dioxin's armoured chest, forcing him back against the thick Plexiglas window. "Dad! Get them out of here!"

Dioxin swung his fist at Colin's face. Colin ducked, the blow barely missing him.

The scarred man aimed his missile launcher at Warren and Caroline, who were carrying Mina out of the door. Colin grabbed his arm and forced it upwards just as he fired; the missile exploded against the ceiling, instantly flooding the room with fire.

The room's two CDH boxes immediately burst open, spraying the entire room with hundreds of white pea-sized pellets. A thick cloud of steam and carbon dioxide gas erupted from the pellets, dampening the fire.

With his free hand, Dioxin jabbed at Colin's stomach, then smashed him in the side of the face with the rocket launcher. Colin fell back on to the smouldering bed, rolled to his feet and leaped again at Dioxin just as another missile struck the bed.

Dioxin ducked down and Colin sailed over his head, crashing heavily against the window.

Got to get out into the open, Colin thought. He knew what he had to do: *Josh told us that the windows are bullet-proof. But can they take a direct hit from a high-explosive missile? I know I can.* He stayed where he was and allowed Dioxin to fire again.

The missile exploded against his chest, pushing him into the glass. He felt the window crack behind him.

Colin concentrated: he could feel his skin absorbing the heat of the explosion, felt the energy surging through his veins and nerves.

"*Die*, damn you!" Dioxin rushed forward, threw himself at Colin, just as Colin created a powerful electrical charge in his fist and slammed it against the glass.

The window shattered; they tumbled out, half-falling,

half-sliding down the sloping side of the building. They sank into the deep snowdrift and Dioxin scrambled to his feet. He activated his jetpack and soared away from the ground.

Colin jumped, stretched his hands out and locked on to Dioxin's boot. He quickly glanced down; already, they were thirty metres in the air.

"Let go!" Dioxin roared, using his free foot to kick at Colin's hands.

Colin saw his chance: he grabbed Dioxin's other foot, then began to pull himself up, hand over hand, his fingers digging into the armour.

Bellowing with rage, Dioxin steered himself at full speed towards the nearby city of Topeka. "Goddamn you, kid! Don't you *ever* give up?"

Through gritted teeth, Colin roared back: "Never!"

"You see where we're going?" Dioxin asked. "We're heading into the heart of the city! So let's you and me make a deal: you let go of me now and I won't start firing on civilians!"

"No deals!" Colin said. "You want me to stop, you're going to have to kill me!"

"Innocent people will die!"

Colin reached up to Dioxin's belt, tore off the spare missile cartridges and let them drop. "How many shots do you have left, Dioxin?" He glanced down again; below, he could see the snow-covered trees that lined the highway. Directly ahead, larger apartment buildings loomed out of the darkness. *Got to stop him before we get too close to the city!*

"Get off me, you little punk!" Dioxin increased his speed and descended, steering straight towards the highway's overpass. He swung another punch at Colin, but this time Colin was ready: he grabbed Dioxin's hand and pulled it down towards him.

Unbalanced, Dioxin began to pitch forwards, head-first towards the overpass. He hit the jetpack's booster controls and they surged upwards once again.

"All of your men will have been captured by now, Dioxin! You've lost!"

"You think so? We have something you will want back, Wagner! You're going to have to let me go!"

Far below, the traffic had stopped as the citizens of Topeka watched the aerial struggle. Directly beneath Colin and Dioxin, a bus driver desperately hurried the passengers from his vehicle.

"I said, no deals!" Colin grabbed on to Dioxin's left arm and tried to tear through the armour.

"You're an idiot, Colin!" Dioxin shouted. "If you're holding on to me, you don't have enough leverage to get through this armour. Whatever way you look at it, *I* have the advantage!"

Colin landed a punch straight into Dioxin's visor. "How so?" he grunted.

Dioxin lashed out with his right fist, striking Colin in the face. Colin's lip split open and he felt one of his teeth crack.

"Because we're two hundred metres above the ground and *I* can fly!"

Holding on to Dioxin's armour with one hand, Colin reached behind him and tore the jetpack from his back. *"Not any more!"*

"No!" Dioxin screamed.

Even as they plummeted, Dioxin continued to punch at Colin. "Let go! Let go!"

Spinning end over end, Dioxin and Colin crashed through the roof of the bus.

Then... silence. Cautiously, the crowd of onlookers began to gather around the ruined bus. A young policeman rushed forward. "Back! Everyone get back!"

"Are they dead?" someone asked. "Who *was* that?"

"Paragon and one of the new heroes!" the bus driver replied.

"Thought they were on the same side."

"Me too."

The police officer yelled again. "I said get back! *Now!* Stay clear! Come on, people! Go on about your business! There's nothing to see here!"

There was a sudden, sharp creak of straining metal,

then one of the bus's windows was shattered by a large, steel-covered fist.

Dioxin pulled himself out through the window. The people ran screaming for cover as Dioxin threw a huge chunk of steel sheeting aside and jumped to the ground.

The policeman stared at him, fumbling for his gun.

"What are *you* looking at?" Dioxin roared.

Then Dioxin felt something hard hit him in the back of the head, knocking him to the ground.

Colin jumped down and landed on top of him, just as Dioxin lashed out with his fist.

Colin was knocked into the air. He spun around and landed on his feet, facing the armoured man.

Dioxin aimed his rocket launcher at the policeman. "Stay where you are, Wagner, or I'll fire."

"Didn't we just go through this same thing a few minutes ago?"

"This time it won't have the same outcome! Try anything and you'll be responsible for killing this man!"

The police officer began to back away from Dioxin.

"If you run, you die!" Dioxin roared.

"Let him go, Dioxin," Colin said. "You know you can't kill *me*. No matter what you do, sooner or later I'll stop you."

Still keeping his eyes on Colin, Dioxin said, "You married, officer?"

"Y... Yes."

"Kids?"

"We have a little girl."

"Be a shame for her to grow up without her daddy, wouldn't it?"

"Yes," the officer said.

"Wouldn't it?" Dioxin roared.

"Yes. Yes, it would."

"You hear that, Wagner? You try anything, and you'll be responsible for making that little girl a semi-orphan!"

"I hear you, Dioxin."

"So what are you going to do, huh? What does the *Hero's Handbook* say about situations like this?"

"It says I should keep you distracted while my partner sneaks up behind you."

Dioxin paused. "You almost convinced me with that one."

Then the young police officer said, "So you're *not* Paragon? You're Dioxin?"

"That's me," Dioxin said, still watching Colin.

"What does the *Villain's Handbook* say about taking your eyes off an armed police officer?"

Dioxin turned to him. "What?"

The policeman had his gun aimed at Dioxin's face.

Dioxin laughed. "I'm bullet-proof, you moron!"

And Colin landed a flying kick into the middle of Dioxin's back.

He ripped into Dioxin's armour, just as Dioxin smashed him across the face with a powerful punch. Colin forced Dioxin on to his back, but the armoured man kicked out, knocking Colin backwards.

Colin crashed into the wreckage of the bus and Dioxin charged after him.

Colin tore the door off the bus and slammed it into Dioxin's helmet, knocking him to the ground.

"This time, *stay* down!" Colin said. "You're beaten!"

Dioxin slowly raised his head. "I'm not beaten. I've *never* been beaten!" He aimed his missile launcher and fired.

Colin jumped forward, somersaulting over the missile, and landed directly in front of Dioxin. Behind him, the missile struck the wreckage and exploded, showering the street with flaming debris that melted the packed ice where it struck.

Dioxin fired again and this time Colin deliberately didn't dodge it: the force of the explosion knocked them both backwards.

Oblivious to the intense flames that covered his body, Colin darted forward and locked his arms around Dioxin, trapping the missile launcher between them. "Fire another missile and it'll blow your own arm off!"

"No!"

"Your armour protects you from the heat and my own skin protects me. But what's protecting the rest of your missiles?" Colin quickly looked about and spotted the young policeman. "Clear the area! When the missiles go up they'll tear the whole street apart!"

Dioxin struggled. "Get away from me! The explosion will kill both of us!"

"No, I'm betting that it'll only kill *you*," Colin said. "And I'm *not* one of those noble heroes who has sworn never to take a life. You burned once before, Dioxin. Now you're going to burn again!"

Screaming, Dioxin reached up with his free hand and pulled off his helmet: the armoured suit immediately powered down and Colin let him go. Scrambling like crazy, the scarred man began pulling off the rest of his burning armour and staggered backwards.

Colin looked down at his own body. He was still burning, but couldn't feel the heat. *Heat is energy*, he thought. *And I can* control *energy!* He concentrated, willing the flames to die out. Then they faded, the heat absorbed into his body. He raised his hand experimentally and a bright spark of lightning arced between his fingers.

Dioxin collapsed to his knees. "You think you've won, Wagner. You're wrong. You might have beaten *me*, but you haven't won."

Colin replied, "Well, I'm pretty sure *you* haven't won." He called to the police officer. "Can you handcuff this guy? And, you know, feel free to beat him up a little if he tries to escape."

The police officer cautiously approached Dioxin, who offered no resistance as his hands were cuffed behind his back.

"Whatever happens, do not take your eyes – or your gun – off that man! I mean it; give him one chance to get away and he's gone! He's responsible for the deaths of hundreds of people – maybe thousands!"

"Are you OK, son?" the policeman asked Colin.

"I will be... I've got to be somewhere else. Can you arrange for a helicopter or a really fast car?"

The officer nodded. "Whatever you say, Titan."

Colin smiled. "My name's not Titan any more. It's *Power*."

28

DANNY COOPER WHIRLED about as he heard a sound outside the door to the machine room. He looked up to see Warren Wagner peering down. "I need help here!" Warren said. He was carrying Mina.

Danny ran up the stairs, followed by Razor and Butler. They saw that both Warren and Caroline were wounded. Butler took Mina in his arms.

"Where's Colin?" Danny asked.

"I wish I knew..." Warren replied. "He tackled Dioxin; last I saw they were in the air, heading towards the city. Razor, what's the fastest way out of here?"

"The roof. It's the *only* way."

"What happened down there?"

"It was Yvonne," Razor said. "She ordered everyone to sleep. I think they're going to be OK, though. A couple of them are starting to wake up."

Caroline said, "That must be what happened to Mina. When the alarm sounded we found her like this in her room."

They heard voices from further down the corridor and ducked into the doorway. "It's all right," Razor said. "I recognise them."

304

Four labcoats appeared, one of them injured and being carried by two others. The woman with the gun said, "We were trapped in the computer room! Renata managed to get us out, but now it looks like *she's* trapped!"

"How many?" Danny asked.

"Three of them."

Danny said, "In the video of the attack on the airport, Dioxin had eight men with him. If he didn't bring any others, then they're all accounted for. The four of them in the machine room and the one Josh shot in his office."

Warren nodded. "All right. I'll go and help Renata. Butler? We'll need your strength to carry everyone out."

Danny stopped him. "No, *you* get the others out; I'll help Renata. And I need Butler with me!"

"Danny..."

"We'll be back! Butler, let's go!"

Butler passed the unconscious Mina to Razor, then he and Danny raced towards the computer room. They stopped when they saw that one of the massive Cray supercomputers had been wedged in the doorway.

"How are we going to get past *that*?" Butler asked.

"Turn your forcefield on!" Danny said to Butler.

"But..."

"Just *do* it," Danny said. "You want to be one of the new heroes, then start acting like one!"

Dumbly, Butler nodded. A shimmering glow appeared around him, close to his body.

"Now extend it forward; push that thing out of the way!"

The translucent bubble stretched out from Butler's body and pressed against the supercomputer. Butler turned pale, shaking from the effort.

"Come on," Danny said. "You can do it!"

The supercomputer creaked; the side caved in and it shifted forward a little, then stopped. Butler swayed and looked as though he was about to collapse. The forcefield vanished.

"One more push!" Danny ordered.

His voice barely a whisper, Butler said, "To hell with you, you goddamn one-armed freak!"

Danny grabbed Butler's arm and pushed him towards the doorway. "Insult me later! Just do it!"

Butler took a deep breath and straightened up. The forcefield appeared around him again, but instead of using it to clear the doorway, he simply charged at the supercomputer and slammed into it with his shoulder. The Cray burst free and crashed to the ground just inside the door.

Butler paused at the entrance, took another deep breath and stepped into the room.

There was a single gunshot; the bullet struck Butler

in the shoulder, spinning him about, dropping him to the ground.

Danny couldn't see any blood: it looked as though the forcefield had stopped the bullet from piercing Butler's skin, but it hadn't lessened the impact.

Butler started to get up, then groaned and collapsed on to his back.

If he passes out, he'll lose the forcefield! Danny thought.

Then... Renata's skin shimmered as she turned back to human and she ran towards Butler. The first gunshot missed her. She grabbed hold of Butler's leg and started pulling him to safety. A second shot struck the wall next to Renata's face.

"No!" Without thinking, Danny ran into the room, then stopped: he could see Renata, Butler and the two mercenaries, but they were all moving in slow motion.

The mercenaries spun about, aiming towards him, firing. Danny watched as the bullets moved past him at about the speed of a paper airplane.

He easily and quickly stepped out of their line of fire.

My God... I'm doing it!

Danny knew – somehow – that he wasn't able to move as fast as he could before he lost his powers and that he'd never be able to attain that speed again. But for now, this was enough. He walked over to the two astonished mercenaries and pulled their weapons from their hands, then quickly tied them up with discarded lengths of cable.

Danny shifted himself back to normal time, to see Renata staring at him in shock.

"Your power's back." She smiled at him and placed her hand on his face. Then she collapsed to the floor, clutching the wound in her stomach.

29

"EVERYONE'S OUT," Façade told Colin as he piloted the helicopter back to Sakkara.

"Are they all right?"

"No fatalities, but some serious injuries. Josh and Renata have been shot. Mina's in some sort of coma."

"God... Why didn't anyone else come to help?"

"When the attack started, the Air Force received an order to assist, but the order was almost immediately rescinded."

"By whom?"

"No one knows," Façade said. "General Piers – the base commander – insists that he was instructed to order everyone to stand down, but he can't remember who gave him that order. They're on the way now."

Colin looked out into the night. "There they are..." He pointed. "On the grounds in front of the building."

"You can *see* them?"

"Enhanced night-vision, remember?"

"Of course. Hold on, I'll set us down."

"No need," Colin said. He unclipped his seatbelt and jumped from the copter, landing heavily in the snow.

He looked over towards his family and friends, then there was a blur and a gust of wind, and suddenly he saw Danny standing next to him, a flurry of snow settling.

"So you've got your speed again?"

"Yeah. I can't move as fast as I did before I lost my arm, but... I'm still a hell of a lot faster than anyone else." They ran over to the others.

"Façade said that Renata..."

"She was shot in the stomach... I don't know what we're going to do. She turned herself solid just after I got to her. Colin, we can *see* the bullet inside her! Your dad says that she needs immediate surgery, but there's no way anyone can operate if she's solid, and if she turns back she could die before they can get the bullet out."

"Colin!" Caroline ran up to her son. "Is everything...?"

"I stopped him, Mum. And... I have something to show you. Later, though." He stepped past her and went over to his father, who was crouched next to Renata, a medical kit open beside him. "Dad?"

"She's in a bad way. At least, I *think* she is. I don't know what to do, Colin. We can't possibly operate on her like this, but being solid is probably the only thing that's helping her. Looks like the bullet is pressing against her spine. If she were to move it could paralyse her or worse."

"If she wasn't solid, what would you do?"

"I'd go in and get the bullet out."

"Is it a delicate operation?"

"Under ideal circumstances, yes. But in an emergency... you just have to dive right in and dig it out."

Colin looked at Danny. "We don't have time to get in touch with Renata's family and ask their permission. So I'm asking *you*, Dan. You're her best friend. What should we do?"

"She can remain like this for, well, probably forever. She was frozen for ten years after Ragnarök's battle. But that was different; she wasn't conscious then. For all we know she could be in constant pain."

"What should we do?" Colin repeated.

"Operate. Get the bullet out."

"All right," Colin said. "She can't hear when she's solid; someone get me a piece of paper and a pen! Dad, what's the procedure? If you're doing an operation like this, how does it go?"

"The bullet's deep, so I'll have to make a lateral incision in the stomach, about four centimetres either side of the wound. Hold the skin and muscle open and, well, just reach in, find the bullet, take it out, then sew her up."

"What if the bullet has punctured her liver or something?"

"It hasn't; the liver is up here," he said, pointing. "There could be some damage to the stomach, the duodenum, the pancreas, maybe the large intestine, too. But nothing as serious as the bullet pressing against her spine."

"OK," Colin said. He looked around. "Where's that paper and pen?"

Razor handed him a torn sheet of cardboard and a black marker. "This any good?"

"Thanks." Colin quickly wrote on the card, then held it up in front of Renata's face for a few seconds.

Danny asked, "What did you write?"

Colin showed him the card: "Dan will operate to remove bullet. When we give signal, turn back to normal."

"What?" Danny said. "I can't do it!"

"You can move faster than anyone else on this planet, Dan. You are *going* to do this! You heard what my dad said?"

"Yeah, but... Col, what if I make a mistake? I might make things worse for her!"

Warren took out a scalpel from the medical kit and showed it to Danny. "Hold it like this, OK? When you're cutting, take your time. Don't go too deep; there'll be a thin layer of fat under the skin and a strong layer of muscle under that. Slice through the muscle, but be extremely careful not to nick her intestines. Once you're through, push your index and middle fingers through the bullet-hole. Look…" He pointed at Renata's stomach. "There's a straight line down from the hole right to the bullet. If you don't move everything around too much, you shouldn't have a problem finding it. Once you have it out, start sewing up the skin. Don't worry about being too neat with the stitches – this isn't embroidery. Just make sure that the wound is closed." He reached into the medical kit again and passed Danny a pair of latex gloves. "Put these on."

Danny held up his left arm. "I only need *one* glove. And I can't put it on myself."

"Sorry, I forgot… Hand out then." Warren stretched the glove on to Danny's hand, then passed him the scalpel. "Ready?"

"No."

Colin said, "Yes you are."

"Wouldn't it be better to fly her to the nearest hospital?"

"You said it yourself, Dan. Renata could be in constant pain. Do it."

Danny closed his eyes and took a deep breath. "All right. Give her the signal."

Colin stood over Renata and gave her the thumbs-up. Renata's body shimmered and glistened, and she became human.

There was a blur and suddenly Danny was crouched beside Renata. "It's done! Change back!"

Renata became solid and transparent once more.

Danny stood up and held up the bullet. "That was... intense! I hope to God I didn't do any damage."

It was then that Colin noticed that despite the freezing weather his friend was dripping with sweat, and his hand and arm were covered in blood. "I'm sure you did fine."

Warren checked the wound. "Looks good, Danny! Well done!"

Colin said, "I can hear more helicopters coming."

"That's the Air Force," Façade said. "Finally."

Colin asked his father, "What about the others? Mina and Josh?"

"Josh is unconscious, but stable," Warren said. "Mina... I don't know what's wrong with her. She's breathing fine, her pulse is strong, but we can't wake her up. All the others woke up quickly enough."

"What do you mean? What exactly happened while I was gone?"

"It's a long story. We've had a hell of a day here."

Colin laughed. "*You've* had a hell of a day? Wait till you hear what *I've* been through! I..." He stopped and looked around. "Dad... where's Solomon?"

30

WARREN ACCOMPANIED RENATA, Josh and Mina in the Air Force helicopter as they rushed to hospital. The others were brought to the nearby Air Force Base while the military rounded up the mercenaries at Sakkara.

The next morning, they were taken to a large conference room on the base, where Joshua Dalton was waiting, his arm in a cast. Next to him stood an old man with four silver stars on his lapels.

A young soldier handed the old man a clipboard and then took out a digital recorder.

"Find a seat, settle down," the old man said. "This meeting will be recorded. I'm General Scott Piers, United States Air Force. As some of you will know, I was in charge of Sakkara until Mr Dalton took over. I've been asked by the president to oversee the investigation into the recent events." He glanced at the clipboard. "Present: Caroline Wagner, Colin Wagner, Daniel Cooper, Butler Redmond, Garland Lighthouse also known as Razor. Absent: Warren Wagner, Renata Soliz, Hector Thomas Millar also known as Façade, Solomon Cord, and Mina and Yvonne, both last names unknown. Renata

Soliz and Mina are currently under medical care. They are being supervised by Mr Wagner and Mr Millar." The general looked at Josh. "That correct, Mr Dalton?"

Josh nodded. "It is. Thank you, General." He looked around at the others. "Before we officially get started, there are a few things you need to know. First, this investigation could take some time. I'm talking weeks or even months. Second, I've just heard that Renata's operation was successful. She's healing extremely fast and is expected to make a full recovery." He glanced at Danny. "Well done. The chief surgeon said you did a lousy job but somehow still managed to save her life."

Danny grinned at that.

Josh continued. "Third, there's no change in Mina's condition. We still don't know exactly what happened to her. Fourth, all of our actions of the past few days will have to be accounted for in full. What that means is—"

Colin interrupted him. "Where's Sol?"

"We don't know."

"What are you doing to get him back?"

"Everything we can," Josh said. "Which to be honest isn't much right now."

"Until we have him back, this isn't over."

The general said, "Colin, isn't it? Well, listen up, boy... by order of the president of the United States of America, the new heroes are now under my control. You

316

will, therefore, follow the chain of command. You will speak only when permitted."

"Permission to speak, General?" Colin asked.

"Permission denied."

"But—"

"I said *permission denied*!" the general roared.

Razor said, "Oh, just let him speak!"

"That sort of insubordination will not be tolerated under my command!"

"Yeah? What sort of insubordination *do* you tolerate, you old fart?"

General Piers turned to Josh. "*This* is how you run your operation, Dalton? It's hardly a surprise that everything fell apart!"

Colin stood up. "I want to know what's happened to Solomon Cord's family, and Danny's mother and brother."

"They're fine. They're here on the base," Josh said. "Façade brought them in this morning."

"Have Sol's family been told that he's missing?"

"They know."

"I want to see them."

"Later," Josh said. "Colin, please... we have a lot to get through today." To the general, he said, "Sir, if you leave this with me, I'll get them to calm down. They're not used to military protocol."

"You have one hour, Dalton," the general said, then

317

stormed out of the room.

"I'm not going to be part of a military organisation," Colin said. "Josh, get the others in here."

"They're not involved in the investigation."

"*Now*, Josh."

※

Colin took Alia and Stephanie Cord aside. "We'll find your father. I don't know how, and I don't know when, but we'll do it."

Alia asked, "What about the men who attacked Sakkara? Have they said anything yet?"

"No. Façade said they're professionals – it's going to take a lot to make them talk. From what he can tell, they never met Cross themselves."

Stephanie said, "I can't believe Josh is going ahead with this investigation while our dad is still missing!"

"I know," Colin said. "*I* can't believe that we're now part of the US military. I never signed up to be a soldier. I don't like this at all."

"Promise me you'll get Dad back," Stephanie said.

"I promise. I don't know how long it will take, but we will get him back."

Stephanie smiled. "If anyone can do it, you can. Dad thinks you're the coolest kid in the world."

"He never stopped talking about you," Alia said.

Warren and Façade entered the room, then Josh called out, "Everyone? Come on now! Settle down and let's get started!"

Stephanie sat next to Colin and put her hand on his.

"We lost a lot here today," Josh said. "But we have some of our enemy's men in custody, including Dioxin. The biggest threat against us is Yvonne. It seems that she has the same kind of mind-control ability that my brother Max used to have. She was using me to feed information to Victor Cross. I had no idea this was happening. Regardless, I feel that I should step down as leader of Sakkara."

"You won't find any objections here," Danny muttered.

Josh ignored that. "Someone needs to take my place. Someone Yvonne can't control... General Piers' men have spent the day going over all the security footage from Sakkara. From what we can see, there were only four of us over whom Yvonne was never able to exert any influence: Façade, Renata and Caroline. Renata is too young, so I'm hereby appointing Caroline Wagner to lead the new heroes."

"I decline," Caroline said.

"Then the only other option is for me to remain," Josh said.

"No, that's not acceptable," Colin said. "Façade will lead us."

Everyone glanced at Façade.

"No," Josh said, "he has a criminal record! He spent eleven years pretending to be Quantum!"

"When Dioxin threw Solomon out of the helicopter, the StratoTruck was only metres above the ground when we caught him. If the StratoTruck had crashed, I would probably have survived. Façade wouldn't. He knew that, but he didn't hesitate to go after Solomon. Façade gets my vote."

"That might make a difference if this was a democracy," Josh said. "But it's not. We're now part of the US military." He paused. "My own role is going to change somewhat. I have a lot of experience and it would be foolish to throw that away. I will stay on as an advisor."

"I don't like the way this is going," Colin said.

"Sakkara's security is being upgraded. We will be moving back there in a couple of weeks. General Piers is currently arranging for a team of specialists to join us. The details are classified right now, but I can tell you that the team will consist of weapons and security experts, and some former superhumans."

"Anyone we know?" Warren asked.

Before Josh could reply, the door to the conference room burst open and a young soldier rushed in. "Got a priority-one message for someone called Power."

"Who?" Josh said.

"That's me," Colin said. "That's my new superhero name. But I haven't really told anyone yet..."

The soldier handed Colin a cellphone. "This was delivered a few minutes ago. The package had the address of this base and your name on it."

The phone rang in Colin's hands. Puzzled, he hit the 'answer' button and held the phone up to his ear. "Hello?"

A man's voice said, "Colin Wagner, also known as Power?"

"That's me."

"My name is Victor Cross. Perhaps you remember me?"

Colin froze. "Where have you taken Solomon Cord?"

"First, I want you to know that this call cannot be traced, so don't even bother trying. Second, I have to tell you how impressed I was with the way you defeated Dioxin and his men. It's a hollow victory though. We got what we were looking for."

"Where is he?" Colin yelled.

"He's right here beside me. Hold on..." A second later, Colin heard Cord's voice, weak and obviously in pain. "Colin... I... I know I can trust you to do the right thing, you hear me, son? You do the *right* thing!"

"Sol! I don't—"

Victor Cross's voice came back on the line. "All right,

Colin. We have Mr Cord here and a number of civilians. Five people. The mother, father, brother, sister and two-year-old niece of your friend Renata Soliz. I also have a man here with a gun."

Colin felt his blood turn cold. He swallowed. "Cross, what are you doing?"

"Two minutes from now, either Solomon Cord or the civilians will die. *You* choose who you want to save. Do not ask for anyone else's help with this decision. If you do not choose, they will all die. The clock is ticking, Colin."

Colin looked around the room. Alia and Vienna Cord were staring at him.

Beside him, Stephanie squeezed his hand.

I promised them I'd get their father back! I can't... But Renata's whole family! No, I've never met them. Sol's my friend, I have to...

No! This isn't right! This isn't fair!

"Cross, you can't make me do this!"

"Life's full of hard choices, Colin."

"You're bluffing!"

"Want to bet?"

"I need more time!" *Maybe if I can stall him long enough, Danny could use his super-speed, track them down...*

"Not a chance. Tick-tock, tick-tock."

Oh God, I can't do this! I can't save one man and allow five innocent people to die!

But Sol is a superhero. If I save him, then he'll probably save hundreds of lives in the years to come.

No, that's wrong! That's just selfish! Renata's niece is only two years old! I can't allow her to die!

"Ten seconds!" Cross said.

Colin looked towards his parents. *I can't even ask them what I should do!*

And then Solomon Cord's words came back to him: "You do the *right* thing!"

Victor Cross said, "Time's up. Who's it going to be, Power? Cord or the civilians?"

Colin knew that he had no option: "Save the civilians."

A single shot rang out, then Cross said, "Solomon Cord is dead."

Colin dropped the phone and ran from the room.

31

COLIN STOOD OUTSIDE the base's south entrance, waiting. Danny and Renata stood next to him.

Stephanie and Alia Cord, and their mother, waited nearby.

Stephanie had not spoken to Colin since the phone call.

In the distance, a small black dot appeared in the sky.

Vienna Cord walked up to Colin and put her arm around his shoulders. "My husband was very fond of you, Colin. He always said that no matter what happened, he could trust you to make the right choice."

Colin nodded and the tears spilled down his cheeks. "I'm so sorry."

"You did the only thing you could, Colin. No one blames you."

Then Stephanie said softly, "*Almost* no one."

Colin looked at her, but she kept her eyes focussed on the approaching helicopter.

"Your father would have done the same thing, Stephanie," Mrs Cord said. "You can't condemn five people just to save one. No matter *who* he is."

"You promised us!" Stephanie suddenly yelled at Colin.

"You promised us you'd get him back!"

"I'm sorry! I thought..."

"What? What did you think?"

"I thought I'd have more time. I didn't think that Cross would do something like this!"

"I wish we'd never met you, Colin Wagner! I wish you'd... I wish you'd never found your way to our house! Everything ended for us that day! You came to my dad for help and because of that, because of *you*, he's dead!"

Her mother said, "That's enough, Stephanie!" She pointed to the helicopter that was fast approaching. "That's your father's body in that helicopter."

A few minutes later, the copter set down in front of the entrance. Warren Wagner jumped out and made his way towards Colin. Behind him, four soldiers lifted out a covered stretcher.

Warren put his hands on Colin's shoulders. "Are you OK?"

"What do you think?" Colin pulled himself free and walked up to the men carrying the stretcher. "Stop!"

He pulled back the sheet.

Solomon Cord's lifeless eyes stared back at him.

"Goodbye."

Colin covered up his friend and watched as the body was carried into the base.

The following week, the new heroes and their families moved back into Sakkara. The building had been greatly transformed: the roof now housed a large radar dish and an automated rocket launcher on each corner. Uniformed guards were permanently stationed on each floor, and everyone – without exception – was carefully scanned and frisked as they entered the building.

Renata Soliz and Danny Cooper sat in darkness on the wall that skirted the edge of the roof, trying to ignore the large group of soldiers who were standing nearby.

"This place is even more like a prison than it was before," Danny muttered.

"You're telling me. My folks are freaking out. They really don't want to be here. They want to go back to Cleveland."

"Like the general said, it's a matter of national security," Danny said. "Nothing we can do about that." He turned at the sound of footsteps and saw Razor approaching.

The older boy sat on the wall next to Renata. "He's still in his room."

"Has he eaten anything yet?" Renata asked.

"Not much. He said he doesn't really *need* to eat any more."

"Stephanie's still not talking to him then?" Danny asked.

Razor shook his head. "Alia's tried to get her to make peace, but as far as Stephanie's concerned, Colin is responsible for what happened to Sol."

"He didn't have any other choice."

"That's easy for *you* to say, Renata. You still have your family. Sol was the closest thing I ever had to a father."

Danny glanced at his watch. "It's almost time." Behind them, more people were approaching, filing up the stairs in twos and threes. He got to his feet. "This feels wrong. I'm going back in."

"You sure?" Renata asked. "You want me to come with you?" She started to move, then groaned slightly and clutched her stomach.

"No, no... You stay here. I want to talk to him alone."

Danny made his way back inside the building. Just inside the door, he met his mother and Façade, who was carrying Niall on his back.

"You're not going to watch?" Façade asked.

"Nah. I'm not really in the mood for it."

The corridors of Sakkara somehow seemed colder and even more empty than before. Danny stopped outside Colin's room and knocked on the door. "You in there?"

There was no response.

"Come on, Col! You have to *talk* about this! I know you can hear me!"

327

The door opened and Danny stepped into the room.

Colin looked pale and drawn, his eyes red. "What?"

"Everyone's up on the roof."

"I know. I can hear them." Colin hesitated for a moment. "I can hear everything, if I concentrate on it. I hear them talking about me. I hear Stephanie crying herself to sleep, blaming me for what happened to her father."

"It wasn't your fault, Col. It was Cross."

"No, it was me. I made the decision."

"Suppose you'd chosen to save Sol and sacrificed Renata's family instead. Would you have been able to cope with that decision any easier?"

"Of course not," Colin said.

"So...?"

"What?"

"So live with it!" Danny said. "You did the only thing you could do."

"And what if he does it again? We have no idea where he is! What's to stop him from picking up more people and forcing me to choose between them?"

"Col, this is *why* he did it! Cross knew he couldn't beat you physically, so he wanted to break your spirit! And it's working! You have got to get over this!"

"A good man died because of me!"

"You think *I* don't know what that's like?" Danny said. "I killed my own father!"

"That was different. That was an accident! Sol died because of a decision I made!" Colin turned away. "Damn it! These powers aren't a gift, Danny! They're a curse! I'm really beginning to wish that we'd just let Max Dalton carry out his plans to strip our powers."

"We would have died!"

"But Sol would still be alive. And so would all the people Dioxin murdered. But now look at us... We're at the mercy of a madman and we don't even know where to *begin* looking for him! We're practically prisoners here. All it will take is one phone call from Yvonne to the US president or some other world leader and we could be looking at a nuclear war! She can make people do anything she wants!"

"So how do we stop her?"

"I don't know." Colin cocked his head to one side, listening. "It's started."

Danny walked over to the window and looked out to the west, towards the elaborate fireworks display that was being held in Topeka. "Happy New Year."

❀

The following morning, Warren took Colin to the roof. Three helicopters were approaching from the east. "Here they come," Warren said, shielding his eyes against the sunlight.

Colin said nothing.

General Piers came out and stood next to them.

The first helicopter touched down, and two soldiers helped an elderly woman down the ramp and lifted her into a wheelchair.

For the first time in hours, Colin spoke. "Who's that?"

General Piers said, "One of our experts. That's Mrs Francine Duval, the mother of Casey Duval. We're hoping she'll be able to tell us more about her late son's superhuman abilities."

"Never heard of him," Warren said. "Who was he?"

"Ragnarök."

They watched in silence as the old woman was wheeled past, keeping her gaze fixed straight ahead.

"Does she know? About me, I mean?" Warren asked.

"Yes, she does," the General replied. "She knows everything."

"That's not good."

Colin glanced at his father, but could tell from his expression that this was not the right time to ask what he meant.

The second helicopter contained a trio of middle-aged men – "Weapons experts," General Piers explained – and a tall, striking woman in her early forties. The woman stopped in front of Warren and smiled. "Titan. Good to see you again. You've aged well."

Warren grinned. "Thanks. You too."

"So this is your son? The man who finally put Dioxin behind bars?"

Warren placed his hand on Colin's shoulder. "Yep. Colin, this is Amandine Paquette, formerly known as Impervia."

"Call me Mandy," the woman said, shaking hands with Colin. "Firm grip. You're going to be a strong one all right." She paused for a moment. "Colin, I'm sorry to hear about what happened to Paragon. I knew him pretty well. He would have done the same thing if he'd been in your shoes."

"Thank you," Colin said.

With a last smile, she followed the others into the building.

Warren watched her go, then – as the third helicopter landed – he said to Colin, "This... This is going to be a tough one for you, but I know you can do it, OK?"

"What do you mean?"

"We need an expert in mind-control if we're ever going to stop Yvonne and Cross."

Colin looked up to see a man with a cane being helped out of the copter. The man had a touch of silver to his hair, deep lines on his forehead and an unmistakable scar on his neck, just below his left ear.

"No!"

"It's the only way," his father said. "We need him."

"For God's sake, Dad! This is about the *stupidest* thing that we could do!"

Limping, leaning heavily on his cane, Max Dalton slowly approached Colin. "I know you're not pleased to see me. I don't blame you. Considering what happened... but they're right, Colin. I'm the best man for the job."

Colin held up his right hand. A powerful bolt of lightning arced around it. "After what you tried to do to us, Dalton, give me one good reason why I shouldn't burn you to a cinder right here and now!"

Max Dalton smiled weakly. "Because you know that would be wrong. You were trained by Solomon Cord. He taught you to always do the right thing. If you want to honour his memory, you will let me live."

Colin looked away and the spark between his fingers faded and died.

Later, when everyone else had gone inside, Danny and Renata came out on to the roof and walked over to Colin. "You OK?" Renata asked.

"I will *not* work alongside that psychopath! We don't need him. We don't need *any* of them! Let's get out of here. The three of us will find Cross on our own."

Then Renata said, "No. Danny and I talked about it all

last night. We're staying."

"Are you crazy? A couple of months ago Max Dalton was going to *kill* us!"

"I know. Look, he'll be watched at all times. Max is still a prisoner. It's just that we need him here."

"No! I won't have any part in this!" Colin said.

Renata said, "I'm sorry, Colin. You just don't have a choice."

"You know something? I'm getting pretty damn tired of people telling me that I don't have any choice! Well, I do. I *do* have a choice." Colin stepped on to the low wall at the edge of the roof and jumped.

Danny and Renata watched as Colin landed heavily on the ground far below and began to run.

"I'd better go after him."

"No, Dan… let him go. He needs to do this. When the time is right, he'll come back." Renata reached out and took hold of Danny's hand. "He'll come back."

THREE MONTHS LATER...

Victor Cross sat in his office, watching footage taken from a CCTV camera. Beside him, Yvonne sat with her feet up on the desk. Evan Laurie pointed the remote control at the screen, pausing it. "That's him..."

"Where and when was this taken?" Yvonne asked.

"Hungary, just east of Budapest. Four days ago."

"At least his hair is finally growing back. Where is he now?"

"We're not sure, but we're getting closer. We've met a lot of people who've spoken to him since he left the new heroes."

Cross said, "When you *do* find him, I want him tracked at all times, but tell the men to keep their distance. Wagner can hear someone coming from miles away. When the time is right, we'll pick him up. It won't be hard to convince him to side with the Trutopians."

"I can do that easily enough," Yvonne said.

"No. The only thing I want you to do is make sure that he doesn't remember you. I definitely don't want him to be fully under your mind-control. I want him to *believe* that the Trutopians are the only way forward."

"You're playing a dangerous game," Laurie said. "After what we did to Solomon Cord, I don't think we can expect any mercy from him. If he discovers…"

"I'm a lot smarter than he is, Laurie. He'll never figure out who we really are."

"But suppose he *does*? Neither of you have any physical superhuman power that comes close to his. If he finds us out, if he can somehow find a way past Yvonne's control, Colin Wagner will tear us apart. We don't have anyone even *nearly* powerful enough to stop him!"

Cross sat back in his chair, staring at the grainy image of Colin on the screen. "Mr Laurie, you have never been been wrong."

THE NEW HEROES

THE QUANTUM PROPHECY

Ten years after a great battle that wiped out all the superheroes, Colin and Danny start developing strange powers. Is this the beginning of a new age of superheroes? Who can the boys trust? And how will they use their new-found powers – for good or evil?

0-00-721092-2

www.TheNewHeroes.co.uk

**And watch out for further adventures of
The New Heroes, coming soon...**